RAPIDS

"A fast-paced, exuberant look at bipolar disorder. It's impossible not to fall in love with Yan."
Tabitha Suzuma, author of _Forbidden_

"Yan is a breath of fresh air. You don't want to miss this story, it will hit you like a tidal wave."
Lucas Maxwell, SLA School Librarian of the Year 2017

"This book nails it—not just the vertiginous flights of bipolar, but also the pure joy of youth . . . Bowles gives us a vibrant, witty, wonderfully weird narrator in Yan, in whose company we cannot help but see the beauty, and the power, of the sometimes disorderly mind."
Marya Hornbacher, author of _Wasted_ and _Madness: A Bipolar Life_

"Authentic, dazzling and a vivid demonstration of why neurodivergent 'own voices' are so important."
Eric Lindstrom, author of _Not if I See You First_ and _A Tragic Kind of Wonderful_

"Witty, inventive and incredibly immersive. Yan is a brilliant, heart-breaking character."
Elen Caldecott, author of _The Short Knife_

"A roller
Dr Rebe

RAPIDS

ANNA BOWLES

For Gill and Jarita,
with love and wonky brains

First published in the UK in 2021 by ZunTold
www.zuntold.com

Text copyright © Anna Bowles 2021
Cover design by Isla Bousfield-Donohoe

A catalogue record for this book is available
from the British Library

ISBN 978-1-916204-232
1 2 3 4 5 6 7 8 9 10

Printed and bound in the UK by
Grosvenor Group Print Services Ltd
Sterling House
Langston Road
Loughton
Essex IG10 3TS

Please be aware that this book contains references to and descriptions of aspects of clinical depression and hypomania including suicidal ideation.

More information on bipolar disorder in young people can be found at the Young Minds website: www.youngminds.org

Adults can find information at the Bipolar UK website: www.bipolaruk.org

AN INTRODUCTION TO NORDHELM

THE KBC NETWORK'S HOTTEST PRIMETIME SHOW!

⊨▷ MEET THE JAARV ◁⊨

These pirates arrive in the chilly land of Nordhelm bent on raiding and pillage . . . only for their fates to become gradually entwined with those of its people and its mysterious lord, Rothgern.

<u>Uskaar</u>
Captain Uskaar has a heart of gold – and a mighty warhammer, Vargsmittar. Huge and strong, Uskaar's secret is that he is a quarter troll.

<u>Yrsali</u>
Uskaar's younger half-sister has had a speech impediment since birth, but nothing slows down the Jaarv second-in-command and her sword Skivare*.

*Not to be confused with Skrivare. That's Swedish for 'printer'. This mistake appeared in one of the early episodes and nobody noticed.

The Crew
Seefar the roamer, Edel the healer, Pug the ship's boy, the enigmatic blue-skinned Navigator and the jovial Alf form the rest of the named Jaarv characters.

MEET THE NORDHELMERS

The peaceful inhabitants of the villages and towns in the land of Nordhelm are watched over by the much more warlike contingent of the castle.

Rothgern
The brooding, leather-clad lord of Nordhelm has been wreathed in tragedy since the death of his wife at the hands of the vittra – until the arrival of the Jaarv drives him to gather his forces and take a stand.

Landnaar
Rothgern's second-in-command is strong, brave and about as smart as one of Nordhelm's thousands of pine trees.

Arngunnur
This wise, elderly advisor does his best to support his lord in the defence of the realm; and generally gets ignored for his troubles.

 MEET ISGA

The three-hundred-year-old queen of the nixxi – a tribe of vampire mer-women – plays by her own rules. She may strike the occasional deal with the humans, but she'll keep it to the letter, not the spirit.

NOT FORGETTING . . .

The Tomtar
(Singular: tomte). These bad-tempered, petty and vengeful pixies will make your life miserable if you don't leave porridge out for them nightly.

The Vittra
Nordhelm's version of trolls are big and slow and really just want to be left in peace. But what chance is there of that?

Ethraig
Life is challenging enough in Seasons 1 and 2, so obviously what the Jaarv and the Nordhelmers need in Season 3 is a telepathic fire-breathing dragon calling to them from across the sea . . .

PROLOGUE

August

The London Eye is turning very slowly – I wish it would spin like a Catherine wheel. Behind me, Big Ben strikes eight times, sinking into me and rippling out to the tips of my fingers and toes. I'm here; I'm a part of here.

I spin round, laughing, to see the Houses of Parliament. Tourists are milling about – between them I catch a glimpse of Chelsea, plodding along the road near the Tube station. I don't want my best friend to be upset, so I wave at her – *Back in a moment!* – and run again, jumping into the road to dodge a huge group of tourists but skipping back up onto the pavement before the big red bus can catch me. It's like being inside a TV show.

London! I've only been here for a couple of hours, travelling round the Tube and popping up in the places I just couldn't wait to see, and already I never want to leave. I wonder if I could do Year 13 here? I want to hop into a black cab, go anywhere! My heart is beating in time with London: *I am Yan.* The sun will always shine. I am rushing through light.

All summer I've been feeling more and more alive. There's a smooth, swift river running through my soul. Sometimes I think I could melt into it, burn up in the joy. Forget the Blip, this is my pure bright beginning.

'Yan, have you gone mental?' Chelsea demands. But she's not really angry – she's glancing all around, excited too. She's sweating her face powder off in the heat, and she's got her green nerd-chic cardigan wrapped awkwardly around her arm.

'Aw, I know you're tired, but we're in *London*!'

Chel can't help smiling. 'I ain't . . . There's just a lot of people.'

'It's OK. You'll get used to it. This is where we're meant to be.'

I grab her arms and do a little dance. She's been my best friend since forever, so she's used to my moods. It's always been the two of us, whether we're bike racing down Hen Hill, jumping cowpats, bingeing *Nordhelm* at sleepovers or trying to figure out how I can get an online hat shop going.

Chel is the one who got Mum to see the unfortunate obvious a few months ago, during the Blip. This trip is our reward for surviving that – ahem – interesting time. Although, officially, the reward is for passing our AS levels (A*s for Chel, of course; Cs and a B for me because of said unfortunate obvious), and a chance for us to inspect universities we might favour with applications. For I am a genius milliner: mistress of lace, wire frames and creative vision. And Chelsea is a genius writer – though she can't exactly show her best stuff at school. She will get a scholarship to University College, and I'll find a famous milliner to make me their apprentice.

'Come on,' she says. 'I'll message my aunt, case she's home by now.'

'I wanna stay here,' I say, pointing at both sides of the river. Though I am also curious to meet Aunt Julie, who's putting us up.

A tourist bashes into my left hand and apologises in

Mandarin. I should shove him right back . . . No. I beam at him instead. I could learn to speak Mandarin properly in my spare time at uni. I could do anything here.

'There's the bit that's paved with gold!' I point to sunlight on the river.

Chelsea's not listening. She's consulting maps on her phone, even though she already checked the route a million times in Brockford. 'Right. We should really get to Swiss Cottage now.'

I have a vision of a little house made of Swiss cheese, with women in red pinafores and mice running in and out of the yellow holes.

'All right,' I concede, and I head off back to the Tube station, trying not to make Chelsea run.

I just want to pack as much as possible into this week. Design studios and Chinatown and the London Eye and exploring little old shops, and nightclubbing and kissing boys and girls, all with my best friend.

And finding my dad, obviously. Mum won't tell me where he lives (lived?) except 'London', so I 'borrowed' her credit card and hired a PI online. The report's due tomorrow. I really should tell Chelsea about that.

CHAPTER 1

Two months earlier: June

I *think* I'm back to normal now. Kind of. I still don't have much energy, and I'm still getting stomach aches as a side effect of the antidepressants, but *not* being flat on my back crying and worrying everyone sick is a win.

I am no longer a zombie.

YAY.

Things changed quickly and then slowly. One Saturday afternoon after I started the pills, I was in bed staring at some dodgy triggery vlog on my phone, and then behind it I saw the closed curtain waving in the breeze. I refocused, and it wasn't just a curtain, but a gorgeous shimmer of watery green. The ray of light poking through and pooling on my *Nordhelm* bedspread wasn't an intrusion but a sliver of returning life.

It was like a switch had been flipped. And from there I gradually seemed to rebuild myself, until now I'm here.

Here in the local hospice charity shop with Chelsea, being inspected by three members of the Brockford granny cabal.

They've got us surrounded. Mrs Cooper's on the till, Mrs Evans is peering out of the storeroom and Mrs Longman is browsing the skirt rack. Meanwhile, Chel's checking the not-very-promising bookshelves and I'm extracting a pair of lace gloves from the accessories box. I've got an idea for attaching a hand shape to the crown and brim of a straw cloche hat . . . Yes, I'm starting to feel creative again. And I need outfits for London!

'You girls have just finished school for the summer, haven't you?' asks Mrs Cooper, the posh one.

'We done our last exams yesterday,' says Chel, and lets herself be told about how schools have their priorities wrong these days, with so many tests. She claims not to mind old-lady lectures. (And then writes the grannies up as comedy vittra in her fanfiction.)

'You'll've got top marks, with your brains,' Mrs Longman tells her.

I'm sure Chel has, too, but I know she hates the 'with your brains' routine as much as I hate the damp sympathy. I'm also sure that I haven't done well. Months of clinical despair aren't good for your grades.

'Your mum doing all right, Yan?' Mrs Evans asks me. Then, in her special sensitivity tone, 'And what about *you*, my love?'

Ah. As of earlier this year, I've got an exciting new label. Previously, people could choose between The Chinese One (the fact that I'm *half*-Chinese is a bit of a subtle distinction for round here), The Nurse's Daughter, That Casanova's Child and The Hat Girl (today: a topper with tiny red silk flowers winding a trail up the crown). Now there's an exciting addition: The Mental One.

At least these particular old ladies call me Yan and not Jan. They don't Speak Loudly and Clearly to me, or look amazed when a local accent comes out of my mouth. Though mine isn't as strong as Chel's, whose family's been in and around north Somerset and south Gloucestershire since humanity crawled out of the primeval sludge. Plus

Mum is always on at me to 'speak properly' because she thinks it makes people take you more seriously.

'My mother's doing very well, thank you,' I say. 'So am I.' I'm tempted to come out with, 'How does your son feel about his wife running off with an estate agent from Bristol?' Everyone knows everyone else's business around here. But I'm not that mean. Today. Instead, I say, 'How's your knee, Mrs Cooper?'

There: Mrs Longman has mild arthritis and Mrs Cooper is up for a knee replacement soon, so that gets them talking about their ailments. And about my mum, who's the local GP practice nurse.

'Your mother's a treasure,' says Mrs Longman. 'So practical, and kind with it.'

Yep, she is, where physical illnesses are concerned.

'You have a nice rest this summer. Don't do nothing too strenuous,' Mrs Evans tells me as the other old ladies chat about their joints and I pay for the gloves and a small blue-sprigged faux-silk scarf. Chel gets some musty Victorian poetry for fifty pence.

'People want the best for you,' Mrs Evans continues when I don't reply.

And the worst thing is, I know they kind of do. As long as there's plenty of gossip involved.

Chel and I make it out onto the market square, where an old couple with cameras slung around their necks are admiring the war memorial. This is the throbbing heart of Brockford, along with the charity shop, ye olde tourist tea shoppe (where Mr Spratt pays me a few quid to sew little hats for the jam jars), an old phone box with a dick scrawled on it, and the Indian takeaway that used to be a Chinese.

'You all right?' says Chel.

'Yeah,' I say, cos it's basically true. 'Let's go back to mine. You gotta post a chapter this evening, right?'

Chel nods earnestly; she takes her fandom commitments very seriously, and her current fic – 'Spirit of Fire' – is getting super popular.

'Any Isga in this chapter . . .?' I venture.

Chel avoids my eyes. 'Aye, a bit . . . Well, no, she don't really fit this time.'

'I know.' I sigh. Chel wants to please her audience, and they're all about Uskaar getting with Rothgern. The ripped (secretly quarter-troll), but kind-hearted pirate captain and the brooding, leather-clad Lord of Nordhelm Castle . . . The show itself plays it right up, though don't expect the studio to admit that. And don't ask *me* to get excited about Uskaar's massive pecs. Which, to be fair, Chel doesn't.

We're walking down bird-tweety Market Street deep in discussion about whether Ethraig the telepathic dragon would win a fight against a nixxi army when there's an interruption. It's the lads who hang around the churchyard drinking tinnies and smoking weed under the yew trees.

'Gonna join us?' Steve Parsons calls. A couple of his friends wave, cheerily enough.

'No thanks,' Chel calls back. It's her they're interested in. English-style pretty, and proper Brockford.

'You can share my beer any time!' shouts Luke Carter, waving his tinny about. He's sprawled on one of the posh tombs from back when there was a lord of the manor here. 'You too, Yan, if it won't fry yer little brain.'

I give him the finger.

'Yeah, thanks, no thanks,' says Chel. She's way better with words on screen than in public.

'Leaving it a bit late to get knocked up, ain't you?' Steve

persists. 'Mia had two kids by your age.'

Mia is Chelsea's big sister – she's got two sisters and three brothers – and what Steve says is almost true: Mia was nineteen. But I've had enough. I stomp into the churchyard, watched by the elderly tourists who've apparently tired of the war memorial.

'Go shove your dick in a gargoyle, Parsons. Wasn't it you Mia dumped to get together with Ryan?'

There's a couple of 'Oooh!'s. Dylan 'Dobby' Dobbs taps the side of his head and pulls a 'mental' face.

Whatever. I can stick sentences together much better than he can.

I turn to Dobby (yes, he actually likes that nickname). 'You fancy the pants off Chelsea. But with that goatee? She rather do it with a literal goat.'

I expect that to just make the lads worse, but instead the others start shouting 'Burn!' at Dobby. Result, more or less, though I make sure to clear off quick and drag Chel with me, before their attention turns back to us.

Her face is stony, but once we get out of sight around the side of the estate agent's, squeezing between the mirror of a black SUV and the rough stone wall, she starts giggling. 'You shouldn't bother with 'em, Yan, you know they're hopeless.'

'Yeah, I know. Anyway, we're going to London,' I say. 'Londoooon!' I poke her in the ribs.

'Loooondon!' She pokes back, grinning, and we head up the road, past the entrance to the crowded estate where her house is, along the row of oaks towards 5 Brock Lane, where I've lived since I was born. The only time I've been away for more than a few days is when me and Mum went to my grandparents' for a month after Dad left.

'Woohoo! Escape to the cit-ayyy!' I shout randomly.

Chel grins and snorts, looking at me side on. Her next words come out suddenly choked.

'Yan, you're so much better now!'

I'm going to have to tell my mum about London: she knows about the plan, but she probably didn't think 'Aunt' Julie – actually a second cousin of Chel's – would agree to put us up. She's not back from the surgery yet, though, so Chel and I head to my room, which is very cool in its own way, with a warped beam across the ceiling, a wardrobe where shoes duel for territory with earwigs, and some interesting wall cracks mostly covered by cut-outs from *Hat* magazine and printouts of Isga fanart, including some of mine. Forget Uskaar and Rothgern: a bloodsucking mer-queen played by Florence Huang is the best thing in the *Nordhelm* universe or any other.

Chel gets down to writing at once; she really should be a professional author, though she won't listen to me when I tell her. I get sucked into some dumb phone game – I still get a bit of brainfog sometimes, I have to be honest, and need something easy to focus on – when I hear the front door opening and closing again, and before long the back door. Mum's home from work, and I see her shiny dark head bobbing down the path of our big, colourful garden to where the little River Brock runs past the end. There, she fills the watering can before heading off to sprinkle water on the raspberries.

Watching her, I get a pang right through me.

I leave Chelsea tapping away and head for the garden. 'How was work?' I ask Mum.

She straightened up when she saw me coming. Now she looks me over: the regular sanity inspection. 'Busy as ever,' she says. 'I saw a kid who started out with hay fever a few days ago and now he's got a real fever.'

'Who is it?' I always try to take an interest.

'Tut, tut, Yan. Patient confidentiality.' Which is what she always says.

'You still going riding with Dr Jones on Sunday?'

'Yes,' replies Mum, with a bit of a smile. She never used to show interest in relationships but lately she's started saying things like, 'Now you're older, I've a bit more time . . .'

I don't think she wants to talk about that, though, nor does she believe I do. She's giving me the fake neutral look that means she wants me to tell her what I'm worried about. I used to, mostly. This year, not so much.

But today's news is positive!

'We're definitely going to London in August,' I say. 'It's all arranged with Chel's aunt. She's going to set up meetings with some English Lit academics for her.'

'Ah.'

I take a deep breath. 'And . . . I'm pretty sure I messed up my exams, but really I don't think I care that much. Being good at science doesn't mean I want to make it my life. If I even am good at it any more. My head still gets fuzzy.'

Mum watches me in silence for a moment. Then she puts down the watering can and frowns. 'Really, Yan? You're letting that . . . that business affect you this much? Even now?'

'I'm not *letting* anything,' I say, a bit sharply.

Nurse or not, Mum could barely deal. Chel had to pester her into taking me to the doctor (a new one over in Bath in an attempt at discretion, hahaha – it was all round the village in five minutes) and then a psychiatrist for the emergency referral. But then I got stuck on a huge waiting list, and the clinic never followed up, and that was it. As far as Mum was concerned I had pills so everything would be fine soon. Because Chinese people just don't go mental.

'Yan!' Mum prompts me now, also sharply.

I scrunch up my eyes. I think she asked me a question. How can my concentration be wandering at a moment like this?

'You *know* I can't have done well in my exams,' I say. 'And . . . I'm applying to art college. Probably St Martin's. For a fashion and millinery course. I'll go look round when I'm in London. Do a campus tour.'

There.

Mum glances off to the side, as if her runner beans might give her support. But she doesn't sound angry when she says, 'Well, I suppose that was inevitable. It's your life. Goodness knows I don't want to be an interfering parent.'

I think she believes that.

'Yes!' I'm relieved she's taking this calmly – not that she really gets stirred up unless there's pustules or petunias or paperbacks involved – but I need her to properly understand. 'You wanted to get out of the city, and I want to get out of the village. You – don't you *ever* get bored here?'

Mum adjusts her frameless glasses and sighs. 'Sunshine girl, I knew from the days when you wouldn't stop eating snails that you'd be a wild one. You weren't going to stick around forever. London's a concrete wasteland if you ask me, but each to their own. Just make sure some good-for-nothing charmer doesn't get you in a pickle.'

'Nah. I think I'm allergic to babies. I might get a girlfriend.'

Now it's the apple trees down the end of the garden that are helping Mum deal with her weirdo daughter.

'That again? I don't think there's anything wrong with it myself, but be sure before you go for it. And *never* breathe a word to your grandparents.'

'I wasn't planning to fill them in on my sex life. And this isn't twenty years ago. So . . .'

I pick at a raspberry bush. Mum's gardening obsession leaves me cold . . . but suddenly I want to ask her every single thing about plants, and everything else I've never even thought of before – and run far away at the same time.

'So?' she prods.

'I'll always love you!' I say, and throw my arms around her, probably smearing soil on my sparkly top.

Mum hugs back. I can sense her smile. Even the slight sadness in it. 'Sunshine girl, go shine bright,' she says.

Chapter 2

August

Now we're in Swiss Cottage and the sun's going down in a pinkish streaky sky and we're gawping at a terraced house with four storeys and a porch with actual pillars. If I lean over I can see down through a barred window into the basement, but the blinds are drawn.

'Wow,' says Chelsea. 'Very wow. Big. You sure it ain't a film set?'

'Nah, it's just your regular fairy-tale palace. With less pink,' I say, and shove her up the steps. Chelsea giggles. Then she rings the bell.

Trinnnnnggg.

We wait.

Julie didn't reply when Chel messaged her earlier. What if she's been delayed? Stuck in some third-world airport? She's a famous TV journalist, and she was only due back from an economic disaster zone this afternoon. She's a pretty big deal to us, as the first Furse to escape Brockford, but I don't suppose we're much to her. She and her lawyer husband might just have forgotten we're coming.

I don't fancy calling Nurse Mum and informing her I'm dossing on some steps for the night, even immaculate marble ones. And because this trip is about her being independent, Chel's told her family not to contact her, and she won't contact them, unless there's an emergency. Phoning them on the first night and saying we have to come home would not be good.

Suddenly the door shoots open. I immediately recognise Julie from the TV, especially her trademark floaty leaf-print scarf. She's on her phone, yakking about some financial summit, and waves us in with a distracted look. She's got a weird face – narrow as the horse that hangs out in the field behind the bramble track back home and tries to eat my hats – and looks kind of knackered under her make-up. You can see she's over fifty.

'Uh . . .' says Chel. Seeing us hesitate, Julie raises her eyebrows and gestures again. We troop in, self-consciously wiping our feet on an enormous doormat with a brown-and-cream patterned weave, then standing there trying not to boggle at the opulent hallway like the plebs we are. There's a curving staircase with a carved bannister, gleaming black-and-white floor tiles and an (empty) hatstand made of dark brown wood that's polished to an even brighter shine than the floor.

Julie informs the person at the other end of the phone that she needs dates 'if I'm going to set anything up for Rome', and hangs up.

'Girls!' she exclaims, and gives Chel a hug. Her plastered-on grin looks mostly false, but I was expecting completely false, so we're OK. Chel seems to like the hug, anyway. Then I get air-kissed, which is very strange indeed. Julie's tall and bony and smells of expensive perfume.

'Lovely to meet you, Yan. And right on time,' she continues. 'I hope you had a good journey.'

'Yes,' I say. I've promised myself I'm *not* going to start burbling here. I need to leave Aunt Julie and Uncle Mark to Chel. For she is a delight and a genius and is going to win the heart of the loaded olds and they will invite her to live here while she goes to uni. I have decreed it, it shall be so! Chel agreed to this plan, though I don't think she's as sold on it as I am.

And she's not starting her charm offensive yet.

'Yes.' She just echoes me in a small voice, eyes darting to a painting the size of a door and consisting of nothing but rough rectangles in primary colours. 'Er . . . can I use the bathroom?'

'Of course! Your bathroom is the second door on the right on the first floor. Your bedroom is the one after that. Mark's working late at the office, but . . .' Julie's phone rings. 'Oh dear, I must take this, I'm terribly sorry.' She doesn't look very sorry, or maybe she does – sorry to leave unwashed yokels wandering around her perfect house. 'Kieran, our youngest, will look after you when you come down. He'll be back any moment. He's kindly agreed to show you around London these next few days.'

Hm. From her tone of voice it sounds like either Kieran's agreement in this matter was not very graciously given, or she's uncertain he'll be back that soon. But within seconds Julie's disappeared through a door that has a child's drawing – of her, I think – with the scrawled words 'Granma's STudy' – at the bottom. Interesting. There's a Granpa's STudy too.

'Oh,' says Chel. 'Right, then. You know I reckon I did meet Julie – Aunt Julie – once, at Great-Grandad's funeral.'

'She seems hard to forget,' I say.

'Yeah, I were terrified,' says Chel, and indicates the stairs. 'Er . . . climb up the Falls, shall we?'

I laugh. This stair carpet is the same blue as the Nixxi Falls from *Nordhelm* and it turns out to be so plush it's like walking on dyed cats (drugged ones, who don't jump up and claw you to death). There's a slight delay as I forget Julie's directions and accidentally find an airing cupboard (the size of a cowshed) but then we're in our twin room. It's pretty amazing. Everything's cream-coloured and fitted to the walls like it grew there. When I dump out my things on the bed they look like fruity bits in a bar of nougat. I do what I can for my clothes – note to self to ask Julie about an iron – then fall backward onto the bed (*boing!*), spread-eagle in the middle and flail my legs.

'God, now we're in the Cream Suite,' says Chelsea. She's referring to *Nordhelm* again, the castle this time. It's comforting.

She's brought three library books with her, which she's now positioning neatly on her bedside table. Chel's got a bit of a tidiness fetish, given the chance.

Our window overlooks a flower garden outside; I bet Aunt Julie doesn't look after that herself. I think of Mum . . . no, I'm not going to think of Mum. Missing home would be pathetic. And I'm not going to dwell on Dad either, not till I get info from the PI. 'Forget the books now. Let's go out!'

'As if Julie'd let us, this late. Come on, Yan, stop bouncing.' Chelsea gives me her long-suffering look. 'We should go to bed early so's we're well rested tomorrow.'

'But what about Kieran?' He is, I recall from our planning, the fourth and last of Julie's sons (all raised by nannies) and only a bit older than us. His brothers have already left to become dentists, bankers and journalists (or maybe just one of each) but he's still at uni, doing Politics. I want to check him out.

'Oh!' Chel actually claps a hand to her mouth. 'Aye, she said – downstairs.'

'Easy to forget, with all this,' I supply helpfully, gesturing grandly around. 'Let's go!'

I bounce up from the bed, take off my hat (lucky I didn't crush it) and we go back downstairs. There's not a lot in the hall, except the deplorably bare hatstand and a set of waist-high shelf-things with handbags and shoes on them. I resist the temptation to peer into Julie's bag, to see what high-flying London career women carry around . . . then I stop resisting, because what's the point?

Inside, there's money poking out of a fat wallet, make-up more expensive than any I've ever touched, a vaping kit and a packet of squashed crisps. Prawn cocktail. How can anyone like fish crisps? And all that money! I need it so much more than the Petersons do . . . I can't resist pinching a tenner, while Chelsea studies a set of photos with Julie's four sons in various stages of posh school uniform, plus a grandchild who presumably perpetrated the 'STudy' signs.

'Look at this place,' says Chel, standing in the middle of the hall and spinning around. 'It's so shiny I'd be scared to live here.'

'Let's find some food,' I say, though I'm not hungry. I want to see what kind of kitchen these people have.

Chelsea accidentally finds the boiler cupboard – there's a theme emerging here – but then we make it to the kitchen, opening off the hall via a particularly grand interior door. It's industrial-sized, chrome-tastic, and shows only minor signs of human habitation (used mugs by the sink). Cleaned by 'the help' no doubt. It's not just a kitchen, but a massive living area, with a huge black table surrounded by heavy-looking dining chairs, and a couple of cream sofas that you could lie full length on.

And behold . . . a *beard*. The front door opens, and the mass of brown fuzz briefly protrudes around it as if floating in the air. Only then does a bloke follow, and deposit a large backpack that I think has some kind of big leaf symbol on it by the hatstand before heading our way.

'Hello,' he says once he's voyaged across the gleaming hallway. I think there's a grin somewhere between the facial shrubbery and the slightly wonky nose. 'I'm Kieran.'

I eye him. Friend or foe?

Chelsea hugs Kieran hello. He seems uncertain at first, but then I reckon he likes it. When he detaches himself, he takes three plates of cling-filmed ham and salad out of the fridge (probably made earlier by the help, aka some underpaid immigrant – I wonder if she lives in one of the cupboards?) and we all sit at a breakfast bar that looks like it was carved out of sparkly bedrock.

'So,' he says, 'first time in the big city?'

'We stopped over for a night on the way to Spain when I were seven,' Chelsea replies. 'Er, I guess that means yes.'

'Chelsea's one up on me.' I shove a huge piece of lettuce into my mouth, then have to talk around it. My stomach feels about the size of a tennis ball, max – trip overexcitement, I guess. 'My mum's not keen on cities,' I add leafily. 'But I've always wanted to come. I belong here.'

'You sound pretty sure for someone who just got here,' says Kieran. Is the smile lurking amid the facial fuzz a little patronising? Only a bit. He spears a kind of ruffly green thing – an artichoke, I think; are we at the Ritz?! – then shrugs. 'Good for you.'

'Your mum's bribed you to nanny us, has she?' I prod.

Kieran looks a bit startled, maybe at how direct I am, but he replies easily enough. 'Something like that. They've agreed to get off my back about uni and stuff for five minutes.' His voice sharpens a bit.

Hmm. I surreptitiously crane around his hulking

shoulders to get a better look at his backpack out in the hall. I recognise the leaf logo – Eco Focus. And the T-shirt, which I hadn't noticed until now due to the weird fascination of the beard – Save Our Forests. I can't argue with that, but maybe his mummy and daddy can?

'It's very kind of you,' says Chel. 'We'll try not to be any trouble.'

Kieran raises his eyebrows. 'Well, that's not very ambitious.' Then he cocks his head towards his mother's study and says in a lower voice, 'Ideally you should avoid getting killed or arrested or taking drugs, but I'm not going to nanny you. You're seventeen. We can just do some cool stuff; they've given me the money.'

Oooh. The magic word. It's not that we think money is wonderful per se, it's that you can't do much without it. Apart from owning our house – Uncle Liko's doing – Mum's not exactly loaded, and there's eight people in Chel's family. Her eyes light up. 'What we doin', then?' she blurts.

He hesitates for a moment – I think it's Chel's accent, and if he snarks about it I will eat him – but then he says, 'I've got details on my phone. Give me a minute to finish eating and I'll show you. Why don't you tell me about you?'

It sounds like his mama's manners are kicking in. Chelsea starts talking about her family, and I start daydreaming about the scene in 'Nixxi's Gambit' where Isga binds Lord Rothgern in kelp fronds . . .

'Yan!' Chelsea is practically shouting, like she's already tried to get my attention.

'What?'

'I'm telling Kieran you're gonna be an international millinery superstar.'

Oh. I hadn't noticed. Why do I find it so hard to concentrate lately?

'Yes. Hats!' I explain to Kieran, who as a bearded Politics student in a brown T-shirt has a sub-zero chance of being remotely interested. I tap my head . . . which is currently bare. Where's the hat I was wearing earlier? Never mind. 'Central St Martin's for Fashion Design – or London School of Fashion for Fashion Design with Millinery. I'm not sure if it's better to take a slightly more general degree, or specialise right away. Well, all right, I'll have to do the Foundation Course first anyway.' So frustrating! 'When I was younger, I was going to study Chemistry, but I didn't do well enough in my exams . . . and anyway art's the only way. Lately I've been able to work in my studio – well, the third bedroom, which is a bit damp, but Mum cleared out the baby stuff and the seed catalogues and now it's miiiine. There's a long bench down one side of the room and shelves for hats on the other. When I was seven Mum forgot to do the washing and made me wear a striped top with a spotted skirt one day, so after that I obviously took matters into my own hands. I've been making clothes since then although it took a couple of years for them to start coming out wearable. I could make you something less horrible than those . . .' I'm not going to look too closely but I'm pretty sure I glimpsed a hole forming in a really unfortunate spot on Kieran's shorts. 'Or a nice tiara to go with your beard? I'm going to sew me and Chel costumes for HelmCon. That's the main *Nordhelm* fan convention in the USA. We *are* going to make it over there one day! So . . . yeah. Headgear world domination.'

Huh, did I go on a bit too long there?

Chelsea's stolidly chomping tomato. Kieran's nodding as if he thinks I'm amusing. 'It's important to know what you want in life,' he remarks. 'You're seriously into that show, then? I've heard of it, but that's about all.'

'I do! I am! We are! Do you think I'm frivolous?' Apparently I care what he thinks. '*The Hollywood Reporter* called *Nordhelm* "Robin Hood in a boat with leather". That's pretty accurate.'

'Well, fangirls aren't harming anyone.'

'That's damning us with faint praise.' I attempt to eat an olive in an aggressive fashion and just manage to bite down on the fork tines instead. '*Ow.* What's your idea of a hobby, then?' I look pointedly at his forest shirt.

'Environmental work,' said Kieran, with a slight emphasis on the 'work'. But when I raise my eyebrows at the sudden solemnity, he grins, and adds, 'In case you didn't notice.'

'I bet Mummy and Daddy love that.'

'Ohhhh yeah,' agrees Kieran with feeling. 'Anyway, that's not your problem, except we're all going out for a lovely dinner on Wednesday, which'll be excruciating, but we'll burn that bridge when we get to it. Otherwise . . .' He gets out his phone. 'Tomorrow, we're going to King's College for you, Chelsea, in the morning. Dad's dug up some academic for you to talk to. And, Yan, I know you're booked on a tour of St Martin's in the afternoon. So I can shepherd you around, and then we'll go to the Globe in the evening. Then there's some other guy they've set up to talk to Chelsea at UCL on Tuesday, and I know Yan's got an open afternoon at London Fashion School at some point, and you want to go around various other places . . . which I imagine you'd much rather do on your own.'

Chel and I nod, almost in unison, which is a bit embarrassing but expresses the intensity of our feelings quite well.

'Right. We've got tickets for the London Eye on Wednesday afternoon, though. And Tuesday night you can come clubbing with me and my mates if you –'

'Whoa, wait, clubbing?!' I interrupt, then curse myself for being such a hick I nearly squeaked with excitement.

'Yeah, just Zippers,' says Kieran, like it's no big deal. 'It's Uma's birthday, from my uni lot. Half-price-drinks night.'

Hm. If that's important to his 'lot', he doesn't move in his parents' circles. I wonder if he'll elaborate on his uni life, but instead he checks his phone, says, 'OK, I've got to fire off some emails before bed.' And now he does sound just a tiny bit like his mum. 'We should aim to get out of here by about nine-fifteen tomorrow, so Chel doesn't have to rush.'

We both nod again, almost solemnly in Chel's case, and say goodnight. Kieran gives us a thumbs up, gets off his stool, grabs some kind of pie out of the fridge and heads off upstairs. Chelsea and I look at each other.

'Kieran seems nice,' she says.

'Yeah, but more importantly he said . . .'

'. . . we can go round on our own some of the time,' Chel finishes my sentence. 'Won't our parents freak out?'

'Hm,' I reply, considering this deeply and subtly. We've assumed we'll be Looked After, because that's how it usually goes, courtesy of my mum and Chelsea's bossy older sister. But . . . 'I wonder if maybe they're expecting this. We're gonna be eighteen soon. They want us to grow as people and make our own decisions and our own mistakes and test our wings and fly and whatever.'

'Wow,' says Chelsea, clearly struck by my insight. 'Freedom. I mean, I want it, but who knew we'd get it?' She pauses. 'This is too good to be true. Something bad's gonna happen.'

She would say that. 'You're a wuss sometimes. Bad like what?'

'I don't know like what, do I?' Chel widens her eyes for

some reason. 'Keep your hair on.'

Did I sound too aggressive, then?

She pauses, then looks determined, which always gives her a dimple. 'I ain't no wuss. We're in London. We're gonna make the most of it.'

We wander out of the kitchen towards the staircase; goggling at this place isn't going to get old any time soon. There's *carved grapes* on the cornices.

Suddenly, Julie sticks her head out of her study door. 'Kieran looked after you all right, did he?' she says.

Chel, taken by surprise, stares back. 'Aye . . . yeah,' she manages to reply.

'Yes, he can be sweet enough when he tries,' says Julie. Her hair is out of its bun, and she looks as if she's winding down a bit; I wonder if she might actually come out and talk to us. She's scrutinising Chel as if considering it.

'Goodness, you do look like your gran!' Julie says, with the faintest tinge of Brocky in her voice. 'But I won't keep you up now. I need to sleep myself. Leaving at six *again* tomorrow.'

Then she does emerge from her study, and shuts the door, but doesn't lock it (interesting: I could have a nose around in there). She heads up the brilliant-blue stairs, and we follow. On our landing, she turns to give us a brief smile then disappears up to the second floor.

'She means you look like your gran *before* she got the wrinkles,' I assure Chel, who gives me a rather dazed-looking nod in return.

Back in our room, I've got so much energy I could power a small city. The feeling doesn't go away when I lie down.

I posted a million photos to my regular Instagram earlier, so I go on my phone to see what the people back at Stanfield High who hate us least have to say about our trip. There's 'Wow'-variety comments from relatively OK people, like Chloe and Tash, who does nail art. I've still got a dolphin on my pinkie. I stare at it for a long moment.

'I suppose it'd be a bit rude to sneak out of the house and roam?' I say to Chel, when she comes back from the toilet.

'Don't be daft. Big day tomorrow,' she says. Pause. 'Seeing Julie is weird. *She* looks like old pictures of Great-Gran.'

'That is how genetics work.'

'Yeah, but to see that *here* . . .'

'It just proves you belong here, then. She's obviously softened a bit already! Next up, start telling her what a great student you are.'

Chel's shaking her head slowly. 'Aunt Claire – that's Mum's aunt, Julie's mum – says she were totally focused on schoolwork as a kid and practically lived in the town library. So obviously we're gonna have some stuff in common, but, Yan, it really ain't likely she'll invite me to move in.'

'We didn't say it would be *easy*,' I say, though maybe I did, once or twice. 'If it's hard to imagine fancypants Julie back in Brockford, then, well, in thirty years' time when you're a Professor of English Literature, it'll be hard to imagine you hunched over your laptop keeping your head down so you don't bash it into your sister's bunk. You can start working on her tomorrow.'

'Mm,' says Chel, not looking convinced. 'All right. I just wanna check my blog before bed.'

We made a pact not to go online too much this week, but some distraction is probably a good idea right now. I go online as well, surfing for rumours about *Nordhelm*'s upcoming fourth season. The showrunners did an interview saying they were always surprised they had so many female fans and wanted to attract a 'wider audience'. We, the narrow audience, would like to know what this entails, but there's no real information yet.

tomtartoes-blog.rabbithole.com
Sunday 22.13

We've arrived in London! It's amazing, and if I start talking about it I won't stop. I promised isga-bites-u that we – I – wouldn't spend the whole trip on the internet.

Buuut I got some DMs asking how long 'Spirit of Fire' will be on hiatus for. I promise it won't be much more than a week, especially as it's almost finished. Our boys are going to get together soon, once they're off the Jaarv ships and into the castle. Remember that four-poster in the bedroom where the ghost appeared in Season 2? I think someone, or some*two*, need to use it. 😊 So look out for that.

I'm going to keep doing Toes' Recs this week, so as not to completely skive off.

- Calming the Sea by lyssapeeps. Sometimes gen fic can be amazing – since Isga made friends with Gunsten the farmer, the seas have calmed down. An adorable friendship fic.
- notyourcrip's vlog on how Yrsali's speech impediment shows how you don't have to be 'perfect' to be a leader.
- Gorgeous fanart of Uskaar and Rothgern hugging by longboat_life. You can really see they feel for each other, even though they're enemies.
- It's time to rec a reclist! Fandom's favourite reccer

vikinghusbands has written a huge <u>list of all the best slow-burn Rothskaar love stories</u>.

Now bitey's reading over my shoulder and saying we should visit an old ship that's sitting on a stand in Greenwich that she just googled.

qwqWe drfinety shou;d, and steal it for the Jaarv!

That was bitey typing!! I've reclaimed my laptop now and I'm closing down to defend it from nixxi attack. I'm basically out of brain cells so going to veg a bit before bed.

When Chel's finished posting, we're still both wound up, so I bounce out of my bed and budge her up in hers so we're next to each other, with her laptop open in front of us.

We need something familiar, so we watch the first episode of *Nordhelm* for the hundredth time. OK, the early characterisation is a bit wobbly, but from the moment Captain Uskaar leaps off his longboat onto a rock wreathed in atmospheric but conveniently not-too-thick mist, and he and his sister Yrsali lead the Jaarv towards the village in Nordhelm Bay . . . it somehow feels like going to seek your fortune *and* finding a home. (Well, after a few episodes spent terrorising everyone and nicking their stuff; nobody's perfect.)

As the credits roll, Chel gives a massive yawn. 'Bedtime.' Then she glances at her laptop again, reaches out a hand – then retracts it.

She sighs. 'I'm *not* gonna start answering comments. We're in London, I'm focusing on that.'

'Absolutely,' I say. Chel sometimes thinks that because she's popular now she has an obligation to provide a public service.

She pushes me gently off her bed before snuggling down, if you can snuggle under a thin summer sheet.

I lie on my own bed and stare at a patch of light on the carpet, which is weirdly compelling for about five seconds, then I sit up and open my mouth to say something else.

Except Chelsea is starting to snore. She has elite sleeping skills honed by years of family-noise training: she nods off mid-sentence, even if you're trying to talk to her.

We really have had a long day, so I try to do the sensible thing too. I lie down again, and almost begin to fall asleep. Then I remember where I am and get so excited about it that I completely wake up again. Well done, me.

I feel like my actual hair is buzzing. Like I'm going to explode with frustration, about absolutely nothing. Am I going mental? Under the buzzing joy, there's a weird little chirp of fear in the pit of my stomach.

I need a distraction.

I said isga-bites-u wasn't going online this week, and it's true. Fandom was a lifeline when I was depressed, but I find I'm losing patience with the drama lately.

However, isga-bites-u is not the only me online. She's just the one people know about.

There's also blackm00ds.

I started this blog for depressive poetry. Not surprisingly my stuff got about two likes and zero comments so I was able to delete it without trace, which was definitely for the best. It also meant blackm00ds could be reborn a month ago, with a new purpose.

I check the replies to Chel's post. It's daytime in the US, so plenty of people are online.

🏛 **22:19 far-oceans:** I hope you guys have fun! Say hello to the London Eye for me – I'll make it there one day, I swear.

📺 **22:41 lyssapeeps:** OMG you recced my fic! tomtartoes RE-COM-MEND-ED MYYY FAN-FIC-TION! Excuse me while I just die a bit here. And I love Yrsali so much, being Uskaar's sister would be amazing. I'm gonna write about her some day.

⊚ **22:51 vikinghusbands:** I wish I had a chance to visit London. It's a wonderful opportunity for you and bitey, and we totally understand that you can't be here for a while. 👻

Huh, that's all pretty reasonable. Chel ships the main Two White Guys pairing, which is uncontroversial. People don't usually kick off in her journal.

Oh, but wait, a new comment appears . . .

🐌 **23:02 shurisgirl:** If your chapter is almost finished, you could finish it instead of blogging? Update, please!

　🔨 **23:03 blackm00ds:** Stop being so entitled.

　　🐌 **23:04 shurisgirl:** I'm not. I was just asking!

　　　🔨 **23:04 blackm00ds:** You were telling toes what to do, in her own blog.

There's no immediate reply. And I really mustn't sit here waiting, because if shurisgirl does come back, or gets defended by some other muppet, then I'll have to make another reply, et cetera.

Chel's said she doesn't like it when blackm00ds fights

people in her blog. Not that she has any idea who blackm00ds is. Maybe I should tell her, but not this week.

I plug my phone in to charge for the night, get up quietly, open the wardrobe, and sort the clothes I've brought by colour, which takes twenty seconds as we're here less than a week. I talk myself out of doing handstands against the wall, and sit on the edge of the bed instead, jiggling my leg like I'm trying to shake it loose. It works off a little of my weird tension – about five per cent. Reading a fic where Isga strikes a deal with Healer Edel and the Jaarv Navigator that leads to her eating Uskaar does for another ten.

Lately I don't feel the need to sleep for much more than four hours a night, or eat more than one meal a day, and I've plucked up the courage to deal with fandom haters, and now I'm on a mission to find my future and my past and truth and wisdom and my father and a theme tune, or something. It's all coming together. I'm taking off into the future. Art college and friendship and life! Perfect.

CHAPTER 3

Waking up after a few hours' sleep feels like firecrackers going off in every part of my body. I practically levitate.

Life! London! *Life*.

Unfortunately, it's not even seven o'clock yet, so I go and lie in the bath – which is the size of a small car – staring up at the little UFO lights set into the ceiling . . . and feeling a tiny bit calmer in the lovely hot water. Or maybe I'm just telling myself that? What's the actual difference? Well, the twitchy-twitchy in my limbs has died down a bit, so that's good.

What's going to happen today?!

St Martin's College! UCL for Chelsea! Culture and sophistication at the Globe open-air theatre. And I shall find out if my father is alive, dead or in Australia. I hope. The name Jim Harris is only slightly more searchable than John Smith, and he was raised in a children's home so it's not like I can ask his parents where he might have gone.

Truly, it's most likely he's in London. That's where he always said he wanted to go, and he sent us one letter from there, on my ninth birthday. It was quite long, and he sounded pretty happy and interested in seeing me again. But my mum burned it – actually burned it – in the garden and I was too young to think of memorising the address first.

I cried, though not as much as I'd done four years earlier when I found Dad's five-line goodbye note on the kitchen table and skipped off to ask Mummy to help read it because I couldn't understand all the words. So Mum spent my ninth birthday rage-cooking apple pies, just breaking off once to tell me to 'stop crying, sunshine girl, that man's not worth it'. That night she wrote back telling him to leave us alone. Then suddenly she was smiley again, and I had my presents and my cake. And a lot of apple pie.

Jim Harris did leave us alone.

I don't believe that I drove him off by being naughty, like I did back then. But he's *my dad*. And I can guess, even if Mum still won't, or won't admit to doing, that he was depressed. Clinically. I inherited it from him.

The water's getting cold . . . and look at that, the UFO lights have a fancy dimmer switch! I jump out and sing the *Doctor Who* theme under my breath in time with twiddling it – WheeUH, whEEEEUH! Yes, I am still five years old.

By eight o'clock I've had enough. Invading Kieran's room is obviously a bit wrong, but it's also too funny to resist. It smells of boy in here, though not nearly as badly as Chel's brothers' room does. Politics textbooks are strewn over the desk, and you can see old bits of tape on the walls where there obviously used to be posters. Footballers? Centrefolds? Oh, and he's got piles of gear with eco-charity logos: Greenpeace, Friends of the Earth, Eco Focus. The backpack, T-shirts, a laptop with stickers all over it. There's even some rolled-up protest banners.

'Come on, come on!' I shout in his ear. 'You've got things to show us!'

'What the . . .?' mutters the lump of bedclothes.

I poke it in what's probably its back, and the rest of its head appears out of the sausage (oo-er), glaring.

'Chelsea's not seeing Dr Abrams until ten,' Kieran says blearily. Then, 'Oh, all right, it's not surprising you're excited. Clear out while I get dressed.'

Imagine being that blasé about going out in London! Imagine having London, with money to spend, as your daily life! Wanker! (Whoa, that's a bit unfair, Yan. Steady on. But still.)

I clear out as instructed, to spare his tender manhood, and wake Chelsea by shoving her wash-bag and make-up stuff into her arms. I almost push her into the bathroom. Then I try on every outfit combination I can manage and decide on the lace-trimmed skirt; then change my mind and experiment with a different hat (blue silk fedora) which is subtler than the first. But nothing is exactly right, and I'm going on a tour of St Martin's, even if it is only a 'general tour' and not an interview. I need to be perfect, and everything needs to be perfect, and what if it isn't?! *Sunshine girl*, I suddenly hear in my head, and go for the yellow sunhat.

At breakfast Kieran slurps down three coffees and grunts when I try to hurry him, so it's nine thirty by the time we get to the Tube. I love the slightly curvy walls and the tiles with 'SWISS COTTAGE' printed on them in a 1930s font above adverts for super-manly shoot-'em-up movies. It's a bit cooler outside today, but once the brief blast of arriving-train air stops it's not cool down here at all, and cramming into a carriage is like playing 3D *Twister*, with bonus briefcases to the backs of the knees and the need to literally hang on to my hat. Kieran's beardy face is practically in mine, and I can see Chelsea biting her lip as she tries to avoid someone's armpit. We're not used to crowds like these, and I know she really doesn't like it. 'It's only for a few minutes,' I try to murmur to her, but it comes out a bit loud.

Anyway, I *do* like it! I feel as if there's a million different types of people here, even though I don't suppose a million people could in fact literally fit in a Tube carriage. No more white-bread Brockford: there's a dreadlocked guy in work overalls; and three bored businessmen wearing practically the same suit like a matching set of black, white and east Asian; and hijabi women murmuring in a foreign language, their eyes crinkling up. Everyone acts like everyone else is just normal.

Back home, rush hour is the 7.29 bus to Brislington. Or it was until the council cut the service.

'I know it ain't – it's *not* a proper interview today, but I really want to make a good impression,' Chel mutters when a couple of people get off and she's able to move closer to me. 'And learn as much as I can.'

Good call. We've calculated that three years of student life here costs *seventy-five thousand quid*, so we'd better be sure we really want to do it.

'Yeah,' says Kieran, shifting as he gets a ponytail fountain of dreads in one ear. 'I think Dr Adams is pretty chill, though. He's the brother of one of Dad's clients, I think, not actually mates with Dad.' He sounds like his dad having mates is about as likely as the queen popping to Tesco.

'Anyway, Chel,' I try to encourage her, 'if this guy doesn't float your boat, you can apply for the Creative Writing programme instead.'

'We been through why I ain't doing that,' replies Chel in her *please stop being so Yannish* voice. 'I don't wanna be totally unemployable. And, look, you know people don't ask you for directions back in Brocky cos they think you're a Chinese tourist? Well, in this place, you'll fit in. But oi looks Brocky and oi talks Brocky.' She deliberately thickens her accent on the last sentence. 'It's making me really self-conscious.'

'Well, screw the stereotypes! I only ended up speaking *properly* –' I put on fake airs for a moment – 'cos my mum makes a fuss. And I'll come in with you, don't worry.'

'Thanks, Yan,' says Chel, sounding relieved although we'd already agreed I would.

I resist the temptation to check my phone, because yes, by now the PI will have opened up shop, and just maybe there's somehow a signal underground . . .

Then I do something amazing. I *switch my phone off completely* (for now, at least). This is supposed to be my friend's morning. As we ascend the escalator, I sense a silken sash embroidered with the words 'Miss Self-Control' settling on my shoulders. Chelsea knows not my noble sacrifice. And Kieran's just picking something out of his teeth.

I gaze around me at the people on the escalators. The scariest and also the best thing about London is that hardly anyone looks at you for more than half a second; you could do anything at all, and nobody would care. Brockford is far, far away and I've got six days to get a foothold here.

Yes, I am like my father in that I've always wanted to come here. Of course, back in the spring, it was mostly because I thought it would be so easy just to step in front of a Tube train. But how things change!

Chapter 4

'That's a nice hat,' Dr Adams tells me, after we've shaken hands. He's wearing sandals and a 70s prog rock T-shirt, and his hair is ginger around a bald patch.

'I'm going to art college,' I explain, though for some reason it comes out as 'cart ollege' and I have to correct myself. 'I'm just here for moral support. Chelsea's the one who wants to study English. Over to you, Chel!' I point to her with a little flourish.

We're in a cramped office with a view of a wall. There's three desks, with name plaques, and shelves full of books and folders. Most interestingly, in my opinion, Dr A's desk is populated by neon-haired trolls, the 90s-style plastic ones, not the online type or the vittra from *Nordhelm*, facing off against the logos on various manky coffee cups. They're not colour co-ordinated *at all*.

We drag over the chairs from the other two desks. Chel's does a strange wheeze when she plonks into it. She looks worriedly round at her arse, then folds her hands in her lap like she's in a BBC period drama, and says in her most refined voice, 'I love the literature of the nineteenth century.'

Aaaand . . . they're off. Yer man's eyes sparkle, and they're both on about the Brontës. I knew she'd be fine. I peer around the place, looking for stuff I like, and spot

Plath on a high shelf with some other poets. As of the Blip, she's my favourite. Cue sneering from some quarters. People should try being a clinically depressed teenage girl before they diss my main woman Sylvia.

Are the trolls an artistic statement? There's one that looks like it's got Kieran's beard on the top of its head instead of on its chin. Maybe it just wants coffee; Chel's dad looks like that until he gets his morning dose. But I'm not going to think of home. Missing home would be lame.

'What do you want to do in the long term?' I hear Dr A ask Chel.

Chel swallows. 'I want to be an . . . academic . . .?' she says, like it's presumptuous.

'She should be a writer,' I say. 'She's honestly amazing.' My mind goes blank for a moment – no, stuff is skidding through it, but it's all irrelevant. Better not mention fanfic. 'You know, she shares a room with her sister and she used to have the top bunk until she fell off it trying to reach across to the bookshelf without going down the ladder. That's devotion!'

'Yan!' Chel's glaring at me. Better than her looking intimidated . . . I think. I know I've said the wrong thing. It's just that the bunk-bed story is hilarious. It's so very *her*, and it's your vibrant personality that's supposed to get you into uni, as much as your marks, according to our admittedly unconvincing school careers advisor.

I want to giggle now. I mustn't giggle. Instead, I consider making a troll hat out of paperclips and Post-its. When I'm done, I'll arrange the trolls by hair colour.

How's Kieran getting on, returning his books to the central uni library?

Must . . . bore . . . self . . . so . . . stay . . . straight-faced.

Fortunately Chelsea and Dr A are chatting comfortably

again, this time about course structure. Then I imagine Dr
A with pink troll hair.

A noise bursts out of my mouth: something like a
giggle, a hiccup, a cough and a snore all at the same time.

Both Chel and Dr A stare at me as I stand up.

'I need the toilet,' I say, and hurry out.

The giggles let up as soon I'm in the corridor, of course.
Should I go back in? No. Chelsea does need to learn to
do without me, whether she thinks she wants to or not.
Particularly if I'm in muppet mode. I really said the wrong
thing in there. But it just popped into my head and then
out of my mouth.

I head down the corridor to a kind of foyer where
there's seats. I sit down, get up, adjust my dress, sit down
again, and switch on my phone. There's not much in my
real-person account messages, except two from Chloe and
Tash back home, saying good luck. I reply with smileys.
Then I message Mum.

10:45 **Me:** Working on warts today?

10:46 **Mum:** Saw some impressive toe-rot.
Bottling the smell for a cold cure.

10:46 **Me:** Urgh, mother! Village wiiiiiitch.

10:48 **Mum:** More srsly Alice Magee came in.
Fell down on street and ripped scarf you made.
Cursed council's lax attitude to road mending
quite inventively. Do you think you could make
another scarf?

My mother is a lot more fun on messaging than she is in

person. She's more fun on her Facebook groups, too, from what I've seen. I reckon it's because she forgets she's trying to be a good Chinese daughter who's bringing me up in a way that won't give my grandparents a heart attack. As for Alice Magee, she's from the flats near Chel's house and one of the few fun people in Brockford. She's in her thirties and dyes her hair pillar-box red and makes rude jokes. And she's so twisted up with arthritis she walks with a stick already.

You've got to grab life while you can.

10:48 **Me:** Course I will. Nhs dismantled yet?

10:49 **Mum:** Nope. Bloody Colic on local radio says waiting lists haven't actually increased, mere docs and nurses just don't understand statistics.

Great. Colic, otherwise known as Colin Carston, local Tory MP, supported the suits who shut down the local adolescent mental health unit before I could even use it. And in general he's Mr Cuts.

10:49 **Me:** Very convincing. I can't wait to be old enough to vote him out.

10:50 **Mum:** Good luck with that. The radio callers were mostly interested in controlling the badger population. Anyway. St Martin's later? Nervous?

10:51 **Me:** Nooo PUMPED!

10:51 **Mum:** Don't bounce off the walls :) I've never seen you so excited.

10:52 **Me:** Way too hot to bounce today.

No reply. She must be with a patient.

I switch to rabbithole, and find a new Isgali fic! Not many people write Isga with Yrsali, and this story is only a thousand words, but it's excellent! I leave a squeeful comment then message my fellow isgababe far-oceans about it. No reply, which I guess is unsurprising as it's so early in their time zone.

But I'm still wound up so I switch logins to blackm00ds. It's weird, but these days I actually go looking for character hate as often as for cool stuff. During the Blip I used to block it, or try to, but rabbithole is such a mess that really blocking anything is difficult. Now blackm00ds intentionally seeks out the foe, and *smites*. Uskaar swinging his mighty hammer Vargsmittar has nothing on me.

And here we are: a juicy little post from some muppet whose username I recognise from a string of admittedly positive but brainless comments on Chel's fics.

castlekeep-blog.rabbithole.com
Monday 07:32

People say I hate on Isga but I'm just telling it like it is. She's a literal predator. She wants to suck our boys' blood! If you support murder, then I'm sorry, there's something wrong with you. 😷

🔨10:29 **blackm00ds:** You're not sorry. You just want to hurt people who like something you don't like. Rothgern's killed far more people than Isga, but you still lose your knickers over him.

I pause for a moment, then edit the comment to say 'skidmarked knickers'. And post.

Mic drop.

blackm00ds' actual blog is empty since I deleted the unfortunate poetry, and that strikes me as wrong somehow. So I do a post that just says, 'fuck you fuck you fuck you', about a thousand times. I'm not even that angry, just kind of compelled. Sometimes, lately, I wonder, *Who's doing this stuff?* Even while I'm doing it.

CHAPTER 5

When Chel comes out a whole hour later, I know the not-a-formal-session went well because Dr A is telling her, 'I think you'll be a strong candidate at interview,' and to remember to look into scholarship funds.

'Was it OK?' I demand. 'It sounded like it.'

'I think so!' Chel's so excited. And I love her so much. 'I'm not sure if it's allowed, but he showed me a bit of a first-year essay, and I could do that, I reckon! I love it here. I so wanna come here. I don't think I said "ain't" at all.'

Hm, if my father's in London, I wonder if he'd have any advice for her on how to get a toehold in the city?

Hang on, Chel's looking at me like she's got something else to say.

'Yan – why on earth d'you tell that daft old story and run off like that?' she asks.

Oh. 'Sorry. I got the giggles. You don't need me holding your hand, see? You were fine.'

'Yeah, I s'pose so. All right . . . I'll see the woman at UCL on me own. I don't want folk thinking I'm pathetic.'

'You are so not pathetic.' Except I do want to shout at her not to be so meek lately. 'We're just different. Come on, we're supposed to be meeting Kieran.'

We sit downstairs in the main foyer and wait for him.

My leg is twitching again. I tell it not to. In my head, I address it sternly as if it was betraying me of its own accord, which frankly it is. It obeys while I'm actually thinking directly about it, then rebels again when other thoughts muscle in. (Ha ha, *muscle*!) I want to go to St Martin's. Why doesn't the PI email?

'You're right. I really ain't pathetic,' says Chelsea firmly. Then she waves to Kieran as he comes through the revolving door with some other guy in tow. Is this one of the mates who're coming clubbing tomorrow?

'Hi,' he says – a solid but not exceptional opening. 'I'm Ras.'

'I'm Chel,' says Chel, as I conduct a rigorous overview of the newcomer. He's kind of stocky, with a sensitive-n-broody vibe going on – in fact, he looks like a darker-skinned, pimplier version of Chel's fave in that embarrassing boy band we might possibly have liked for five minutes when we were nine. He has a kind of clean, earnest look to him too, and I like his deep voice. I wonder if I should take this opportunity to practise chatting up London guys, but this question is quickly resolved when I see Chel's eyes bugging out of her head.

'This is Yan,' says Kieran. 'I bumped into Ras here and I invited him to join us so nobody else would have to put up with him for a bit.'

Ras makes a vaguely obscene gesture in Kieran's direction, but he's mostly looking at Chelsea.

Hmm. I'm busy eyeing her too, as she looks like she wants to grab more than lunch. This is quite a rare phenom. She's really pretty, but she's usually got no time for flesh-and-blood boys – too busy writing about fictional ones. She once snogged one of the non-moron guys in our class, who now hangs round at a distance, pining, and she did have a proper boyfriend last year, but I don't think they actually got down to it. She'd have told me. His main advantage was being one of the rich kids whose parents drive them to school so they don't have to get the bus – otherwise he was just a loser who smelled of pot.

'Oh my God, Ras is cute,' she mutters as we leave the building.

'Get in there!' I urge her, deliberately cheesy.

'OK,' says Chel, and nods. 'I'm gonna be impulsive.'

I'm not sure if it counts as being impulsive if you say it is, but I reckon this is part of the London experiment, so I'd better be supportive.

I give her a furtive thumbs up and she moves ahead to walk with Ras.

'Kier says you're here on a kind of college recce,' he says, as we head up a road that's as wide as a dual carriageway but lined with shops.

'Yes, just for a few days,' replies Chel in the same fancy voice she used on Dr A. 'I think I want to apply to do English at UCL.'

'That's what I'm doing.'

'You are?' Chel sounds so excited I wince slightly. 'Wow, that must be amazing. I've looked at all the London colleges online, and the first-year syllabus there is the best. I – well, I'm weighing my options.' Chel pauses, suddenly cool again.

'It's a lot of work,' says Ras. 'And I don't actually know what I think I'm going to do with a degree in English, but you've got to do what you love.'

'Aye!' says Chel; then clamps her mouth shut and blushes. But Ras doesn't seem to have noticed the Brocky moment, because he's busy nodding.

'Iwannabeanacademic,' Chel blurts.

Ras pushes his hair back from his forehead. 'Mum and Dad wanted me to be a doctor –'

I don't hear any more, because an ambulance is wailing and squawking its way down the road, the packed-in traffic trying to get out of its path. When it's gone, Kieran's talking to me.

'So how are you finding London?' he asks, as we watch a man in a grey suit bolt unwisely across the road and nearly get run down.

'Don't patronise me,' I snap, then smile quickly to show that I was joking. I fling my arms out. 'It's the capital! It's great! People! Buildings! Academics with troll collections on their desks! One had your beard on its head, but purple!'

'Really?' Kieran smooths the fur.

'Well, if you like beards, yours is a good one,' I concede, because I have manners. 'Anyway, I love London! Don't you?'

He cocks his head to one side then the other, considering. 'It's great if you don't mind the racket and pollution . . . Guess I take it for granted, living here.'

'Well, I won't! I want to do everything!' How could anyone not relish being here? 'Anyway, look, do we need to flank them so they don't walk into the road?' I point ahead to Chel and Ras.

'Yeah.' Kieran's boggling a bit. 'Not your nanny, like I said, but talk about getting straight in there! Last night she seemed like the quiet one. She's not beating around the bush today, is she?'

'She's kind of set fire to the bush,' I agree. 'That's usually my style, not hers.'

'Mm. Ras isn't generally that big on girls, either.'

'Oh, you mean he's gay? Or that he wanks five times a day but has no social skills?'

'No! Bloody hell, Yan.' He gives me a slightly odd look,

which I do not deign to notice. 'He's been known to have girlfriends. I just meant he's really into his course and works two jobs. He's with his family a lot, as well – they're close.' Kieran looks a bit wistful. 'Right – I'll get sandwiches, and we can take them to the square.'

He steers us all swiftly into a deli. I like him. I want to experiment further and see if his claim that he can cope with us really holds up.

Kieran takes our order and goes over to the counter while the rest of us lurk by the door.

While we're waiting, I listen to Chelsea and Ras for a while, then when there's a sudden silence, like they've both suddenly got self-conscious, I say blandly, 'You guys are getting on well.'

'Ras is doing cataloguing work at the UCL library this afternoon,' says Chel, sounding only marginally less excited than if she'd met someone off *Nordhelm*.

'I'm filling Chelsea in on the English course,' says Ras. He's got a faint accent I can't place, but it's nice. 'You two are from the West Country, by the sound of it?'

'Yeah . . . the north bit,' I say, suddenly aware of my accent. If he makes a Wurzels *oo-arr alroit moi luvver* crack, I'll smack him one. 'We just don't fancy staying there.'

'London is the place to be,' Ras replies earnestly. 'I've been here since I was little, and never get tired of it.'

'He's easily impressed,' Kieran puts in as he comes over with the sandwiches and we head out. 'He grew up in a cave in the Afghan mountains and escaped from the Taliban by riding across the desert on a donkey.'

'Cos your mum wouldn't give me a lift in the news helicopter,' says Ras, and gives him the finger.

Ah, bromance. I'd guess they go through that script about once a week.

'My grandparents came over in the Seventies,' I say to Ras. 'They opened a takeaway in Manchester. Then my mum was determined to get out of the city, and there's good bonus pay for nurses willing to work out in the arse-end of nowhere . . . So, yeah, me and Chel grew up in Brockford and this week is part of Operation Get the Hell Out.'

Ras nods sympathetically, but doesn't reply. I don't think he wants to talk about the alleged cave, and though I'm sometimes up for all-immigrants-together-even-if-I-am-third-generation-mixed bonding, I don't want to end up spilling my guts about my dad, so I manage to shut up for once.

Anyway, he's supposed to find Chel fascinating, not me.

I inspect my ham-and-pickle baguette – I skipped breakfast, so I've got room – and Kieran obviously tries not to inspect Chel and Ras too closely. I wonder if he's jealous. He hasn't got a girl/boy/whateva-friend, or if so he hasn't said.

I stare around: taxis, coffee chains, a pair of monks in orange robes who nobody seems to think are weird and – hey, a *single*-decker red bus.

'The poor thing!' I exclaim to Kieran. 'It's stunted! Or is it a baby?'

Kieran looks horrified until I explain I wasn't talking about some passer-by but a bus, which has by now gone around the corner. Then I tell him about the buses back home, which is actually a deeply boring subject, but I'm really struck by the colour differences and apparently have to tell someone.

A few minutes later we flop down onto the grass in a lawnified square the size of a small field but with fewer animal droppings, and Chel 'stumbles' onto Ras so that when she sits down it's rather close to him. Subtle, Chelsea. But Ras isn't running away. They're still yakking.

'Brockford is . . . nowhere,' Chel's saying. 'It's like mud. When you grow up in that sort of place, it's hard to pull out of, like. People want you to stay. I'm here to try, though.'

'Ah, you can do it,' Ras assures her. 'Families can be a pain. You should've heard my parents when I dropped Medicine.'

'Wow. That was brave of you.' Chel fiddles with her earring and gives a little half-smile. Though frankly I doubt they've got that much in common. Her family thinks nobody should achieve anything and his probably thinks he should win the Nobel.

I raise my voice to call to them, 'Yeah, she's all about being brave today.' I sound bitchy, but it *is* a little bit much, the way she's pretending to be impressed by – well, apparently actually *is* impressed by – some guy. This is supposed to be *our* trip.

Chel shoots me a hurt look; I mouth *Sorry*, because I am. Ish. She says to Ras, 'Is – is there really an eighteen-storey library here?'

'Yeah, that's Senate House, the central library. You've probably seen it used as Evil HQ in films,' confirms Ras. 'Um. Would you like to see it?'

'I – we're going to look at an art college for Yan this afternoon, and then the Globe,' replies Chel. 'But, er, yes! When I can.'

This moment is apparently so charged that Ras has to head for the nearby public toilet. I scoot across the grass, or rather sort-of hand/bum walk to avoid trashing my skirt, towards Chelsea. 'Way to put the moves on, I'm impressed,' I tell her. 'Though unless there's something you haven't told me, you've never actually got right into a guy's pants before. If you come on much stronger to this one, his head'll catch fire.'

It's not that I disapprove. I mean, I want to have sex at the first opportunity. But in spite of her fic, and three older brothers on the other side of a paper-thin bedroom wall, she's all about waiting and making it special. She likes to plan, my BFF does.

Usually.

Right now, she just scoffs.

'We're here to have a good time.'

'Yeah, but to you that usually means reading George Eliot.'

Another scoff. 'Ain't he cute? And smart. He reckons I'll get into UCL easily.'

'So he's brighter than Mrs Mayhew.' Our English teacher is nice enough, only she keeps saying Chel *is a very bright and hard-working girl*, but *you do understand London colleges are very selective*. 'Good. Just remember my mum got bowled over by a dark and glamorous mystery boy, and look what happened there.'

'That was completely different.'

'Well, yeah, all right. Look, you don't have to come to St Martin's with me this afternoon. They won't let you go on the tour anyway. You and him could . . .'

Chelsea bites her lip. 'Hey, I don't actually wanna run off with him. I just wanna go with the flow for once, like you do.'

'Too right. And I'm going to get properly started when we go clubbing, I promise. I'll kiss – four people. Maybe I'll go a bit further with one of them.'

Chelsea stares. 'That's . . . ambitious.'

'Well, I'm experienced. I was in a Proper Relationship

with Cameron from Year 12 for a week.' Though the circumstances of that are best left unremembered. 'And I kissed that girl in Bath, after that party.' For a couple of weeks I got a sort of flirty email thing going with dora_theroarer, another of the isgababes, too, but she's in Oregon and it petered out.

'Whatever, you loony.' Chel shakes her head. 'I do wonder what you're thinking about half the time lately.' Pause. When I don't reply, she says, 'Just leave me this one guy, OK?'

I roll my eyes as if she's being greedy. 'Oh, all right.'

Chel giggles. Then stares intently at the public toilet from which her heart-throb will emerge any moment.

I mock-flounce off, crab-style, on hands, feet and arse, to where Kieran is flat on his back, staring at the sky with his hand shading his eyes, still munching on a ciabatta, which is probably bad for life goals like not choking to death.

I lie nearby and resist the impulse to flail my legs around. This guy's presence is kind of weirdly restful, when I seem to be permanently buzzing my tits off.

Clouds drift across the sky, and if I tilt my head I can see grand old houses around the square, upside down. Maybe I've offended Kieran and he's ignoring me. Or maybe he's asleep. While eating. I can hear Chelsea and Ras again, but not what they're saying. There's a baby crying in a pram to my left, and a bunch of twenty-something blokes in suits on some benches to my right. One of them thinks he's just clinched the best deal ever. Apparently, he sells pencils.

Kieran finishes his lunch and looks at me sideways without really turning his head. I think he's about to speak but I get there first. 'So what's your mum and dad's deal? Are they in your face all the time?'

'Not *all* the time,' he says. 'Ah, they're less evil than some. But they want me to follow in my brothers' footsteps – win awards for dentistry, like Matt. Life goals, eh?'

'I could do with a cash prize even if you couldn't. But you want to save the whole wide world. How come you're not wearing biodegradable cardboard pants?'

'Cos they're uncomfortable and dissolve in the rain. Anyway, recycling your bottles and all that stuff's good so far as it goes, but it doesn't help that much. Most environmental damage is done by businesses.' Suddenly he sounds really animated, starting to talk faster. 'And you get to *them* by mobilising online, showing them that people notice what they're up to and that it'll cost them. I can send you some links if you're interested.' Just as he's getting going, he pauses. 'Though I bet you're actually not.'

'Huh . . .' I *want* to be interested . . . It's just that stuff whooshes through my brain so fast. Weirdly, though, it's actually easier talking to Kieran than to Chel right now. I tip my broad-brimmed hat over my face so I suddenly can't see anything but yellow light. 'I bet they tell you things can only change slowly.' That's my mum's approach when it comes to getting the hundredth-generation Brockies to accept someone called Biyu.

'Ohhh yeah,' he says, then parrots in an obvious mimic. 'Be realistic, Kieran! Become a lawyer or a journalist or a civil servant – or all three at once! – Kieran. Get inside, be patient, change things slowly.'

'Uh-huh. I hear that. Bleh.' I drum my heels on the ground a couple of times. I'm actually being unfair to Mum. My grandparents, who run a takeaway and scrimped and saved so Mum and my Uncle Liko could get on in life, pretty much disowned her when she dropped out of doctor training. They only got in touch with her again when Uncle Liko became an eye surgeon, and successful enough to soothe the family pride.

I just feel like *everything*'s restricting me right now.

'Do you think I'm mental?' I suddenly ask, into the warm, stuffy air filtering through the woven straw over my face. Inside the crown, I can see a tiny hitch where I messed up the weave. 'At home, people say I'm mental cos I'm loud.' And, all right, because I was actually depressed for a bit. And want to be a vampire mer-woman, though I don't tell everyone about that. 'And also because I'm obsessed with hats. It's not like they're a vital part of modern life.'

'It's a bit of a leap from "hats" to "mental". Chase your dreams, that's what I say. My ex was at dance school, you don't get more impractical than that.'

'Yeah. Even if I get Fs on everything and St Martin's art college says my portfolio looks like a drunk did it, I'm moving to London.'

Kieran snorts. 'You've got a way with words.'

These days I have.

My phone buzzes.

AAAAAaaaaaaHHH!

I scrabble madly for it . . . and see a spam text from the phone company. I'm irritated, and irritated at myself for being irritated. I shove my phone back into my bag, but now there's a message sound –

12:54 Mum: Good luck, sunshine girl xxx

Argh. I love her, but I just want to hear from the PI. They'll probably email, but what if they call? I could call them; except I need to avoid drawing attention to me not actually being the owner of the credit card I paid with.

Why are my thoughts all over the place?

I must concentrate. I think Kieran said something, and I should reply . . .? But I've no idea what he was talking about.

'We'll be late!' I snap, and jump to my feet.

'No, we won't,' protests Kieran lazily, peering up at me from the ground. Chel and Ras are still eating. Slowly. I think he's making her a map of the Globe auditorium with bits of twig. I guess he's got a certain charm.

'I want to be at St Martin's early,' I tell Kieran.

'We're only half an hour's walk away. Look, we'll go in fifteen, OK?' He lies back, pillowing his head on his arms, revealing armpit hair like mini versions of the beard.

Apparently, I have to accept this. I check my make-up in my pocket mirror. It's as good as it can be, considering the temperature's about a million degrees even in the shade and the moment I start moving I'm going to melt into a puddle with a lacy skirt and a straw hat floating on top. I'm so antsy I wish I could insist on going alone, but I can't do that to Chel.

So I wait. I am martyred. The air itself is the scorching Breath of Ethraig. I am stretched upon the rack of time beneath the blazing sun of wrath.

Not much of Kieran's fifteen minutes is left when Ras scrambles up. 'I'm going to be late for work,' he says regretfully.

Kieran cranes to look up at him. 'Are you joining us tomorrow night?' he asks. 'Zippers, for Uma's birthday? She's laid-back enough to put up with you tagging along.'

Boys.

Ras hesitates for a moment. I get the distinct impression clubs aren't really his thing. But Chel is gazing up at him . . .

I expect him to come back with something cool and blokey, but instead he says, 'Yeah, sure,' with genuine and clearly Chelsea-fuelled enthusiasm. 'I can swap shifts at the bar.'

Then he throws a long look at Chel. She nods and lies back casually, then kind of leans up on her elbow to watch him go, and he looks back and sees it, and cue general awkwardness combined with puffs of hormones as thick as school kitchen steam.

Once Ras is gone, I grab Chel's arm and haul her up off the grass, and mutter, 'He's so into you.'

I expect her to demur, but instead she actually looks a bit smug. Now we're both giggling.

Then I think: *St Martin's*.

'Forward!' I declare grandly.

Kieran comes up behind me, takes my shoulders, and gently turns me around. 'Better chance of being on time if we go in the right direction, Yan.'

CHAPTER 6

There's rows and rows of little fountains in front of the huge converted warehouse that is Central St Martin's College. Through the middle there's a path, and as I walk up it a strange thing happens: all the fountains stop, and then start leaping and falling together like they're beating time. A drumroll!

An admin-type lady in a green skirt so unfashionable it's probably *de rigueur* on Neptune comes and takes the names of the half-dozen people in the tour group. She is our leader.

'What do you hope to get out of today?' the Neptunian asks us, while we're checking each other out. I'm not sure if other potential students are competition or allies. One girl says she's a potter – clearly not a rival, then. I like the conviction in her voice, too. Her hands are all calloused and she's got clay down the sides of her roughened nails and doesn't seem to mind. She's got a gauzy pink top – and, when we stand together waiting for the turnstile, I can see through it; she's got raised lines on the dark brown skin of her arms – scars, the deliberate kind, some of them pretty recent. OK, I've never done that . . . But maybe it means my me-ness wouldn't bug her out, especially as she's obviously confident enough to not hide herself.

'Cool top,' I say, and try to smile in a way that explains what else I mean. I think she gets it. 'Hi! I'm Yan.'

'I'm Abena,' she says. 'I love your style.' She points at the lace on my pocket that's the same as the brim of my hat. She noticed! Nice eye for detail.

Nice melty brown actual eyes, too. Ooh!

'I . . .' I stop myself from saying I'm sure I'd love everything she makes, because that would be stupid. I can't pull *here*.

I look up instead. St Martin's is a canyon of light, pouring through the glass roof. The space above us is criss-crossed with walkways. You can see the structure of the old warehouse in places: bare brick, scrubbed and worn little wooden tiles.

Neptunian Tour Lady tells us that there are no undergraduates here right now, just summer schools. Up the stairs we go, and warrens of corridors open into silent metalwork, woodwork or pottery studios. Abena spins around to examine a gleaming clay tree, its sculpted grey surfaces waiting for colour, and finger-smeared tubs of glaze. We tunnel through the centre of a jewellery summer class. Metallic screeching comes from a room behind a glass wall, and I see a girl in protective goggles leaning into her work, with spray bottles and tools on a desk behind her. What's she making?

Beyond her there's a store of canvasses stacked like hanging files, and a huge half-finished painting of a blue-tinged naked body that looks oddly like the Jaarv Navigator is leaning against the wall. There's an actual textiles library here, with a thousand different materials each dangling from its own little hook, rough and scratchy and woven or squishy in the hand, purple silk and eggbox things and slick sheets whose names I don't know until I read the little labels. Already we have to move on. There's a paper library with every back issue of *Vogue* in a fancy binding.

'Does the St Martin's fashion course give you a good general grounding?' asks a girl who's with her ancient father, noisily weighing up an Art degree versus a safer option (looking at him, I'd guess he wants her to be either an accountant or . . . another kind of accountant). The Neptunian's roboting out a polite stock response when I interrupt: 'I need to choose between Fashion Design here or Fashion Design with Millinery at London School of Fashion – but I can't.' It comes out really loud. I put my hand over my mouth. Everyone looks.

'Everyone here starts with the Foundation Course,' says the Neptunian tolerantly.

I know that but it's so slow . . . And the tour is short but also slow, and the people on it are slow. I do not want to see the damn lockers. We make it, at last, to the fashion studio, where there's bales and reams of cloth and a clutter of ribbon and wool still spread over two tables in the white-beige space, and dozens of dummies with lightbulb-shaped bumps for heads. There's dresses on a rack, and I hold one up to the skylight radiance; it's a blue-checked scoop-neck design that would suit white-n-rosy Chel. I finger it. I catch Abena's eye – she's examining the wood of a loom – and for a moment I feel like we understand each other completely, while not being sure what I understand. I like it. I'm irritated by it. It's not what I'm here for! I want to make friends. But not now. Everything's too much. I turn away.

'Hey, don't touch the students' work,' grumbles the Neptunian, removing the dress from my hands. She doesn't notice me pinching a roll of thread from an open box and shoving it into my pocket as a talisman. Finally, an older woman strides past us, wearing an intense, pinched expression and a long, pleated turquoise-and-indigo skirt. Faculty. She doesn't look at us. She doesn't stop and offer me a scholarship on the spot. If I touch the floor with my fingers, maybe I could root myself into the building. Or burrow into a bale of fabric or seep into the paintings downstairs and not leave. Who could go crawling back to Brockford after this? Lace and felt and form and colour will flow through me. Ground me here.

Why exactly am I this excited? Sometimes Mum says to me, 'They're just hats.' Of course they're just bloody hats; only I . . . want. Hats have shape, and so the energy is channelled, and doesn't burst and break.

Here, behind a glass door, is a room full of students making hats.

We get to stare for about five seconds while the Neptunian exclusively reveals that this is the millinery studio, and a summer school is in progress so we may not enter, and the tour is almost complete anyway – blah blah blah. She leads us on. But I duck back down the corridor and peer through the glass door again.

There's a woman with a blond ponytail and a blue designer overall in here, teaching. It's Kathy Maynard; I recognise her from *Hat* magazine! She's quite ordinary to look at and has a bumpy mole on her nose but she goes by the name KayEm and her recent 'Outré' collection is beautiful weirdness rendering the military helmet as transformative art. Right now, though, she's teaching basic stuff. Three women and two men are slowly and incompetently stitching or cutting or despairing over their own work. Looking at the mess they've made, there's good reason for the despair. I should go back to the tour group and make sure I get to say goodbye to Abena . . . Instead, I burst into the studio. It's like some external force is driving me. Again.

'I'm Yan,' I announce, and point to my straw hat with its dyed weave and tiny chains. 'I made this. Can I sit in for a bit?'

KayEm appears surprised, but she takes a good look at my hat. Her dough-faced students stop destroying their materials and stare too.

'This is a closed class,' she says, and pushes a stray bit of hair out of her face.

I need Chel here to smile persuasively and make it clear that I am funny and charismatic and not alarming.

'I'm enrolled for next year on the Foundation Course. Then I'm going to specialise in millinery. I just want to watch,' I say. Come on, Kathy. You're a daring artist who should support exciting new talent. 'I'm not in town for long.'

'Well – OK,' says KayEm, pointing to a chair in the corner. She's got a nice smile, and her eyes look tired, and she's wearing too many necklaces, but I like her. I sit and look around at the hundreds of hat blocks on the shelves, in subtle ranging shades with varnished wood all whorled and worn smooth. The nearest woman's making a hash of stitching on a brim. Her hat block looks better bald than it will when she puts that monstrosity on it. I jump up and go over.

'Hold the needle like this,' I explain, taking it out of her hands. She's surprised. I demonstrate a proper stitch. Now she's annoyed . . . Screw that. I'm helping you, you daft old bat!

KayEm comes over. 'OK – Jan, is it?' she says. 'Are you after my job?'

She sounds mostly amused. I want to tell her yes, because clearly this lot could learn plenty from me. 'Sorry,' I say. Then, 'It's *Yan*.'

She looks appraisingly at my straw hat again, then reaches up to gently finger the brim, where I wove in the thread of blue. 'You've got talent and your own style, if not much sense of the orthodox,' she says. 'Well, that never got anyone anywhere worth going.' She laughs at her own words and says, 'Have you got a portfolio?'

Yes, indeed I do! I whip out my phone and show her pictures of my hats. I babble about my favourites. I'm talking too much. I'm a motormouth. A shoutermouth.

'Mm,' says KayEm, paying close attention. I'm agog. *Praise me, now!* But all she says is, 'OK. You're a bit over-excited, but I remember being your age. This is not the place for a chat, however.' Indeed, students are giving me dirty looks, as I steal their learning time. 'How about you come along to my studio in a couple of days?' She consults a little diary. 'Wednesday at one?'

AAAAAAAAHHHHHHHHH! I can hardly breathe. What's she inviting me for? Is she going to hire me as her assistant? No, she'll just want to give me maternal pointers. Adults do that. Maybe I can talk my way into something. Maybe I can't. I can do anything! It's a start.

'Yes!' I say, and take the business card she holds out to me. 'I tont to wy and –' Damn it, I'm so excited my words are coming out wrong again. 'I mean, I want to try and –'

But one of her students comes shuffling up with a question. It's probably a stupid one, but I'd better not interfere. I should go. The Neptunian will be cross that I've run off . . . Like that bothers me, but Chel and Kieran will be wondering too, and I do care about that; more than I would have expected. I must be driving them mad. I really need to slow down.

Today I met that academic I told you guys about last week. I know some people said I should talk to him about writing fic but in the end I didn't. I think that's the right choice. It was far more likely to turn an old guy against me than impress him.

He took me seriously when I talked about becoming an academic, and it felt amazing. 😎

Right now, me and Cousin K are waiting for bitey to come back from a college tour. (I'm drinking something called a triple mocha latte that K bought me. It's . . . interesting.) I've had a bit of time to think, and I'm wondering what I should write after 'Spirit of Fire'.

I love writing Uskaar as a softy who melts Rothgern's hard heart. Like everyone says, Uskaar might have a really big hammer, but he never actually kills anyone unless they attack him, and he doesn't steal from people who are penniless. In 'Low Tide' he gave his loot to that poor family, for example.

But there's only so many things a writer can do with those characterisations. Uskaar brought the Jaarv to Nordhelm in the first place to pillage it, and we know they terrorised the coast further south before that. And in canon, Rothgern's characterisation can be a bit wobbly depending on the scriptwriters. Sometimes he's just a tyrant, other times he's a sharp operator who'll do anything 'good' or 'bad' to keep the kingdom running.

That might be a starting point for something a bit different . . .? Darker . . .? I could go with a hard-hearted Uskaar, and a Rothgern who's really pragmatic. And how about they both stayed that way, rather than getting romantic? That would be kind of interesting in the bedroom (rigging, keep, dungeon . . .) and when it came to psychological stuff. I could put some Isgali in the fic too, for bitey.

Oh, she's coming back over.

Chapter 7

As I cross onto a high walkway heading for the stairs down to the exit, I'm physically slowing down.

My mood is plunging like a lead balloon.

I can work out where the address on Kathy Maynard's card is later; if I dare. I've made a fool of myself, charging around like a tomte on spiked porridge, running away from the tour guide.

The Neptunian is down in the sterile central foyer now, glaring at me. (Everyone else is gone, thankfully including Abena.) When I get to her, I lie that I needed the toilet. She leads me to the turnstile, checking me over in case I'm hiding a stolen sewing machine in my handbag.

'How was it?' demands Chel as soon as I'm in earshot. She and Kieran are sitting on stools in a fancy student coffee place that's part of the entrance to the building.

'Uh, lots to see,' I say.

'But you liked it? You still want to come here?' Chel persists.

'Yes, of course, I just need time to process.' I walk out of the building, so she and Kieran have to follow. I really don't want to talk about it. I was like a hyper toddler in there – and now I want to kill someone, if only I could be bothered. It's like I'm itching on the inside of my skin, and

I can't scratch because people are looking at me.

'You didn't scare anyone by Yanning at them?' asks Chel. When I don't respond, she says, 'How was the millinery studio?'

'Leave me alone just for a bit, OK?' I snap. I don't need to be humoured. The sun is trying to set fire to us as we trudge past hoardings and road cones and men in hi-vis jackets.

'Fine.' Chelsea's staring at me. She says to Kieran, 'Ignore her, she's in grumpy-guts mode. It happens sometimes.'

I am not *depressed!* I mouth at her, but she looks puzzled then has to pay attention to Kieran when he says something to her.

I don't bother pointing out that she's channelling her mum with the 'grumpy-guts mode' comment, I just half-listen to her and Kieran talking. He's on about a family holiday to the Maldives that was apparently unsatisfactory in some way. It doesn't seem to register with him that it sounds like complaining about having to spend a fortnight in heaven.

I trudge. Kieran is now telling Chel about the dinner-n-choral concert Aunt Julie's taking us to later in the week, to wash our brains out with official culture or something. Choral music. Thrilling. I mean, *Hallelujah, hallelujah, hallelujah* . . . Oh, guess what the next word is?

'It'll be interesting, won't it, Yan?' Chel suddenly asks. 'Yan?'

I check my email so I can pretend I haven't heard.

There's one from the PI.

I almost drop my phone down a hole in the pavement. (Why is London ninety per cent roadworks?)

The email says . . . there's been a problem with the credit card I used to pay for the investigation, and they can't proceed until that's sorted out.

Disaster.

Mum must have checked her online statement and queried the transaction.

Yet I expected it, didn't I? Really?

That explains why I started feeling so crap – I knew this was coming.

At least Mum can't have guessed it was me. But what am I going to do now?

We will be happy to restart the process if you're able to provide alternative credit card details or a cash payment at our head office, says the email.

Huh. Cash in person.

When I got a random inspiration and looked into this last week, I discovered private investigating is a lot more mundane in real life than in the movies. You find a website, tell them who you're after and they do a basic search for a flat fee. I just pretended to be Mum on the phone and read out her Visa number. It was as simple as that.

But I do not have an alternative credit card. I do not have three hundred pounds in cash.

Though could I maybe get the cash? Borrow it from Chel's relations? Then I'd have to tell them why I need it . . . Fat chance they'd agree.

Oh God. Maybe I should just forget it. Maybe this is a lucky escape. What the hell did I think I was going to do, waltz into Dad's kitchen accompanied by a soap-opera soundtrack? Whatever he's doing now, he doesn't want me. It's many years since I stopped thinking that Mum was the meanie and he was the fun one, except when he had his moods.

When he was depressed.

Even if he doesn't live in London any more, I have to know one thing: that he's alive.

Suicide runs in families.

If he . . . *that*, then maybe it would actually be worse to find out.

Kieran's debating with himself where to get fish and chips. We walk down another half-dozen sun-blasted, overcrowded streets. Chel's going on about how we must visit the British Museum on our last day here. Thinking of the sheer amount of junk rammed in a place like that – half of it blatantly stolen from other countries – makes me exhausted. I give robotic answers when she asks if I want to see a costume exhibition there.

Chelsea looks at me more and more oddly and I want to shout at her that *this isn't my bloody fault – I can't help it . . .*

But what is 'it'? The disappointment about the PI, surely. I can't go into that, not with Kieran here.

Luckily Chelsea's distracted by a message from Ras; apparently they swapped details. She informs us that he says it was nice to meet her, and blushes up to the roots of her hair.

'Yeah, it's great, he's into you,' I tell her. 'Really great!'

I do care. I just . . .

It doesn't matter what my problem is, I have to stop harshing my BFF's squee. Maybe I'm getting a summer cold. I say the weather is tiring me out, which is entirely believable. The sun finally goes behind the clouds, offering a bit of relief, and Kieran takes us onto a footbridge across the Thames. There's a railway bridge next to it. Trains rumble across. Tourists take selfies.

I stop halfway across the river, kind of stalling inside. Staring at the grey-blue water that flows and flows, with a billion ripples, all the same; exhausting.

'There's a nice breeze up here,' says Chelsea, walking

nearer to me. Kieran tactfully doesn't follow; it's like they've slipped into some Yan-management system by Fursian instinct. Do they think I can't see? 'Look – are you all right?'

'I . . . barged into a millinery class,' I finally admit. 'It was Kathy Maynard. I got a bit in her face; maybe too much. I showed her my portfolio.'

'Wow! KayEm!' exclaims Chel, who's looked through my copies of *Hat* magazine enough to know a few names. What she doesn't say is, 'Oh no, I'm sure you didn't make an idiot of yourself,' because we both know I did. 'You, well, like you've said, it's no good being a shrinking violet if you wanna get on in life.'

'She gave me her card and said I should visit her on Wednesday.' I pull it out of my pocket.

'Yan, that's amazing! We can go after we've seen Goldsmiths.'

'It's *not* amazing,' I snap. A child pushes between us, chased by his father, so luckily Chel doesn't see my sneer. Just in time, I get my face straightened out. Back in that giant greenhouse I thought it was amazing, yeah, but really – what's the actual bastard point? Who except me and the queen wears any kind of hat except woolly ones in winter? And Chel once said KayEm's designs look like putting shoes on your head.

Sort it out, Yan. There's only one thing that would make you more of an idiot, and that's taking this mood out on your best friend. 'There's a lot happening,' I say. 'I'm trying to let it sink in.' Is that the problem? All of it? I haven't felt this crap since the Blip. But I'm not flat on my back in bed now, dreaming of death. I just feel kind of tensed up with indifference.

Chel laughs. 'Aye. *So* much happening,' she says, and

happily feigns a kick at one of the mad-eyed London pigeons. 'I love it!'

Apparently my personality's defected to her for the afternoon. She's welcome to it.

A few feet from us, Kieran's messaging again, and grinning. Planning something.

'Some of the Eco crowd are going to a protest tonight,' he says. 'Course, I couldn't possibly leave you all alone, after I promised Mum . . . but I did wonder if maybe you'd rather catch your Shakespeare with Ras?'

Chel's face lights up. 'Yeah! Cool! I mean . . . if he's not too busy, with two jobs?'

'Well, that lot are always trading shifts,' Kieran says. He's already messaging again. 'Rashid says,' Kieran informs us in an arch tone a moment later, 'that he saw *A Midsummer Night's Dream* last month, but he could cope with seeing it again.'

Now Chel's eyes are sparkling.

'He's a great guy,' Kieran continues, looking slightly amused. 'I've known him since sixth form – he was on a scholarship. His parents are both doctors, but they had to give all their money to the people smugglers, then work as cleaners and build up from nothing. The whole family's super-smart.' Kieran sighs.

Chel's eye-sparkle intensifies. I feel sick.

But anything that keeps her happy – and occupied – is fine with me. We spend some time – who knows how long – staring at various buildings, then get burgers (I surreptitiously drop half of mine in the river), and, by the time Ras pitches up, there are crowds moving towards the Globe, with us among them. I grab my phone and stick my nose into the comments on Chel's last post so as not to interfere with their bonding.

🎮16:05 **vikinghusbands:** We're proud of you, girl. I'm sure that academic didn't deserve your truth. Stay with the people who understand you best. 🙈

🏧16:19 **ships-kitty:** So true!

🎰16:29 **lyssapeeps:** Yeah, toes, go for it! Wherever your heart takes you. 😉 I'll read anything you write.

🍶17:01 **far-oceans:** Yeah, you probably made the right call. That guy might have been chill about the fic, but he might not. (And triple mocha latte is god tier, is what it is.) I'm loving your fic idea. DM me if you want to bounce more ideas around, especially for an Isgali storyline.

🍶17:22 **tastyriceballs:** toes, have you read my new fic? Throne for Two.

🎮18:31 **vikinghusbands:** OK *deep breath* I'm sorry for the comment-spam, and I understand that you're not replying because you don't want to waste your precious London time. But I had to come back and say this, because it's been niggling at me. You say you want to write 'darker' fic – I've been slightly concerned over some of the comments you've been getting on your stories, from people who want you to pander to their kinks and unhealthy ways of looking at the characters and their relationships. You're allowed to keep writing the stories and the characters in a way that is comfortable and safe for you.

🍶18:32 **far-oceans:** Er, by 'people' do you mean me by any chance?

🎮18:32 **vikinghusbands:** Amongst others, yes. You have to realise that many fans are much younger than you, and be responsible. I saw your post about your favorite kinks.

18:33 **far-oceans**: Yeah. It was under a cut. With a 'no-under-18s' sign slapped on it.

18:33 **vikinghusbands:** I'm sure toes read it anyway. That's what teenagers do.

18:34 **far-oceans:** Bitch, that is my fault how?

18:35 **vikinghusbands:** Teens shouldn't be subjected to that kind of temptation.

18:36 **far-oceans:** Temptation to do what? Teenagers are going to go out and abuse octopodes because I recced some tentacle porn??

18:38 **ships-kitty:** Thank you for protecting us, @vikinghusbands!

18:41 **tammyisadisaster:** come on! i can choose not to click on a link like i can choose not to raid my mom's wine stash (though I wouldn't do that cuz its foul lmao)

OK, this is not great. I love far-oceans, they're like my and Chel's fandom big sibling, though they're in the USA (they're a marine biologist and might get a research trip to Southampton one day – fingers crossed). I should defend them, and definitely defend Chel, against vikinghusbands, who thinks cleaning up fandom is her mission. Which pretty much misses the entire point, IMO.

But my brain won't start. My fingers won't move.
Whatever.

CHAPTER 8

Am I feeling better, or have I just acclimatised to the spiky fog rolling around my head? I still feel like my brain's vibrating, and, for some reason, my left hand has clenched up. I unclench it. As soon as I forget about it, I realise I've done it again. But I don't stare at it accusingly, because that would be mental. I stare at the Globe theatre instead. It's an almost exact reconstruction of the one that burned down in Shakespeare's time, only presumably this one is fireproofed.

From outside, it looks more like a cake or a weird cloche hat than a theatre. Once we're through the gates and the archways, though, we're standing in the little sawdusty circle with the galleries all around, as American tourists shuffle in to join us, squinting at the sky, which luckily is clear. I've got a plastic bag to protect my hat, but it'll hardly be enough if there's a downpour.

Ras is telling Chel about Persian literature in translation, quoting in two languages. She's nodding along, deeply interested, eyes wide. She does that a lot with people, but you can tell when she's faking because her cheek tenses up and twitches. Right now her jaw is almost slack. It's kind of adorable.

Ras is moving onto Shakespeare. 'The original Globe

was built in 1598. This is the groundling pit, where all the commoners stood – well, I'm sure you know that – and heckled the actors, and chucked orange peel and nutshells at the stage. Poor people sometimes went to the theatre a couple of times a week because there wasn't much else to do.'

'It's like people sitting down for *Corrie* or *EastEnders* every night,' reasons Chel. 'Except . . . that's a bit – well, soaps aren't broadening their horizons, I suppose.'

'You want to talk about broadening horizons?' says Ras. 'Shakespeare gets credit for adding hundreds of words to the English language, and maybe he genuinely added some, but a lot of it was introducing existing working-class vernacular to a wider audience.'

'That makes sense,' says Chel. Her eyes go sparkly sparkle spark.

Ras sounds a bit like he's quoting from an essay, but I'll give him a pass because it's interesting. I believe he's actually as geeky as Chel, which is just not a thing she gets from Brockford boys. He's probably not used to nerd-girls as conventionally pretty as she is, either. Though looking at her now, I can't help seeing she looks, I dunno, definitely working class. Maybe her ponytail's scraped back too tight? Above those searching eyes she's got, and the half-cardigan. Nerd-chav fusion, that's her look.

Now Chel and Ras are talking about the possible inspirations behind Shakespeare's conception of Puck.

'Sounds like the tomtar!' I interject when they start talking about folklore goblins. 'These mental *Nordhelm* pixies with blue-and-orange hair – well, copper, really . . .' But Chel doesn't seem glad of my contribution, for all that it supplies a convenient opportunity for her to start talking about her writing and thus impress him, so I shut up and stare around. Everything's made of wood, of course, white or deep brown with a hint of red, and all that real thatch up on the roof. I love the galleries, with the steep benches going almost round the back of the stage. People further in front of us in the groundling pit are actually leaning their arms on the stage. The sky overhead is doing that weird thing where it's perfect blue but shading to grey and somehow manages to look heavy, even though you can't see any clouds.

I tune in when Chelsea's voice turns a bit tentative and she asks, 'Anyway, Ras, have you put yourself out, just for us? I mean, this were – was completely last minute, and you must be busy.'

Ras shrugs, a bit too carelessly if you ask me. He totally did it just for us – as in, just for Chel. 'People at the bar will always swap shifts if you take on a weekend for them.'

'Oh, OK, that's good.'

'Everyone's busy at uni, you learn to juggle stuff,' Ras explains.

'Oh. Yeah, I can imagine that,' says Chelsea. 'Yeah.'

Really profound conversation.

This is getting yawnsome. They need to have a more meaningful exchange to deepen the bond they are forging. It's my duty as BFF to get that to happen. And I know exactly how! He's the perfect person to persuade her to study what she really wants to study . . .

'Chel needs to keep time for her writing, though,' I say.

'Yan!' Chel exclaims.

'You write?' asks Ras.

'I – a bit,' Chel says, blushing. Liar, liar, major conflagration taking place in pants! She's got about half a million words of mad popular *Nordhelm* fic out there. 'My writing is – personal.'

'She could study Creative Writing,' I suggest. 'It's a course at UCL, right, Ras?'

Chelsea actually jumps, then laughs nervously. 'Yan, I really ain't . . . No. I don't write that much.'

Ras can see she's uncomfortable. He clears his throat and says, 'I'm a poet myself. But I won't bore you with that.'

Oh no, what have I done? That is surely the prelude to him boring us for the rest of the evening. But now *he* looks awkward.

'I'm definitely interested,' says Chel.

Well, I'm not.

'I like Sylvia Plath,' I announce. Then I go on, because he can probably cope with something not completely English, 'And Xiaolu Guo, though she's not a poet as such but her *Twenty Fragments of a Ravenous Youth* is, well, fragments. And it's about getting the hell out of the countryside to follow your artistic calling, and getting a boyfriend . . .' I side-eye Chel, then remember the said fictional boyfriend is a violent nutter, and stop.

'I like that one too,' says Chel.

Ras hesitates, then nods. 'Yeah. Write the name down for me, Yan? I'd like to read it.'

CHAPTER 9

Instead of a rainstorm, just before the play finishes, we get a spectacular free lightning show, the whole sky flickering above twilit purple clouds. People stare at it instead of clapping. The air's full of ozone and a little taste of autumn, and as soon as the encores are over, we *run*. We just make it under the stone-carved entrance to 'LONDON BRIDGE UNDERGROUND' when the rain really comes pouring down. People giggle and shove in around us, chattering. Then Chel and Ras lean back against a wall to get out of everyone's way, and look at each other. *Oho*.

'I think the portrayal of Puck was overdone,' says Ras.

'Oh, I dunno, I like that level of physicality in a performance. I couldn't tell the difference between the courtiers, mind,' says Chel. 'But that seemed to be the point in this interpretation.'

'It's in the original text. The rustics are individuated while the courtiers represent a class,' says Ras.

Their eyes meet, and . . . an old guy grumpily shoves between them because they've pushed away from the wall to stare at each other and are now blocking the way.

Ras suddenly looks extremely self-conscious, turns on his heel and heads for the escalator.

At the bottom, we stop by a big sign with arrows pointing left and right.

'I'm getting the Northern line,' says Ras. 'You need to go down there for the Jubilee line.'

'Oh,' says Chel. 'Yes. Yes. I see.' She nods like his interpretation of the sign was Shakespeare-level insight.

He really hasn't mastered pulling, has he?

'Invite her home with you!' I say.

That gets them unified. They're both staring at me in horror. Come on, guys, you want to shag! I want you to shag, and how cool would it be?

'You really should make a move on her right now,' I advise Ras. 'That guy over there is winking at her.' Actually he's just rubbing his eye, but it feels like time for an intervention.

'*What?*' demands Chel, looking aghast. There's a moment's silence, then she relaxes a bit. 'Oh – God, Yan, you meant *winking*.'

'That's what I said.'

'Er – no you didn't,' corrects Chel, with a strained grin.

Ras's eyes are fixed on his trainers.

'I did not say "wanking"!' I protest. Except when I play the words back in my head, I realise I did. 'It was a slip of the tongue. Who cares?' Except I suppose I trashed a tender moment there.

'No – look – no. No,' Chel continues, to me, to Ras and possibly to the world in general. Oh dear.

Silence. This is getting dull.

'You're coming clubbing with us tomorrow night, yes?' says Ras finally.

'Yes!' agrees Chel, all relieved smiles.

'You can't chat in a club,' I point out.

Ras nods, with an expression that says he's determined

to forge on in spite of me. Rude! 'I'd love to continue this conversation . . . Oh, but you're visiting UCL tomorrow, aren't you? I'm working in the library, job work, I mean, but the hours aren't set exactly, as long as I get everything done. I can take a break to show you around.'

Ooh, nice one. Chel agrees eagerly and they make the necessary arrangements before she hurries me off as if I'm the one who wants to linger.

'Er, whoops! Sorry about the winky-wanky thing,' I say, as we walk towards the westbound Jubilee line platform. 'It's just, I can see you really like him.'

'Yeah, well, you couldn't help misspeaking. But maybe sometimes you could *not* speak? What are you playing at?'

I consider that question. It's a bit harsh by her standards, but maybe not unfair lately.

'Well, I ain't gonna be angry,' says Chelsea as we jog down a short, echoey staircase, 'because we're having a good time, and I'm not going to spoil it.' She pauses. 'God, I sound so much like Mum.'

'So what?' I really do want to be supportive.

The train comes almost immediately, and I skip aboard and spin around a yellow pole: *whee!* The Tube's not so rammed at this time of night as it is in the daytime.

Chel's still talking, half to herself. 'We're in London, we need to make the most of it.'

'Exactly!' I agree. I'm going to be a good Yan now. 'Enjoy your instant cup-a-romance!' Especially as I'll be stealing all the hot guys at the club.

'Charming description,' says Chel, but she's reluctantly grinning.

A woman gets on the train and I nearly whack her *en* circular *route* round the pole as I chant, 'Do it, do it, do it, do it, do it, do it, do it!'

Chel gives me a long stare. 'A few months ago you was flat on your back droning like a robot, and now you're babbling so fast your words come out wrong.'

Yeah, well, a few months ago I wanted to die. Let's not focus on that. 'Cheat!' I say. 'We're talking about you, not me. So, is Ras really as clever as you? He can regurgitate stuff he's read, but what if his poetry's awful? Do you like his arse? Did you see he's got Poe from *Star Wars* on his phone case? Maybe he knows more about fandom than he lets on, not that you even properly told him. Can he give you interview tips?'

Chel looks a bit stunned for a moment, but then starts answering most if not all of my questions. The term 'intellectual wavelength' comes up, and we suddenly discover that *Star Wars* episodes seven through nine are a nuanced critique of contemporary masculinity and not 'boring' as she pronounced them when she borrowed her cousin's DVDs and I low-key pretended to be Rey until she gave up and turned on her laptop to write.

'And he must be so brave, escaping a war zone!' she concludes dreamily. 'On a donkey!'

'Ah yes, a donkey.' I think of the flea-bitten specimens in the field near my house. 'They're essential for romance.'

Chel tries not to smile, and fails.

Earlier this year, when I was, to put it in medical terms, completely screwed, Chel sat there in my room's window seat writing and doing her revision. If I wanted her, there she was, and if I didn't, she sensed it and left without me needing to say.

I *have* to be a good friend to her now.

CHAPTER 10

When we get back to the Swiss Cottage mansion, Aunt Julie is on the stairs, turning the corner from the landing just as Chel's foot hits the bottom step. She's wearing an actual silk kimono, and slippers with a flowery pattern that wouldn't be entirely out of place on Chelsea's mum.

Chel, who's been half asleep since we got off the Tube, jumps like a tomte bit her on the bum. We advance to meet the lady journalist halfway.

Chel's gawping a bit. Because of awe, nerves, uncertainty or what, I don't know, but I have to clutch my poking finger in my other hand so I don't reach over to push her jaw shut. Julie herself is looking a bit awkward, but it kind of softens as she regards her 'niece'.

'Did you have a good time, girls?' she asks.

'Oh yes.' Chelsea scratches the back of her neck, elbow aloft, like a teenage boy failing to talk to a girl. 'The performance was extremely . . . extremely . . . er . . .'

'Okafor's interpretation of Puck has been well reviewed,' says Julie impersonally. The flash of human interest I saw in her face is starting to lacquer over, but she continues. 'Are you interested in theatre?'

'Well, I dunno much about it,' says Chel diffidently. 'Been a couple of times in Bristol with school. We did

DNA by Dennis Kelly for GCSE.'

'Gosh, that's a bit modern.'

'Well, there were – was – *Merchant of Venice* as well. And we went to see *Julius Caesar* at Bath Playhouse. Too much scenery-chewing, I reckon. Caesar ain't – is not a Hollywood villain.'

Julie looks like she's remembering something. 'Yes . . . Not much has changed there, then. You should have seen their production of *Jane Eyre*, in what year was it . . .?'

'Oh, you've seen *Jane Eyre* as a play? How did they stage it?' asks Chel, suddenly excited.

'Yes! Well, it was many years ago, obviously, but . . .'

And they're off. Julie's hand has gone slack on the bannister again as she does her bit of rather hazy reminiscing from the Stone Age, and then Chel spills forth what I trust is erudite commentary on the fundamental qualities of the novel version of *Jane Eyre* and how they might translate into other media, which gets an eager response . . .

Maybe I should just sneak upstairs and leave them to it, but they're blocking the way now and I don't want to interrupt the flow.

Eventually the lit-speak peters out. I'm pretty sure Julie's registered the time, as there's a clock opposite the bottom of the stairs. I think she's going to make her excuses, but instead she says, 'Oh, was Dr Abrams helpful?'

Sadly, now her brain is out of the literature zone, Chel reverts to er-um territory. 'He was very helpful. But KCL's just the first place I've seen. And I don't wanna . . . well, decide too quickly. It's a lot!'

I surreptitiously squeeze her arm. *Come on, Chel, you've done well so far.*

Julie's regarding her with some slightly patronising but identifiably human sympathy now. 'Hm, I do remember what it was like, arriving here after a life in Brockford,' she says, then turns simultaneously misty-eyed and grim. 'If your parents are genuinely behind you you'll have it easier than I did, at least.'

'What did yours do?' asks Chel.

'Oh . . . Nothing really bad. It's more what they didn't do. If you want to step outside that tiny world, people fundamentally don't get it. Or most don't. But your mother seemed to have her head together, on the phone.'

'Yeah,' says Chel at last. 'Mum's cool.'

'Well,' says Julie rather briskly. Her eyes flick to the clock again. 'I've been up since five. Just wanted a – snack, then I could just about pass out. You know how busy Mark and I are but we're all going out on Wednesday night, and we can have a chat over dinner.'

'Yeah!' Chel manages to sound enthusiastic. I agree: it'll be worth dozing through a choral concert to get her a whole evening with the olds, showing off just how great she is so they'll invite her to live with them on the spot. Judging by this little talk, stage one of the plan is already complete.

Julie turns her head as if the conversation is over – and notices me with a start. I've been severely lurking, to give Chel centre stage.

'Oh, Yan! How rude of me! How do *you* like London?'

'It's great,' I say. 'Great great great!'

I'd planned to say something more intelligent than that . . . but I need to get somewhere I'm not being looked at *right now*, because it is suddenly absolutely imperative that I spin around on the spot many times.

'Lovely,' says Julie, and sweeps down through the space Chel creates.

'Well,' mutters Chelsea when we reach the door of our

room. I take a moment to stare around at the hallway of white silk-striped wallpaper and paintings of horses and a wooden chest weirdly like the one Uskaar barfs into, that time the Jaarv sneak into the castle drunk. Then we enter the bedroom. 'That were – something.'

'You were bonding with her! Winning her heart so she'll invite you to live here!'

'You think?' says Chel, half-hopeful, half-incredulous. 'Well, yeah, I know you think that. But – eh, d'you really think it *could* be real?'

'Yes! Yes yes yes!'

Chel pulls her top off, sniffs the armpit and shoves it squeamishly into her laundry bag. 'We was only talking. But I s'pose it's possible . . . Ugh, anyway, I'm too tired to think about it now. I oughta shower, but . . .' She lowers herself onto her bed with a sigh of relief. 'I need a moment's wind-down.'

Chel picks up her laptop and I take the opportunity to dash to the bathroom and spin round randomly on the spot for five minutes because . . . well, I'm not sure I can explain half of what I do at the moment.

CHAPTER 11

When I get back to the room Chel is, of course, fast asleep.

Sleep is clearly a good idea. Unfortunately, although my mind is fuzzy, I feel like I'll never be tired again. I lie in bed for a while, wiggling my toes, letting my fist clench since apparently that's a thing now. I feel like a caramel river is bubbling through my head . . .

Ugh. No way am I going to sleep. Maybe I'll explore the house? But as Julie was roaming around out there, I'd better leave it a little while, until I haven't heard anyone moving for, say, twenty minutes.

I check the blog post I guess Chelsea was making while I was in the loo. It's short.

tomtartoes-blog.rabbithole.com
Monday 23:58

I need to sleep but I just wanted to stop by here because I saw the replies to my last post.

Um, @vikinghusbands, I'm really sorry if I made it sound like I was going to write something skeevy? Everything that happens in my fics is always consensual. We all want our boys to be happy. ☺

I know writers have a responsibility to readers. Nobody's pressuring me to write anything in particular.

I'll try to come up with some better story ideas.

Anyway, riceballs, your fic looks adorable!! And I'm going to read it and comment just as soon as I can. 𓆩♡𓆪

Oh dear. I should have realised that she'd have a wibble when she saw those replies on her last post. I'm half-tempted to wake her up just to tell her not to listen to numpties. But she needs her sleep.

Let's see what comments she's getting. It's teatime in the USA, so they're already coming in.

🍶 23:59 **tastyriceballs:** Ok! Don't forget to comment! I can't wait to hear what you say!

📟00:02 **lyssapeeps:** I know any fic you write will be SO SO SO SO HOT *flails madly* And I know you can't put up a new chapter of 'Spirit of Fire' for a few days so I'm rereading your fics. This bit from 'Rothgern's Curse' is my favorite:

As Yrsali jumped from the rigging, slashing her sword Skivare towards the terrified Nordhelm warrior, Uskaar glimpsed Rothgern standing in the flaming boat bobbing at the side of the *Langskip*, roughly bandaging a wound on his own arm.

In spite of Uskaar and Yrsali's efforts, the Jaarv were being pushed gradually back towards the prow of the boat, with nothing at their back but the fierce grey water of Nordhelm Bay. Uskaar swept Vargsmittar in an arc before him, pulping the heads of the foremost

Nordhelmers, but at that very moment Rothgern tied off the bandage and looked up, seeming to sense that he was being watched. He gave Uskaar a savage, bloodstained grin.

Uskaar's gaze met the lord's, unflinching. Here was a challenge, then! And it occurred to him, fleetingly, that here, possibly, at last, was an equal.

Sorry, toes, I didn't mean to just copy and paste your actual fic BUT IT'S SO GOOD WHAT ELSE CAN I SAYYYYY. There's so much sexual tension I almost shrieked out loud on the subway to work. I can't wait for our boys to get together.

🛡️00:03 **duskietta:** I needed an excuse not to vacuum my apartment this evening and rereading every fic you've ever written is it. Can't believe you're so young and write so well.

Damn it. For once, there's nothing that really deserves savaging. Where's vikinghusbands when you actually want her?

🔨00:04 **blackm00ds:** @lyssapeeps You've got good taste, but how about you come up with something yourself rather than just cutting and pasting the whole thing back both here and in the fic comments section, hm?

Huh, reading that comment back, it's kind of mean. lyssa's a bit vacant but nice enough, and she says she knows pasting a quotation was lame.

It would be far too off-brand for blackm00ds to apologise, though.

Aha! I have an idea!

I switch to isga-bites-u, and post in reply to my other self.

♩ 00:05 isga-bites-u: @blackm00ds, lay off lyssa! She's right, toes' fic is just so good that it speaks for itself.

It takes me a while to hit 'post', because I've started laughing, and I have to double over to avoid waking Chelsea. I said I wasn't going on as isga-bites-u this week because I didn't feel like her, but I forgot, and now I just argued with my own sock puppet! I mean, come on, self! Though it's probably OK because I'm a hundred per cent in the right.

I need another distraction.

I'll message oceans. They'll be home from work. And suddenly I really want to speak to them. oceans is a firm anchor (lol pun) even if nothing else is. Sometimes they set their account so you can't see if they're online or not, but right now there's a green dot.

00:08 **isga-bites-u:** Us two are having the MOST AMAZING TIME IN LONDON and now I can't sleep. Whatcha doing?

00:10 **far-oceans:** Hey, bitey! I'm just chilling at home with Hannah and Pixie.

00:11 **isga-bites-u:** Doing what?

00:11 **far-oceans:** Oh, it's really exciting stuff. Spirited Away's on Netflix, Hannah's knitting, Pixie's messaging their Star Wars friends, and I'm on here.

00:12 **isga-bites-u:** Life goals! You're my OT3. 🖤 🖤 🖤

00:13 **far-oceans:** Heh, thanks. So, London. You aren't blogging the trip?

00:13 **isga-bites-u:** I'd rather tell people about it direct!

Except somehow, now it comes to it, I don't like the idea. As if it might give away something I don't want even oceans to know. Wtf?

00:14 **far-oceans:** . . . So?

00:14 **isga-bites-u:** Um, it's almost too much to talk about. My brain feels a bit all over the place.

00:14 **far-oceans:** You need to take it easy. You went through a really hard time this spring.

00:15 **isga-bites-u:** No way am I taking it easy this week! Hey, so I saw vikinghusbands getting on her bullshit in toes' blog.

00:15 **far-oceans:** Yeah, well. toes is really popular now, and her writing's relatively vanilla, so of course the fandom police want to recruit her for their purity crusade. Especially as she comes off as a bit unsure of herself.

00:16 **isga-bites-u:** The fanpols believe they can convert her? When us Isga-loving pervs are her bff and her online bestie?

00:17 **far-oceans:** You're doing the Lord's work with your bracing influence on toes. And, yeah, it looks like self-appointed Chief of Fanpolice vikinghusbands does think that. Tell toes to be careful. v.h. is dangerous.

00:17 **isga-bites-u:** How so?

00:19 **far-oceans:** Uh, where to start. She's been in other fandoms, under different names. In *Star Break* fandom she hassled anyone with a hetero ship for being homophobic, which was quite a trip when she's cis straight and the Dan/Olivia shipper she went after the most was going through top surgery while this was happening. Didn't stop star_turn – her old name – whipping up hundreds of minions to hate-spam him until he left the fandom.

00:19 **isga-bites-u:** Oh nice.

00:20 **far-oceans:** Yeah, it was real classy. Sometimes though, you've just got to laugh. You know v.h. doxxed me when Nordhelm fandom was still small, just before you guys joined?

00:20 **isga-bites-u:** WHAT

00:21 **far-oceans:** I couldn't prove it was her at first, but then one of her minions rebelled and left her little cult and told me. I did a drawing of Isga drinking blood from Yrsali's thigh, and vikinghusbands emailed it to uni and my dad.

00:21 **isga-bites-u:** THAT DOES NOT SOUND FUNNY

00:22 **far-oceans:** It whipped Dad up into a new frenzy of praying for my soul, and I was still seeing him at that point. But the research team at uni? We literally talk about octopus sex all day. The guys thought it was hilarious and I ended up showing the rest of the team all the NC-17 Arctopus fanart I could find.

00:22 **isga-bites-u:** 😂 😂 😂 OMG THAT IS FUNNY. But what is the sad cow's deal? You can tell from her tone that she's got serious probs of some kind.

00:23 **far-oceans:** Eh, who knows. I guess she needs to feel powerful or something. And to be fair, she *does* kind of support the kids she draws in. As long as they do what she says.

00:23 **isga-bites-u:** We don't all use our issues as an excuse to dump on other people. You don't.

00:25 **far-oceans:** Hey, I just realized what the time must be in the UK. You know sleep is the number one thing for mental health. You don't want another Blip.

00:25 **isga-bites-u:** You sound like my mum. Except she'd never voluntarily say 'mental health'.

00:26 **far-oceans:** Haha well, I got reasons to know about it.

00:26 **isga-bites-u:** You can always talk to me about your personal stuff!

00:27 **far-oceans:** Maybe some time. Look, I'm serious about how you should get some sleep. And I should probably get my leg out from under Pixie before it falls off plus we all starve to death because nobody's made dinner.

00:27 **isga-bites-u:** 🦊 You could

oceans' little green dot turns red as I'm typing, so I stop . . . and suddenly I'm angry. Because oceans is amazing, and they draw the BEST fanart, and they went through some heavy stuff with their stupid dad after coming out as trans and poly, which is still going on even though they're twenty-three and live with their partners. I think they have depression, too.

So I'd like to support them, but they obviously see me as just a kid. They slap 'no under eighteen' signs on some of their posts. Is that aimed at me and Chel? Telling us to fuck off?

No, that doesn't make any sense. far-oceans is just complying with rabbithole rules to protect teenagers from adult content. I can choose to break those rules, and I do, because if a queer teenager can't talk to queer adults about anything to do with sex, then, uh, I'm not seeing how that's protection.

far-oceans just won't tell me what's up with their brain.

Well, fine. It's none of my business if they don't want it to be.

I've clearly got a more important mission right here. I hadn't quite realised how dodgy viking . . . what's her name? vikingcupboard? vikinghungry?

Why can't I remember her name?

I have to make sure Chel doesn't wibble her way into trusting . . .

I can't remember her name.

Why am I randomly forgetting things?!

Rage surges through me. I chuck the phone down on the bed hard enough that it almost bounces off the covers.

oceans went on about the Blip. Why do people keep reminding me of the Blip? And they keep inspecting me like I might – well, what do they even expect? I'm supposed to be away from all that, away from Brockford, and now even fandom friends on the other side of the world are giving me hassle.

It's coming back. Right now. The terror.

No, it's not. Of course it's not. I've been so happy lately!

I scrunch up my eyes.

People don't even know how bad it was. I didn't tell Chel all the details, and I certainly didn't tell Mum.

But this I do remember.

I wanted to die. I wanted it the way you want water. I couldn't put any of it on my fandom blog, and nobody read blackm00ds when it was just bad poetry.

I thought a) I was broken, b) I was dirt, and c) I deserved to die. And not committing suicide, as in deliberately moment-by-moment not committing suicide, is the most boring thing ever, on top of the soul-dissolving anguish that makes you want to do it in the first place. *Put the imaginary rope down, brain. No, you can't go and get a real one from the shed. Here's a compromise: you can fantasize some more about stepping off a chair and choking to death, as long as you don't actually do anything. Deal? Mmkay? Meanwhile, Mum's downstairs making some dinner you'll*

upset her by not eating, and here you are dreaming about –
well, bitch, you deserve to die for that. You deserve to die for
thinking you deserve to die. You deserve to die for being stuck
in this pathetic cycle. Ooh, brainwave – there's a way to get
out of this: suicide! Hm . . . wait . . .

Depressive logic: minus ten million out of ten, would
not recommend. It's drip, curdle, drip; learning every
crack in the ceiling, attaining ultra-master level on every
brainless app you can find. It's obsessing about whether
crying makes you an evil person when it's all theoretical
because you can't cry anyway. And the sun comes up and
goes down outside the window. Drip, curdle, drip. I don't
think I'll ever forget.

'I feel grey sadness,' I told Mum. 'I don't have enough
energy to move.' Though in fact I hauled my arse to school
quite often – only nothing I heard stuck in my brain. Then I
came home and sat holding myself in, while black thoughts
seemed to howl around the room, as well as inside me.
Even when Chelsea came around, I often couldn't feel her
presence. I was just ashamed of wasting her time.

I will never let that happen again.

It was when I was just pulling myself together that Mum
persuaded me to read *20 Fragments of a Ravenous Youth*.
It's short enough that I could get it into my fuzzy head, and
I think it was Mum's way of telling me she understands I
need to follow my dreams. But in the book it takes Fenfang
years and years of playing Three-Hundredth Woman on
the Left before she sells a film script. I'm not going to be
Three-Hundredth Woman, ever. I'm going straight to the
heart of all things.

Except not right now, because it's the middle of the
night, and my brain is squawking like a fire alarm.

A cash payment at our head office.

The words from the PI's email come to me in a searing flash of colour. Of course! That's what's making me antsy: I've been in denial about what I need to do. I've been avoiding thinking about it, but it's been bubbling away in my mind, and that's why I can't sleep.

These poshos are not going to miss a few quid, right?

I slip out of bed.

First I sneak up to Julie and Mark's floor, partly to check all is peaceful – yep, nothing but some gentle snores from their room, and Kieran's – then to check out the main bathroom, a fabulous green-and-white event with a freestanding, carved-foot bath, because after this *I really will need to sleep*. And I'm in luck! Sleeping pills – a prescription for the mysterious husband Mark.

I knock back one sleeping pill, then another because I need the bloody things to work, then I sneak all the way down to the main hall.

It doesn't take me long to find money – in Julie's study, in the bags in the hall. I guess, to the Petersons, twenties are pocket change. I take about a hundred quid from each place, to make it less obvious. It's an amazing thrill.

I'd never normally do anything like this, but once you realise there's no actual reason to follow all the rules, it's easy.

Buzz, rush, ecstatic static in my head. I'll pay the PI in cash tomorrow. I'll find a way to get to their offices, it shouldn't be hard. I remember the address – it's near where Chel and I are going tomorrow morning!

This has to be fate. I go back to the bedroom and lie down, grinning so much it hurts. Fandom, Fenfang, father, death . . .

After a while, the rush of traffic blurs with the rush in my head. The sparks are finally dimming . . . and there's a train thundering through my brain. My thoughts are decoupling and churning along on their own. A quarter of my mind stays awake, floating above the rest, rushing and rushing on.

Weird, huh?

CHAPTER 12

Everything's shit, and if it's a thing that moves I'd like to kill it.

I'm a moron who took some random sleeping pills I found in someone else's bathroom, and clearly this is the result. It's half past eight in the morning and I'm showering, and I'm itching out of my skin, and when I shake myself afterwards to try to work off energy I bash my elbow. I'm done with today already.

But I *can't* be. We've got a brilliant schedule, and I'm going to get Dadquest back on track. I seem to have still not quite told Chel about this . . . I need to park her somehow for an hour first, and slip in a visit to the PI while we're in the right part of town. Fortunately we'll be on our own, exploring in Shoreditch and Chinatown, until it's time for UCL and Ras – then clubbing in the evening. We're seventeen and nobody's watching us.

When I get back from the bathroom, Chel's at her laptop, doing an online quiz called 'Is it a Thing from *Nordhelm* or a Piece of IKEA Furniture?' Or pretending to – when she ticks a box to say that Landnaar is not Rothgern's bumbling second-in-command but actually a wardrobe, I know she's not concentrating.

'So, about Ras,' she announces a bit too brightly,

shutting the lid of the laptop. 'I've slept on it, and I think I definitely like him. And look!' She triumphantly thrusts her phone in my face, with a message from Ras saying, 'See you later. ☺' Not quite earth-shattering.

'Excellent. What did you reply?'

'Um, nothing yet.'

While I was gone, she's painted her toenails to match the lavender streak she had her little sister Ruby, who wants to be a hairdresser, dye into her hair last week. I sit on Chel's bed, mirroring her cross-legged position, and seeing the drying varnish flash on her nails makes my own toes wiggle. I hold them still with my hands so I'm in a kind of half-yoga, half-*Twister* shape.

'That's no good, Chel! Be brave. Though, of course, he's probably going to want to show you his poetry. Could be dangerous.'

'Well, maybe it's good,' she counters immediately. 'Maybe I *will* show him my fic.' The determination dimple appears for a moment.

'Really?' I doubt she means that – the dimple only lasted for a second – but I can't be sure. 'Go for it! People should see how talented you are. How about – uh . . .' I cast around for the name of her sexiest fic, just to be funny, but I can't remember it.

Chel hesitates for a fraction of a second, then sighs. 'Nah. You know I won't. Anyway . . . how do you know if you're in love, Yan? I mean, if you ain't a fictional Jaarv with a soundtrack to give you a subtle hint?'

I consider. 'I think it's one of those things you just sort of know. So, if you *don't* know . . . I mean, Ras is a massive improvement on your tragic pothead ex, but he's still a mystery man. Except today he becomes our exclusive guide to the secrets of UCL – and then our gateway to the night.'

There. I sound like me now. I'm shaking off the weird pill hangover, ready to snog my way around the hot young folk of London town, providing I can make it through today's UCL visit.

'Gaah, it's all complicated!' Chel falls back on her bed, while I take the opportunity to manically wiggle my toes without her seeing. 'Right! I'm gonna message him!'

'And say what?'

'I dunno!' wails Chel. 'There must be something clever . . .' She pokes at her phone a few times, typing and deleting stuff. 'I can't just say "great", that's lame. But if I say too much it'll look like I'm trying too hard.' She groans, then goes bippety-bip-bip on her phone, then jabs the 'send' button hard. 'Right! I sent "Looking forward to it." And I added a kiss. Oh God, why'd I add a kiss?'

'It'll be fine,' I say. I want to get involved, because this is important to her, but I'm using all my willpower trying to keep my toes still.

'*VARGSMITTAAAAR!*' roars Uskaar's voice.

It's Chel's message notification, the audio she only turns on when she wants to get something right away. She actually squeaks. 'Oh my God, Yan, a reply! It says, "Me too!" But no kiss. Did I come on too strong? Or is Ras trying to be cool?'

'Listen,' I say. She really is all over the place . . . but look who's talking. 'Worst-case scenario it's a horrible disaster and you'll look back on it and cringe for the rest of your life. But there will be absolutely no practical consequences, because we're here less than a week.'

'Oh, that's very comforting, thanks.'

I grin, and she smiles a little too.

Chelsea goes to the bathroom. I shuffle round on my arse, and end up facing across the small gap to the head of my bed. There's a tiny nick in the cream-painted wooden bedside table. I bang the flat of my hand against it, just once, so it's not strange, just a random movement. Then I pick at a little splinter. You could probably get all the paint off if you did this for long enough. I imagine sitting here for a week, just doing that. Like being depressed but wired. Well, that would suck like a duck in muck.

Also, everything's wonderful! The sun erupts inside me. Again.

'It's a beautiful morning!' I trill when Chel comes back, and I bounce up and pull back the curtains. The jaded yellow light that was showing through the material turns to day. 'Get your knickers on and let's get out of here.'

CHAPTER 13

Less than an hour later, I've kind of run away from my best friend.

We're in the City, the land of shiny skyscrapers that nevertheless borders on hipster Shoreditch. Chelsea was standing there on a corner in the full sun, squinting at a map on her phone, turning it upside down and cursing when the screen flipped round too. After lengthy and weighty cogitation I still had no idea how I was going to explain making a detour to the PI – so I just thought *screw it*, ducked into an alley and headed off.

'Gone to look at something. Message you in an hour xx,' I fire off to Chel, just as a message pings in from her: 'Where the hell have you gone?' Then I get another one, presumably replying to mine. I don't read it.

It should be about fifteen minutes from here to the PI's office in Shoreditch. I want to get there right now. I'm walking so fast and I'm so tense that my ankles hurt, but it's not fast enough. There's not much point getting on a bus in this traffic, though. I'm nervous; I'm sweating – well, nobody's going to think that's odd in this weather. And I'll only be half-lying to the PI: I am *a* Ms Harris. Just not, technically, the right one.

A smell of piss and a yeasty blast from a pub cellar;

muscly guys rolling barrels from a van through a trapdoor in the street. *Clang, rumble.* Newsagents advertise cheap calls to Africa; and here's Kirby Investigations, in a two-storey row of peeling sash windows above a minicab office. It's not *Jessica Jones*, but it feels right somehow, like a place that just gets on with the job.

I ring the bell, thinking, *Be glamorous and confident, Yan.* No, maybe not glamorous. It wouldn't exactly fit in with what looks like it's going to be a rather scuzzy establishment. Competent, then. Older, for sure. I smooth my floaty scarf. There's a rough *buzzzz* and I'm in. A receptionist sits at a desk at the top of the stairs – she's on the phone. Next to her stands a strangely long-leaved rubber plant, as big as me with a sort of perky, bordering-on-sinister look, like it fancies a bit of strangling and might have a go at me if I turn my back. I smile my lipsticky smile. Desk-woman half acknowledges me. She's about as noir as a hairdresser. The vibe is basically run-down dentist's reception, except there's a honking great CCTV camera right over the receptionist's head, pointing straight at me. Nice.

And there are posters all around. 'Are you worried your spouse is cheating on you?' demands the one with a picture of a woman frowning at a smirking man getting into a car. 'Debts recovered!' promises another in big text on a black background. I just want to recover my dad.

'I'm Ms Harris,' I announce when the receptionist's off the phone. She stares politely but blankly. Of course, Yan, you idiot; this place must get far too many cases for her to remember them all by name.

'I engaged you to find the address of a James, or Jim, Harris, but I was told there's a problem with my payment,' I say airily. At least I'm sweating less in the air-con. 'I can't imagine what's happened, but I've brought cash.'

Only now does it occur to me that popping up here with a cash payment, and my out-of-London address and country accent, might seem odd. Well, too late.

Just take the money, Reception Lady. But she *is* looking at me funny now. I want to shout at her that this is my dad; that I'm not under any illusions, I know he dumped my mum and ran off, but I have my reasons, OK? Instead, I stare back. I will myself to be charismatic.

The receptionist says, 'Uh huh.' Then she taps on her computer and takes my money.

Of course she does. What do these people care as long as I can pay? This is the adult world.

I like it.

'It should take about two days. We'll email you,' she says, and hands me a receipt, and immediately looks away as if she's forgotten me already. That's just as well, as the grin that's currently breaking out on my face is probably not the most chilled expression ever. Then I make myself turn around and go down the stairs, out into London again. London. London. I breathe it in. It smells hot and stale. There's pigeons.

It's not much more than half an hour since I left Chelsea. I've got a voice message from her, and I duck into an alley beside a giant blue wheelie bin to listen to it. 'Where the hell have you gone? I thought we were gonna explore together?'

We were, Chelsea. We will. I know I'm not being a good friend. I just need . . . Well, I can't always tell her everything, can I?

OK. OK. I shove my phone in my pocket and look around. There's three red buses nose to tail, spewing out fumes, and a plastic bottle rattles to the kerb as it spins away from a car wheel. There's a smear of ex-pigeon on the tarmac, with feathers sticking out of the mess at jaunty angles. I love everything. Two white artist types pass me, with piercings and leggings and dreads; a Chinese woman with a briefcase stops to check her phone, and I almost wave, like she might recognise me. Cos here's me, Yan Harris, a future student in my future home.

Chapter 14

'See, you've been fine without me,' I say, when Chel and I finally manage to meet up on a street corner by a market stall selling Indian fabric. Bales and bales of scarlet and turquoise and even tartan, all jostling as someone unrolls a stretch of paisley, *bump bump bump*.

Chelsea doesn't look impressed. 'Where did you go?' she demands, hands on hips.

'Bet you've been messaging Ras.'

A tiny twitch at the corner of her mouth gives me my answer. Then she repeats. 'Yan! Where did you *go*?' She's using her mumsy, steady, I'm-not-angry-*except* voice. But I don't want conversation, and I don't want to stand still, so I set off, towards where there's supposed to be vintage shops.

Chel has to follow. I march and she scampers. Then I slow down, and she comes up beside me.

'*Yan!*'

'We're not joined at the hip,' I snap.

I'm being a bitch. *Why am I being such a bitch?*

My legs speed up again. They seem to know what they want without asking the rest of me.

'No, I know,' says Chel from behind me, and her voice is meek, and I hate it. 'I been going on about myself too much this morning, ain't I?'

I don't reply. She *has* been talking a lot, and it's not to do with Ras: it's stuff like whether she wants to go to KCL or UCL, whether Ethraig the dragon will be back in *Nordhelm* Season 4, and whether her eldest brother Wayne's going to finally settle down with a girl he's met.

I like it when Chel gets a bit rambly. When you're the fifth in a family of six, you don't always get listened to much at home. So that's my job.

It's really not hard!

Usually.

'I just needed a few moments to myself, OK? I'm not used to being with people twenty-four/seven like you are.'

I have to let her think she drove me off, because it's that or tell her the truth. *So why can't I tell her the truth?*

It's like my lips are sealed unless I want to say something mean.

And I have, as intended, managed to shut Chelsea up. I'm probably going to that Christian Hell place where they have a whole circle especially for people who hurt their best friends.

I've got to make it up to her. Have some fun. *Make her stop staring at me.*

'Shoppering time!' I declare brightly.

'Oh . . . yeah!' Chel responds in a sort of wobbly brave tone 'Let's.'

I'm awful.

But hey, I'm going to find my dad!

Shoppering is when you poke everything and buy nothing: window-shopping, only up close and personal with the merch. It's good fun when you're skint, but opportunities for it are limited in Brockford unless you're into poking artisan loaves in ye olde picturesque street of tourist shoppes, which I know from experience can lead to the baker phoning your mum.

We pass through a covered market as big as an aircraft hangar, full of people selling carpets and neon bags and saggy velvet hats to other people in saggy velvet hats and painted jeans. I'm over that look. Today I'm on a mission to check out the vintage stores. I can see myself mixing it up in a Fifties puff dress with a Harajuku bow. I've already got a Sixties hippy skirt off eBay; when I last visited my grandparents and Grandpa saw it, he offered to take me to Manchester Primark if I couldn't afford new clothes.

On the other side of the market is the full-on white-people zone. You can tell, because the number of nose rings doubles and there's a pub claiming fish and chips for twelve quid is a bargain. There are also design-agency offices, galleries and studios. I recognise some of the names. Why don't I just knock on the door and ask for a job? No. Be a cool dude, Yan, not a mad, grinning teenager. I have an appointment with Kathy Maynard tomorrow. I got this.

Here's a vintage shop: blazers and bow ties in one window, flapper kit in the other. A shop dummy with the head of a fox: freaky. I head in as Chel peels off to some other place a couple of doors down: fashion is not really her thing, especially when it's experimental in any way. When my mum took us to Glastonbury for my birthday last year, Chel grumbled about 'floaty woo-woo' and went back to the car to read.

The old lady behind the counter has winged glasses and white hair with a pink stripe in it, and she's examining an old smoking jacket some guy is trying to sell to her.

'There's a worn patch here,' she says critically, holding the rich purple jacket up to the light and smoothing her hand gently down the lapel. 'But this style is quite in demand.'

'Yeah, it absolutely is,' says the bloke trying to flog it, a greasy type, very thin. I bet he's a junkie. I thought junkies were supposed to nick and sell people's phones, not vintage clothes? Well, anyone can branch out.

They start debating price, very involved and frowny-faced. I head round a display of scarves to the jewellery. There's a row of brooches on a threadbare plush display, and one has a bit of emerald glass set in a silver weave design. It's similar to the clasp Rothgern fastens his belt with . . . in fact, it's almost identical. It's clearly meant to belong to a *Nordhelm* fan. Chel would love it.

It's like I was drawn in here on purpose.

'We did have something similar in last week and it went quickly,' says the counter lady, and the probably-a-junkie keeps nodding earnestly at her. Nobody's looking this way. Another customer wanders between me and the sales desk, his back to me, sorting through a rack of trousers.

The brooch is fifteen quid.

I bet it's not worth that – places like this are out to milk hipsters. In fact, there's a bunch of them standing in the middle of the floor, loudly chatting about whether one of them should buy a dressing gown, a red waistcoat, a plaid waistcoat, or all three. It's so unfair, when there are people who actually appreciate things but can't always have them: namely, me and Chel. But I feel powerful now. Powerful enough to just take what I need.

So into my pocket goes the brooch. The shop won't go bust because of that. I grab myself a pair of deep-blue velour gloves hanging off the rack next to it, too. What a rush! Nobody's looking at sweet little me as I walk back outside and head for Chel's shop, which does vintage too, though it looks like mostly bric-a-brac and not clothes.

Chel's at the counter buying something when I go in. The layout here is kind of open-plan, so I decide not to nick anything, and just wait to follow her out again. She's got her purchases in a little bag. Book-shaped, of course.

'Big spending,' she says, waving the bag. 'I've blown about six quid.'

Life is just *wrong* sometimes. Kieran's rolling in so much dosh he doesn't even think about it, and now Chel's sorting through coppers to find out if she's got £17.70 or £17.80 left. My mum gave me much more than that for the trip, if still not a huge amount. Chel saved up her Christmas and Easter job earnings for ages to get a laptop so she could more easily write fic without her family knowing, then had to start saving again from scratch.

'I've spent nothing,' I say. 'I got you a present, though.' I hold out the brooch.

'Spent nothing?' Chel frowns, then she realises. 'Oh my God, you didn't . . .'

'Yes!' I prompt. Chel's not reacting the way she's supposed to. I point at the brooch with my free hand, and nod so that my hair jerks and swings in front of my face. Motion, energy, fun! I keep doing it. 'That shop takes stolen goods anyway.'

'How on earth d'you know that?' Chel swallows, glances all around like she thinks the back streets of Shoreditch are being monitored by MI5, and hustles me round a corner.

'Don't look at me like that,' I go on. 'There's no danger of me getting caught. Like you said, I don't stand out in this place –' there's a guy with three-inch fake eyelashes and major stack heels on the other side of the road; I'm underdressed by comparison – 'and everybody knows Chinese girls are too well-brought-up to steal.'

Chel peers around again. 'That ain't the point! I don't believe you, lately. Jesus, imagine getting caught. What'd Julie say?'

'She doesn't actually care about us.'

'I thought the point was you wanted her to care about me! And if we get arrested she'll start, pretty quick.'

'Oh, come *on*, you really think we'll get arrested for nicking this?' I'm still holding out the brooch. She still doesn't take it. Fine. I go to put it on my own blouse. Then Chel grabs it. And shoves it into her pocket.

'I dunno, do I? I don't know what the local police do about –' she lowers her voice nervously – 'shoplifters.'

'Chel, you're such a Brocky.' She needs to calm down. Why doesn't she get it? We're supposed to be doing this together. There's so much we could share if she'd open her eyes.

'Fine. Whatever. Actually, I got – that means *bought* – you something.' She fumbles in her plastic bag, and now she's holding a book out towards me. 'If it's exciting enough for you. I mean, obviously you got it already, but this is a really gorgeous edition. I think it were cheap cos the spine's wrecked.'

It's *Ariel*, by Sylvia Plath, with a tattered spine, but also a beautiful, abstract design on the cover.

My friend's bought me a present. I don't know why she has, because I'm a cow. I also have the weirdest feeling that the book will burn into my hands if I take it. It'll fuse with my flesh, and twist into something I can't control. I can't refuse it though – and I don't actually want to – so I accept it from her, and leaf through the softened old pages.

I am the arrow, writes Sylvia. *At one with the drive.* I feel those words. More than that; they are me. Teachers smile patronising smiles if you quote Plath at them. But I need poems like blunt scarlet that stab into my heart.

I need to say something to Chel – but what if it comes out loud and inappropriate, however I intended it to be?

'Look, it were only one pound fifty,' Chel says, opening the cover and tapping the pencilled price. To her, that's a bonus point in a present – the Furse girls and their mum compete with each other to find the best bargains.

'Thank you,' I say, and hug her. See, I can be normal and not a muppet. Except things between me and Chel are shifting, so fast I almost can't follow. There's a wall growing up between us. It's getting thicker – and at the same time she just pierced a hole in it.

I feel like we're drifting somewhere raw and secret, where I'm usually alone. And right now, I need to be alone.

I go stiff in the hug, though I don't pull away. I wait for her to do that.

'You're welcome,' she says, a bit formally.

The wall is intact again.

I lead the way to more shops, where I buy an old top hat, ostentatiously, with money. I even forget about my dad for a while. But I can feel Chel waiting for me to explain myself.

I can't.

Chapter 15

Before UCL, we go to Trafalgar Square for some proper touristing. I climb on a huge lion statue, gawk around so much I'm lucky a pigeon doesn't poo in my mouth, and make victory signs.

Then we walk up Charing Cross Road – once home to a million second-hand bookshops, Chel says, but there's only about three left – and here we are in Chinatown.

I run full-tilt down the main, paved road, just managing not to bang into people. I take selfies of me and her with tourist shops with lucky cats, vivid red lanterns dangling everywhere even though New Year was months ago, a genuine London phone box with *Fuck* scrawled on the door and cards advertising prostitutes wedged inside it, and English signs and Chinese signs and racks of silk clothes I wish I could afford. Dead, plucked ducks hang in windows, cooked brownish-orange, and Chelsea flattens her nose against the glass and peers in at rows and rows of buffet spring rolls and noodles like a Charles Dickens orphan till I whap her on the ear. There's an intricate pagoda-like fake roof, high above the street. And a person in a panda suit, dancing for money.

And the east Asian faces! Biracial faces! People just strolling along. Nobody staring and thinking I'm too white to be Chinese or too Chinese to be white, when actually I'm the best of both. I'm a million billion miles from Brockford.

I stand still and just look around me. A Chinese family in *Harry Potter* T-shirts wanders past nearby, and the children smile at me and Chel. '*Ni hao!*' I call – hello, one of my half-dozen Mandarin phrases.

They shout, '*Ni hao!*' back.

'Ugh, the heat's wearing me out,' Chel says after a while. 'And it's not too long till we're meeting Ras. Is it all right if we sit somewhere and eat?'

'Somewhere' turns out to be Russell Square, which is near UCL, and, Chel says, where Virginia Woolf and her mates used to hang out. We get a patch of shade by lurking nearby then pouncing when a bunch of office workers leave, and flop down.

Chelsea produces the sensible little package of sandwiches she made in Aunt Julie's kitchen this morning.

'Bleh. Not really hungry,' I say.

'You never are, lately.'

I could lie . . . but I'm doing enough of that already. 'Yeah,' I agree, straightening up and tucking my sweaty hair behind my ears. 'I'm not turning anorexic, I promise. I just – I'm just really not hungry.' It's as simple as that. 'It could be the weather. Or tapeworms.'

Chel rolls her eyes. 'Let's assume it's the weather. All right, I admit Cheddar sandwiches weren't the best choice for today. It's what Mum always makes.'

'A fridge full of hundreds of exotic delights, and you went for the Cheddar?' I ask.

'Yeah. I really like the stuff.'

'Should I mention I live on a council estate?' Chel asks Ras as we wander down an alley and past the UCL Egyptology

Museum (every college should have one of those).

'Oh so very cynical, young Chelsea,' I comment. Most of her questions have been more refined, of course; stuff about the English department's strengths in particular subject areas, et cetera. She's actually got a written list of queries, mostly answered by Ras already and later to be re-put to Dr Trent, another of her aunt and uncle's friends of friends.

Ras has a think. 'Depends on who you're talking to. Some of the admissions tutors are into diversity. Others go on about impartiality. A few probably do still just think poor people are icky.'

Chel nods intently, taking it all in. 'Was UCL your first choice?'

Ras glowers for a moment, then sags a bit. 'Nope. Oxford.'

Oops, sore point. Chel and I exchange a look.

'They don't even give us the Oxbridge application info at Stanfield,' I say.

'Nah, they did,' says Chel. 'The bloke as did the careers talk held up a couple of prospectuses for two seconds. Obviously not for the likes of us.'

'Well, that's just ridiculous,' says Ras sturdily, then sighs. 'Enough about philistines who don't appreciate our –'

'I write fanfiction,' interrupts Chel.

Wow. I didn't predict that one.

Hm. Being in my own little world all day probably had something to do with that.

Yan Harris, pay attention to your best friend RIGHT NOW!

She has her chin raised. Ras is eyeing her, but he doesn't look freaked out.

'Fanfic?' he says. '*That's* what you write? Well . . . OK, cool! Just don't mention it at interview. Especially if it's – oh, I can see it is – *that* kind of fanfic.'

He smirks. Chelsea's clammed up.

'Mum caught my sister Suraya reading some once,' Ras supplies.

'Er,' says Chel. 'Well, I haven't written all that much. What fandom's Suraya in?'

'Marvel Universe. She only really likes . . . what do you call the clean stuff? Gen fic,' says Ras. 'So you write the sexy stuff?'

'Um. A bit. It's mild.'

'Oh, come on,' I put in. She started this, and I'm going to support her. 'Chel's got three brothers! She knows plenty about boy bits. She gets hundreds of comments every time she posts a chapter and it's about the quality not the rating. She's very, very good.'

'Yeah,' says Chel, raising her chin again. 'I am.'

I get the impression Ras isn't sure if he's daunted or turned on. I notice he hasn't asked Chel which fandom. 'Well, good for you,' he says. 'Fanfic can be really good practice. But you know it's a writing ghetto. It won't get you far.'

'Like you can talk about that,' I protest. 'A) you're a *Star Wars* fanboy yourself.' I point at the Poe phone case poking out of his pocket. 'And b) I bet you haven't got ten thousand hits on your poetry, if it's even online.'

'No, I haven't.' Evidently Ras is not going to be offended. 'So I know it sucks not to have any readers. Also, everyone likes *Star Wars*. Suraya got me the phone case.'

'Yeah, but I do get readers,' Chel puts in loudly. 'Yan said ten thousand hits cos that's what I gets on my stories. I got about two hundred comments last week.'

'Oh . . . Wow . . . That's very good, I suppose,' says Ras. Those numbers clearly did whack him in the ego. Hah. 'I'm – working on a long-form poem about refugees at the moment. What it's really like to be one.'

I'm not sure I approve of him yanking the conversation his way, but Chel seems relieved.

'That must be so difficult,' she says.

'More and more people have to do it. Hiding in lorries. Leaving everything. Crossing the Channel in tiny boats and drowning, and they call us terrorists!' Ras scratches his head, messing up his hair. 'A damn poem, though. Who am I kidding there's a point to that?'

Oho. Angling much? But on the other hand, his poem sounds like some real talk, the kind people need to hear.

'If it makes just a few people think, it's worth it,' says Chel.

Ras grins. 'Yeah, I tell myself that. I'll – you can read the poem if you like?'

'OK!' says Chel.

Ras's grin widens. 'Well, then. Do you want to see UCL library?'

'Yes!'

As Ras leads us down an alley to the main quad, Chel grabs my arm. 'Oh my God, Yan. What did I say all that for?'

'I don't know,' I retort. 'You tell me! I thought you were going to take your secret to the grave and all that.'

'Well, you're impulsive, aren't you?'

'So?'

'So I can be too!' Then Chelsea's voice cracks into a bit of a wail, only half-joking. 'I'm not completely timid and dull, right? This trip shows that.'

'I really doubt he thought you were in the first place. Now you've scared the poor boy.'

That makes Chel snigger a bit. 'What, with my big throbbing readership?'

'Most definitely with that. Look, don't worry – he'll just forget you ever said it. And you were right earlier; maybe his poetry's actually good.'

At that, Chel doesn't look entirely calm, but nor does she seem to be full-on panicking, so I guess I've done what I can.

Ras continues to give us a tour, sneaking us into the impressive library with his summer-job pass, and telling us about how UCL was the first place to let in women and non-Christians. I've got to admit, this place may be worthy of Chelsea.

Then, when we step through a door into yet another anonymous lobby, Ras and Chel are somehow holding hands.

This is my cue to get interested in my phone. Mum's updated me on the state of her sunflowers, and the fact that some thief apparently cloned her credit card details but she noticed it before they spent anything, and froze the account. Cool: she has no idea what really happened. I message back that I'm OK.

It's still quiet here, but my brain seems to be lurching around my skull. Everything I saw in Shoreditch and Chinatown is still banging around inside me. Ras and Chel are murmuring together.

There's a corpse in a glass case in front of me.

For real! Perched upright on a stool in a dubious ruffled shirt, smirking serenely under a creamy-yellow sunhat that has a bit too much in common with a mushroom cap for my tastes. According to a plaque, it's Jeremy Bentham, a philosopher who said in his will that his dead body should go on display. It's actually a cop-out, though: it's only his skeleton covered in wax and dressed up.

He's not looking at me, but past me in that way people do when they want to make it clear they know you're there. And here's me, digging my nails into my palms again, about twenty seconds after I made myself stop. I wonder if getting taxidermied in a case in a university gives you deity status like some pharaoh mummy? Might as well try praying to Jeremy to help me *calm the fuck down* . . .

I used to think that praying at statues of gods and prophets was how you got stuff. One day when me and Mum were living with my grandparents at the takeaway after Dad left, I stood in front of the statue of Zao Shen the kitchen god and started chanting, 'Chicken nuggets, chicken nuggets.' Grandma came and explained that this is not how religion works, then she tried to cook me some herself. But the ungrateful Yanlet grizzled because they weren't from McDonalds. Not my finest hour.

All right. All right. I am calm. I am not five years old and making a fool of myself in Manchester. But it's all real in my head, all at once, and this is a dead body, and I wanted to be dead, and there is glass between me and the dead body. *Glass between me.* So I thump the glass before I can get a fucking grip on myself . . .

And Chel and Ras don't even notice. They're completely engrossed in the kind of looking-everywhere-but-at-the-other-person that is one hundred per cent about that other person. I do believe they scared themselves by holding hands.

Chel glances around at me, and grins sheepishly. I grin back half in encouragement, half in relief that they didn't notice what I was doing.

Chel checks the time on her phone. 'I better get to Dr Trent's office, like you said?' she prompts Ras.

'I'll show you the way,' he responds. Unseen, I make a brief shooing motion at her. She needs to do this. Also, I need to get the hell out of here. Maybe I can walk off this incredibly weird, almost painful energy.

'I'll meet you back at Julie's,' I tell her, and *move*.

I don't actually know where I'm going, and I don't properly run; it's just the sound of my feet on paving stones, the spinning world under the blue, blue sky. Out of the college gates, and down side roads; I want to find something hidden, some kind of secret heart of London. 'Hope it goes well with Dr Trent. No need to hurry back to Julie's. I'm giving you and Ras pace,' I message to Chel, and only notice the typo once it's sent.

There are lumbering, thrumming buses with the huge shiny bodies of film stars on their sides. An old lady with the sun in her tight white curls. Sandwich shops with placards about paninis. Tiny, intricate alleys, shops with dark windows and white sills, second-hand books, a thousand hand-sewn cushions. I pass Great Ormond Street Hospital. A gaunt little girl, looking thoughtful in a wheelchair, cocks her head as I pass. The bag with the balding topper I bought in Shoreditch bangs and bangs against my legs. It feels like guilt.

I stop, look around. A little less frantic now.

I've reached a shrubby little square with pigeons and ankle-high railings. I only bought the hat so I could unpick it and examine some interesting stitching, so I sit on a bench and do that, then cram the thing into the mouth of a bin. There's a little shiny man painted on the side of it, enclosed in a perfect, precise circle. I need perfection too, so I get up and keep walking. Images are pumping through my head like there's a valve stuck open. Trees, buildings, sky, future, past.

Am I too much?

Not long before we came here, I had a Talk with Mum while I was helping her tie up plants. In the slightly-too-mild tone that means she's short on patience, she said, 'Yan, if you don't want people to think you're strange, don't court it.'

'I don't,' I protested.

Mum bent over an underweight-looking tomato plant. 'I suppose I'm jealous,' she said. 'When I was your age – oh, listen to how old I sound! Anyway – Liko and I had to do three hours' homework a night, then work on the tills. You take everything so lightly.' She paused, probably remembering the Blip. 'I *want* you to be able to take things lightly. I'm happy with anything that makes you happy, and it's been a while since I could do that by swinging you round on my feet singing "You Are My Sunshine".'

'But . . .?'

Mum picked an insect off a tulip. '*But* what I just said about courting trouble. Oh well. Kids and flowers: you can't force either of them to grow the way you want.' She looked at me sideways, taking in my pink eyeshadow and low-cut purple top. 'You can choose a sensible colour scheme, though.'

'Oh, Mother, you don't understand my art.'

One of our old jokes. But the rest of it wasn't. She worries about me, and I understand why. She couldn't solve depression by rationalising about exam stress and cooking my favourite long-bean stir-fry, and she can't protect me from crashing grades or incoming squillions of student debt or raging hormones with motherly advice about social camouflage. There's a point in my life where she stops, and can't go on. But I have to. I wouldn't even want her to try to understand, because nobody could. I feel like I could twist my hand in the air and create beauty from nothing. Like a shimmer of light would flow from my fingertips, Disney-style. Half-naked summer bodies curve in the air around me; metal and angles of traffic and sinuous human flesh.

I've been walking/running for a long time. I think I've come in a circle – there's the School of Oriental and African Studies. I could do a degree in Mandarin there, maybe a part-time one so I could fit it around my St Martin's or LSF classes. There's posters on a noticeboard; I read them, except my eyes keep jumping ahead and I have to go back. They're forgotten as soon as read.

A bubble of random rage is travelling up me like indigestion. At home, wood pigeons will be cooing in the trees. Rich incomers will be driving their kids home from school in the nearby towns and backing up their four-by-fours in the market square. Everything will be pretty – everything dead.

I feel like a bubble just popped in my mind. And . . . relax.

I'd better go back to Julie's.

CHAPTER 16

Arriving at Julie's, I wonder if Chel's going to give me a roasting for running off twice in one day, and whether I can stand still long enough to deal with it.

I'm about to duck into the ground-floor bathroom for a preparatory wee when I hear voices coming from the sofa part of this open-plan kitchen-living-room-million-pound-show-home.

Chel's sitting on the sofa with her 'uncle'. She looks surprisingly happy to be there. Like she's been settled in place for a bit.

'. . . all the local families are crammed on our estate, or they moves away, and the pretty bits of Brockford are for the incomers now,' she's saying. I was thinking about incomers just earlier, is there a connection? Of course not, how could there be? Where did that idea come from? Chel breaks off when I appear and says, 'Hi, Yan,' a bit distractedly.

'I . . . went for a walk on my own for a bit,' I say. But she doesn't seem to be annoyed. My excuse – giving her space with Ras-boy – was actually a decent one. Or maybe she's just thinking about something else.

Cos this here is Mark. My idea of him as a big fat lawyer was on the money. He's big on curves – of a non-sexy kind – and short on functional follicles. But he's wearing beige jogging bottoms instead of a suit – I guess he works from home sometimes – and he doesn't look as evil as I expected. I mean, he's paying attention to Chelsea.

He's noticed me, too.

'Ah, you must be Yan. Hello,' he says in a deep, posh voice, and I prepare for some further pleasantries on the subject of me being me and him being him, but he doesn't bother. He turns his attention back to Chel.

'And how many jobs do you reckon there are in Brockford, anyway?' she continues. 'My dad's a carpenter, a good one, but he can't do work as ain't there.'

'That just reinforces my point,' replies Mark. 'There's a need to build on greenfield sites. Affordable homes for local people and jobs in construction. And that does come at the expense of the environment. It's a trade-off.'

'What, a trade-off between decent living standards and not destroying the planet? That's a false dichotomy, and it makes poor families the villains. The actual problem is that just about every house in Brockford over fifty years old is empty cos they're "second homes" for rich folk.'

Chelsea actually makes air quotes. And doesn't mention my house, which has a few too many genuine rustic features – such as spiders, subsidence and attempts by the river to get indoors – ever to have been gobbled up by landlords.

Mark nods slowly. 'Julie and I rent for holidays, we don't own a second home, though I doubt that will impress you. There's no denying that house prices are grossly distorted, compared to everything else. The only realistic way to amend that – or at least to slightly ameliorate it – is a substantial increase in the housing supply.'

'Aye? But what do property developers build when

they do get hold of the land? So-called luxury retirement flats.' Chelsea is now waving her mug of cold-looking tea around. Her accent's getting stronger.

Mark takes a moment to uncross his legs and wince as he lowers one foot to the ground. 'Not as young as I was,' he murmurs drily. 'All right. While I'm not a fan of government regulation in general, ensuring new builds are suitable is one area where it could be more effective. This is not a question with a simple answer. Few large-scale social or political problems are.'

'I'm not saying they are. I'm saying, if nobody takes responsibility cos they'd rather take money, then nothing changes, ever. That's what your generation are up to, and mine's gonna have to sort it out.'

'That's true. So you'll need a plan that goes beyond simple outrage. We tried that in the Sixties. So what is that plan?'

'Give us five minutes! Nobody wants to take your fancy house away –' Chel pauses. 'All right, my dad probably does, to be honest. But we've just gotta start looking for ways forward that aren't about money. And if people don't see that, they're part of the problem.'

'This is something you feel very strongly about.'

'Well, yeah.'

'Yet I think you've said you want to be an academic? In an ivory tower.'

Chelsea falters a little. 'I know . . . But believe me, there's no more ivory towers these days. I know I can't do it without some other job to live on, at least not at first.'

'Especially in London. Have you thought of any other options?'

Chel bristles. 'I've thought about my own life quite a bit. I'm good at thinking, that's the point.'

Mark smiles. It's patronising and annoying, but there's something else there too. That's just as well, or I'd thump him. 'Nicely put,' he replies. 'I didn't mean you shouldn't come to London. I meant you'd be quite capable of completing your BA in English Literature and then transferring to Law.'

There's a very weird silence.

Chelsea boggles, as do I. 'You're telling me to be a lawyer? And help oil companies dig up Africa, like you?'

'That's not my point,' Mark continues, a little less warmly.

'It absolutely is *the* point!' If Chel gets any more vehement, that cold tea is going to splash all over Mark's pot belly. 'I want to do something that makes the world better.' She stops waving the mug and stares into it instead. 'Which I know being an academic won't. So maybe I don't want to do that! Maybe I don't know yet, really, I suppose. It's all new.'

'Yes, it is. You have time.' Mark sighs, and looks almost sad for a moment.

'If the world don't end cos of what you Boomers been doing,' mutters Chel. This makes them both laugh, though as far as I'm concerned it's true and Mark should be squirming.

He leans a little towards her. 'I'm just saying, you have a lot of options, and you're no sillier than I was at your age, if in a different way. Aim high. If you become a lawyer you could work for a crusading organisation if that's what you want once you've got some education. Give yourself the option.' The sad look is back for another moment, then he checks his wristwatch. 'Well, I've enjoyed talking to you, but I do have to get back to work now. I've a conference call with Lagos.'

'Right, right. And I'm – well, we're going out. Er, good to talk to you too.'

They nod at each other, as if this really has been some kind of business meeting, then Mark's on his way out of here, nodding to me as well on the way, giving me a searching look, though I don't know what the hell he'd be searching for.

Major BFF consultation time.

As soon as Mark's in his study, I leap over Chelsea – who half-wails, 'Ohmigod, whatwasthat?', flops backward on the sofa and covers her face. After a couple of moments, an eye peers out at me from between two lavender-nailed fingers. 'Was I just patronised to hell, or complimented?' she demands.

'Both at once,' I say. 'What's his deal? How long were you talking?'

Chel sits up again, and looks at the clock. 'Blimey, ages! Let's go upstairs, it's less weird up there. Well, slightly less weird.'

Once we're in our room, I punch the air, dance on the spot and try not to shout. Standing still, even for a couple of minutes, did not agree with me. 'This is amazing! Our plan is going *swimmingly*,' I say in a probably crap imitation of Mark's posh accent. 'You're the model studious poor relation. He lurrrves you. Kieran won't behave like they want but he thinks you might!'

Chel sits on the bed. 'Yeah, apparently he does. Why? Cos I definitely don't wanna be a lawyer. That was quite enough confrontation for me.'

'What counts is, your performance worked.'

'Performance? Worked at what?'

I roll my eyes. 'Making the olds think you're the daughter they never had, so they'll invite you to live here.'

Chel laughs shakily. 'Oh my God, Yan, I'd totally forgotten that. Anyway. I'd just got here and was getting biscuits in the kitchen when he went to the loo, I think, and then he comes to, well, maybe *inspect* me is the word, and then we got talking.' She frowns. 'You should've heard him at first, asking me about my impressions of London. Talk about up yourself. '"UCL is no Oxbridge,"' she parrots in an imitation of Mark slightly better than mine. 'That got me going. Who wants Oxford? London's where everything happens! Where you'll be!'

'Well, you really held your own.'

'I'm as surprised by that as you are.' Then Chel's eyes go wide. 'Oh, I know what he was playing at,' she exclaims. 'Trying to bring me out of myself, like. Some smart adults do that, don't they? Needling you to see what you think, and if you won't just agree with them. Remember that temp English teacher in Year 10?'

I nod. It's a convincing theory and fits most excellently with our plan. 'I bet this family are like that all the time.'

Chel snorts. 'I doubt Kieran likes it. It's almost . . . nice of Mark, though?'

'In his evil lawyerish way,' I concede.

'Phew, well. I think I need to clear my head now. Did you have a nice wander round on your own, then?'

Yes. No . . .

'So what about Ras? Are you still really into him?' I demand.

That change of subject was way too abrupt, so I think she won't go for it – but she does.

'Yeah, let's think about something a bit fun for a moment,' she says. 'He read me part of his epic poem! It's genuinely good. Here . . . *On the road through the heart-land/ing far away . . . Wheels shake beneath crouched feet . . .'* Chel's good at orating. I can hear the emphases and line breaks. She continues, 'I'm not sure you can really use "crouched" there, though, with "feet". I see what he's getting at but it's a bit forced.'

I nod, loyally. This is a very Chel idea of 'fun'.

'Did you tell him that?'

'Of course not.'

'Really? You were just showing off your big brain to an old guy, surely a UCL sex bomb deserves it more.'

'Don't call him that!' But she's laughing. 'All right . . . I need to chill before we go out.'

She rolls over and takes refuge in her laptop. So I go online myself, as an alternative to twitching all the way up the wall.

tomtartoes-blog.rabbithole.com
Tuesday 18:06

OK, I'm away from my 'real' family, but you guys are my family too. 🐾 And there's a couple of things I'm chewing over that I know you'll have good advice on.

The old guy we're staying with said I'm smart enough to be a lawyer! Very kind of him, but I reckon if I'm smart enough to be a lawyer then I'm smart enough to not want to be one. The academic I saw the other day seemed to think I could do his job. Then I was talking to someone who writes poetry, and I actually mentioned fanfic. He came out with the same line as my English teacher about fic (not that I would EVER tell her about my writing, she just spoke to the class). You know, the one about how it's a good way of getting practice . . . but you have to stop practising at some point.

What am I saying? Well, it's nice to get taken seriously, I

suppose. I don't get it at school, that's for sure. And I guess I COULD write original stuff as well as fic? Apart from there not being enough hours in the day.

I don't think I really have the urge, though. I couldn't handle the rejection letters. Thinking about getting turned down by unis is enough. But if I did write original stuff, I could put darker ideas in there, where people couldn't stumble across it, like @vikinghusbands says. I don't know. I can't imagine not wanting to write fic. It's just nice that people think it's possible I could do something else too.

I can see Chel's updating her blog. She's got the determination dimple and it's funny and I'm half-tempted to take a vid of it and upload it . . . No, that's not really compatible with the whole thing where we keep our fandom identities secret so people at home don't hate us even more. I message Tash and Chloe some random nonsense instead, and I'm lucky, they're on, and they reply.

But after standing and watching Chel and Mark without getting involved I need to let rip. I'm just logging in as blackm00ds when Chel finishes on her laptop, reaches across and grabs me by my dangling hair.

'Whatcha looking at?' she asks.

'Er, fanart,' I say, hurriedly swiping to my favourite pic of Isga uncoiling her purple-black tail and slipping off a bone-strewn rock into the sea.

'Wanna watch a couple of episodes before we go out?' Chel suggests.

'Absolutely.'

I let Chel choose and, she goes for some comedy: 'A Mess of Pottage', when some clueless Jaarv eat the porridge the villagers put out as protection money for the tomtar, and the little buggers go on the rampage.

A lot of people find the tomtar annoying. They give zero shits, and every last one of the little maniacs is called Kaos, because they think individual names are for snowflakes. According to ettkaos, one of the few actual Swedish fans, they all have ADHD, like she does. I'm starting to relate to the amount of ants in their pants.

That's one of the best things about *Nordhelm*. Human or not, the characters feel like real people, and you can see yourself being them, and know you're real whether anyone else sees you or not.

Chapter 17

Watch party over, I nick extra condoms from a bathroom cabinet, put on my skinny shorts, glitter sandals and glitter cowboy hat – real, not plastic – and rev up to become Sex Yan.

And an hour later, here we are. Not in the West End – too likely to get IDed – but heading for a warehouse club where the door guys don't ask questions. We get off the bus – a big red London bus, with a curvy staircase at the back! – and walk through a street of annoyingly ordinary houses that might as well be in one of the small towns back home. Ras is wearing a button-down shirt that shows his chest hair, and a pimple is Everesting out of his chin. He keeps looking at Chel as they talk, and I have to approve; it's like he's looking inside her, just the right distance so he's actually seeing what's there.

Tonight, they are to snog. Chel resolved on it, all on her own, after we finished watching *Nordhelm*.

'Are you sure you're OK about us coming with you?' Chel asks Kieran for about the fifth time (as if encouraging him to back out now is a sane idea). 'We appreciate it, lots.'

'Like I said, if Mum wants you chaperoned, she can do it,' Kieran grunts. He's already annoyed because tonight's supposed to be his mate Uma's birthday thing but she's got a stomach ache. 'But don't run off on your own.'

Sticking with Ras, who met us at the bus stop and immediately initiated a rerun of the handholding incident, is clearly not a problem for Chel.

I pretty much have to walk beside Kieran, and he is definitely judging my cowboy hat (cream, with a pink glitter sash). Perhaps he thinks it's tacky – or that I'm overdressed, in a special way that involves not having many clothes on.

'What?' I challenge him. He's been giving my hot look the side-eye all the way here.

'Subtle outfit,' he says.

'You think I look like a country girl overcompensating.'

'Your words, not mine. Best to get it out of your system, I suppose.' He raises a hand, palm out. 'Hey, you dish out the honesty, you'd better take it.'

'Fair enough. You're looking better than usual, tonight,' I say. He's got a kind of retro black thing with silver buttons that somehow manages to suit him.

'Well, thank you,' he says. 'Now let's have a good time.'

We've reached a deeply unglamorous industrial estate. Plumbing supplies; a stationery wholesalers with a giant 3D envelope over the door; and, at the end of the row, a big, dark, anonymous shed with a neon sign: *Zippers*. None of the letters are broken, so it must be classy. The bouncer gives Ras a careful look, as if he can smell the nerd vibes, but otherwise we sail in as promised. And . . . We. Are. In. A. London. Nightclub! At first there's just a lobby with who-knows-what smeared on the floor, but beyond that an industrial double door opens and closes on waves of heat and noise and surging light.

Kieran leads us towards the bar. While he buys us a drink I gawp, because *woo-hoo!* Look at this place. Undulating bodies flash red, blue, white, the floor is throbbing, the air is throbbing, I'm throbbing, I want to run straight into the crowd and grab the hand of the boy in the sweat-stained T-shirt with the huge sun on his chest . . .

You're not supposed to do that, and Kieran *might* chase me. Instead, I find a Chinese guy chatting to his mates nearby at the bar. He's a little too skinny even for my usual type, but how would it feel to wrap my arms around him? His face is delicate, and I think he's got even more eyeliner on than me. We lock eyes like you do when you spot someone you don't know but sort of recognise naturally. He turns away from his friends.

'So, do you come here often?' I ask – a line so lame it's obviously deliberate.

He's hooked, anyway. I'm good at this! I'm good at everything. It takes me about two minutes to get in there, via a discussion of his musical aspirations, and then . . . urgh.

I smell fags. First there's the gust of foul breath, then it's lips and tongues and *eww.* I hate the smell, and now I know the taste is worse. I yank myself away, and Mr Skinny gives me a questioning look. I eyeball back: betrayal! You looked so pretty, and I was *almost* interested when you told me about your band.

'You stink,' I inform him. I'm angry, and he needs to know.

Mr Skinny protests, predictably enough. I think he says my hat is stupid – it isn't, but I might have been stupid to wear it in this sweat-bath. Maybe there's a cloakroom. No. That would take too much time. I'd better get back to the others.

Kieran's watching me as I head over. He's on his phone – probably wondering where his mates have got to – but he's got me a drink, and shoves it along the bar at me. 'Classy,' he says, nodding over at Mr Skinny. 'Freaked yourself out, did you?' Now he sounds all kind. He must think I baulked at my own unladylike forwardness, not the fag stench. Fine, if it keeps him happy. I stick out my tongue.

I wonder if Chel's going to give me a hard time, but she's busy with Ras, who's telling her about his family holiday in Normandy.

'Uh . . . we go to Weston-super-Mare some years,' says Chel.

'Oh. We can wave to each other across the Channel, then!'

'Weston's on the *Bristol* Channel,' I point out, before realising that this probably doesn't help with the Awkward McAwkwardness. How to save this one . . . 'Do you get to go back to Afghanistan and see family?' I'd like to visit Uncle Liko in Guangdong . . . Which is not a war zone. Hm, I may have been insensitive to Ras there.

'That would be slightly difficult,' says Ras, so drily it'd shrivel a cactus, but I can't really blame him.

'It's gonna be amazing, amazing, amazing!' I sing along to the music, perfectly in time. 'What's going to be amazing? Well, something!' Mr Skinny still looks pretty from the back, and so does the big-bum woman next to him. 'I fancy everyone! Is that a bit tasteless?'

I turn around to get Chel's and Ras's vital opinions, but Ras is off. He's spinning Chel onto the dancefloor, finding room somehow. Chel almost stumbles on her heels, but then she's into it. Ooh, Ras is a nice mover! Who'd've thought?

'Whoa, he's good,' I tell Kieran.

'Yeah,' Kieran replies, and there's an awkward moment when I suddenly wonder if he's going to ask me to dance, which he'd probably do Jane-Austen-style or something . . . but he doesn't, and the moment passes. Phew. That would be only one step up from doing it with Chel. I've thought about that of course. My best friend . . . no, no, nooooo. Hashtag YanFail.

'Right, Chelsea's safe with Ras,' says Kieran. 'My crowd are at the other bar. I think you'll like Erin and Paul. Mario stayed home with Uma, but Leah's joining us. You're cool with trans women, right?'

'Of course,' I say, rolling my eyes. Well, all right – I haven't knowingly physically met a trans person, cos there's not exactly a rash of them in Brockford, but I live on the internet.

Kieran sets off around the edge of the dancefloor. I wonder if Leah's cute? He said Erin-and-Paul like they're a couple, though. Maybe they're wonderful, but I don't want to get it on with two virtually-marrieds (I'm not that adventurous *yet*), and anyway Kieran probably wants to hang with his mates and not me, so on second thoughts . . . I'm off again, behind a pillar and into the crowd. Oh *yeah*.

The pounding in my veins syncs with the bass. Everything is wonderful wonderful wonderful . . . Someone grabs my arse; I dodge. In the space between backs I hold up my phone and snap the dancefloor and Instagram it for the Brockies: 'I'm here and you're not, sux to be you.' To hell with them. I sashay – excellent word – through the crowd and put my arms out, both because I am fabulous and to protect my hat. I get some glares for shoving people, who deserve it for being in my way. Music screams: remixed death metal with howling vocals, pounding drums. The music is in me now.

There's a really nice-looking guy leaning against a pillar chatting to a mate. He's kind of wiry as well as thin: just right for me. I hover, and smile, and soon enough he senses someone's looking at him, and spots me, and smiles too. I'm in there!

Except I'm not. He goes back to his conversation, and doesn't look up again when I get nearer. So I shove in even closer, practically brushing him with what a comedy character in a particularly cheesy *Nordhelm* episode calls my 'advance guard', and he gives me a pained look.

Huh, probably gay. Forget it. I can and will do far, far better than Mr Skinny or Mr Wiry. I toss my hair, which Mr Wiry ignores, and I spin away again, for a while, I don't know how long, I just spin, bodies to bodies, beat to beat, banging into some people who bang back, others who shrink away. I've only had one drink . . . I'm high on life and music and sweat. Once I glimpse Chel and Ras, but I don't go near. Me and Chel don't have to be together all the time. I want her to be happy. I can pick from everyone else in the world!

I've made my way across the hall, I think. There's Kieran, with a couple of people who are probably his mates. Apparently I've been kind of looking for him, because I suddenly feel very strongly that familiar faces are nice. With familiar faces, I won't quite spin off into the void . . . or something.

He scowls and takes a few steps forward to meet me. 'I said, don't wander off! I was about to come and look for you.'

'You really think that's necessary?'

That really is quite a scowl. 'Yes! You're bloody hard work, Yan.'

Whatever . . . I can guess which of his friends are which just from looking at them. Erin and Paul are definitely involved – you can tell because right now they're so clearly on the verge of becoming uninvolved I can practically taste the foul vibes as I rock up to them. Erin's tall and skinny, a ginger girl in a really unfortunate yellow dress peering down at dark little Paul like a short-sighted vulture. He's completely ignoring her in a way that shows he's actually completely not. Another tall girl, in glasses and a tiger-print blouse, who must be Leah, is slurping a blue cocktail beside Erin. She looks at me meaningfully (how does she know who I am . . .? I suppose if Kieran described me, I'm kind of distinctive) and jerks her head and rolls her eyes at her friends. Ooh, me and her are getting front row at a car crash.

'Hey!' shouts Kieran over-cheerfully, through the bass, and quickly introduces me to everyone. When it comes to his friends I should probably not go for absolutely *everyone* . . . Thinking about what I normally like, Leah looks sweet but a bit mousy for me, tiger blouse notwithstanding, and Erin's murderous expression is probably a no even if I was into gingers, but I like the look of Paul, who's short but has squeezably narrow shoulders in a tight T-shirt, and soft-looking lips. I could go for him if he detaches himself from Erin, which is clearly a thing that could happen. I am a femme fatale. I am fatal.

Everyone's glad to see me, too, possibly because Erin is about ready to knee her boyfriend in the bollocks and I'm a distraction. We all shout things at each other, and hear about half of them. Kieran manages to get Erin away from Paul and she cheers up as they start joking about something.

I think I'm having a conversation with Paul and Leah about the Tube, but it might be boobs or lube, I'm not actually sure because of the level of noise pushing in behind me. I lace my hands behind my head and stretch, turning deliberately in Paul's direction. And stay that way for rather longer than you would if you were just trying to loosen stiff muscles.

'Whoa,' says Leah, giving me a funny look. I go back to standing normally, but it's worked, Paul's eyes are on my chest. I grin at him. Bad Yan, with his girlfriend right there! Well, it's all just too fascinating.

Oh, and Erin's noticed! She pushes Paul in the back and he turns around, and I think he's trying to look innocent and offended, but Erin takes a swing at him.

Whoa! He's fast enough to catch her arm, but her elbow knocks Leah's drink out of her hand. Kieran's straight in there with a hand on Paul's shoulder; Leah's accidentally bashing random bystanders as she flaps at her soggy blouse.

It's all in slow motion, though. Everything is, compared to me, even the pounding dubstep, and the security guy who appears after half a minute and looms over everyone. Green light washes over people's faces, making them look ill. I detect that Erin hates me, which is hilarious. Just because I'm the prettiest girl in the room.

Then, after the bouncer retreats, something really weird happens – Erin puts her arm around Paul, then they talk to Leah a bit, then off the two of them go as if they were in tru luv 4eva.

'What the hell?' I ask Kieran and Leah.

'Oh, that's just them,' says Leah, shrugging and wiping down her blouse one last time. The mess doesn't really show in this light. 'But why'd you shove your tits at Paul, girl? You're lucky Erin didn't whack *you*.'

'Yeah, what she said,' says Kieran. 'What *is* it with you?'

'I didn't mean to do it,' I insist, trying to look innocent, which doesn't seem to convince either of them.

'Hm, whatever. Kids these days,' says Leah, who looks a maximum of twenty years old. Then a new thumping beat starts up. 'Oh my God, I *love* this one. Come on.'

Kieran says something, but it's lost in the noise. And then we're off! Leah beckons me, and she's cuter when she's dancing – she gets a sort of Chelsea-intense face – and K-boy's not bad, in a flaily way. Working off a fair bit of tension, methinks.

All hail alcohol. It's surreal. Paul and Erin were surreal. Everything's surreal. Anything can happen. Maybe romance between Leah and Kieran. I should get out of the way. Nah, that's an excuse. I just want to GO.

Leah's got her hand up in a dance move. I startle her by slapping it in a high five, and plunge back into the crowd. And there she is. The girl I realise I was looking for. She's got a kind of Afro undercut and little glinty gold earrings. Swelling hips under a bare belly above low-slung jeans – *sinuous* – and taller than me, with little breasts in a sweat-stained white top. Diamond in her belly button, which I want to bite and pull at gently with my teeth. A bit of a snooty expression, which is well justified. And she's dancing on her own. Waiting for me.

She senses me, and gives me a bit of a sceptical look. I don't think she likes my hat; huh. I doff it like a Victorian gentleman, and that gets a smile. We're behind some speakers; I think we'll be able to hear each other talk.

'Well, you're new,' shouts Undercut. 'Here with your mother?'

What? 'I'm with my bestboy – best friend and her boyfriend,' I say, right in a quiet bit of music. Oh God, what a lame thing to come out with. And mixing my words up again. Get it together, Yan!

'Fresh from the countryside,' shouts Undercut as the track blasts out again. 'Sweet.'

OK. Fine. Patronise me. Her Essex accent isn't the smoothest thing I ever heard, either. But her body language is saying something better. She moves forward and slips her fingers under my chin. I chuck the hat aside – who needs it? Everything I've made is so limited. I'm going to start again, I'm going to shape fire and thought under my fingers.

'You look so intense,' says Undercut, still patronising but curious too. She's right. I'm throbbing so hard there's about to be an explosion splattering bits of Yan all over the walls, and then I'll rise into the crashing waves of light . . . How am I supposed to look, if not like me?

She kisses me.

Soft breasts, wide hips brushing mine then nestling together in a way that's new to me, hard teeth nibbling my lip, which is *extremely good yes please more* . . . Undercut gets a hand round the back of my neck and strokes it. I do the same with her, then move my hand down to play with the ribbon-straps of her top. I'm thinking too much, but my body doesn't care.

Then, out of the corner of my eye, I see a fat woman come up next to us, holding two drinks. Oh God, of course. It's Undercut's girlfriend. A woman as fine as this one wouldn't be alone.

The girlfriend's smiling, though. She's rather pretty, too . . . Watching, relaxed. I'm a show. I don't care. Tonight I love everything. I'm expanding, into myself and the rhythm of kissing, grinding. My shorts are wet, and I wonder if Undercut's fingers will creep downwards; but no, eventually she pulls back, and gives me a little prod on the nose with her forefinger as if to say, 'Cool it, sweetie.' Damn it, she thinks I'm a kid. Then she grabs her drink and guzzles it thirstily, which is understandable . . . Should I suggest going home with both of them?

Someone taps me on the shoulder. 'Yan!'

It's *Chelsea*. Can she not see this is the worst time ever in history? Undercut's getting wrapped up in her girlfriend – literally – and Chel is tugging on my left arm, demanding, 'Bogs! Now!'

Bloody hell. I could refuse to go, but it's obviously too late to get back in with Undercut, so I let myself be dragged off into a smelly, sticky-floored bog. There's a sort of shelf in the wall under a dark window, back a bit from the row of twitching arses and reflected open mouths that is the make-up zone, aka the sinks. Chel sits on the shelf, tapping her lavender nails on the chipped green tiles.

If she's going to lecture me for running off, or ask where my hat is, or make a big deal out of me snogging strangers, she'd better get on with it.

'Ras is so sweet!' she says. 'We kissed!'

'Oh, right, cool,' I say. Chel keeps watching me, like she's expecting me to question her, even though she's only done what she said she'd do. I've got plans of my own, the perfect body to find, but I'd better come up with something. 'So – uh – you've left him out there?'

'Yeah. I just needed a rest from dancing.' Chel fans herself. 'God, it's boiling. And loud.' When I don't say anything else, she goes on, 'You was eyeing that girl out there. You like?'

Aha, I think Chel's trying to be worldly. I guess she didn't see me kissing Undercut with such enthusiasm or she'd probably have flipped. She doesn't need to know.

'Ah, I just fancied her. We snogged!' OK, apparently we are talking about it, because my mouth has a mind of its own.

Chelsea frowns. 'OK. That were *really* quick. Guess you wasn't joking the other day. And you – ah – just walked off?'

'So what?' I say, annoyed by her tone. She's the one who dragged me here. 'It's not a big deal, I just fancied her. I'll tell you more later. And I know that's not what you grabbed me for, anyway. So, you kissed Ras, great! Now why don't you look happier about it?'

That's got her. But she wavers.

'It's only the second time you kissed a girl. That *is* a big deal,' Chel persists like she thinks this is a safer topic. 'So you really know you like girls now?'

Er, no. We are not having that conversation. 'Come on, Chelsea. It's hardly the millionth time *you've* kissed a boy. And then you ran off to talk to me.'

Chel kicks the green-tiled wall. I can smell the booze on her breath. 'I just needed a time out.' Pause. 'Ras freaked me out!'

Aha. Thought so. 'By doing what?'

'Well, kissing was brilliant, kind of, but then he started telling me about, oh, it's difficult to juggle study and two jobs and his Persian literature study group and seeing his family sometimes, and a relationship on top of that would be tricky but we could make it work.'

'And?'

'Yeah, most of that is fair enough.'

'But?'

'*But*, a relationship? Does he think I'm like Steve and his mates says?'

'Huh? What's wrong with a relationship?' I have to think through the logic for a moment. The losers in the churchyard scoff at the women in Chel's family for supposedly being slappers, not committing to sensible –

Then it dawns on me. 'You mean getting knocked up and living on benefits?'

'Yeah!'

'That still doesn't make much sense. I mean, from Ras?'

Chel plucks at her neckline and makes a feeble attempt to fan herself with her blouse. The wall is getting a proper heel-drumming from her sparkly sandals, but she looks reassured. 'No, I suppose that ain't the first thing a boy like Ras thinks of,' she concedes. 'Oh God, it's me, not him! It's all so . . . I just don't want the whole relationship thing right now. I need to figure out myself first.' She pauses. 'You think I'm pathetic. That I don't know what I'm doing. Can't make me mind up.'

I think she's being boring, and she's slowing me down.

'Of course not. You're just a bit drunk. You need to tell Ras this stuff, not me.'

'And what if I brought a brown guy home? What would my family say? I mean, most of 'em are sensible, but you never know with –'

OK, that really *is* enough. I raise a hand. 'Chelsea Furse, you are *not* laying that on me.'

She looks down at her swinging feet. 'Sorry. All right. All right. I'll go back to Ras if you'll come with me.'

Urgh. I want to be supportive, *but*. 'Chel, you've got to talk to him yourself.'

She looks daunted, but I don't let up with the stern and sensible advice, and soon enough she gets it.

'Yeah, all right,' she concedes. 'Um, but, please, just come over to start with, and we'll say I been sick or something. That'll at least give us an excuse to get out of this dump.' She gestures towards the door as it opens and a wave of trance surges in, along with three screaming drunks who look younger than we are.

'Leave the club? Then you'll sober up and never talk to him properly,' I point out. And no *way* am I being dragged out of here yet.

Chelsea continues drumming her heels, but more slowly now. I'm having trouble staying still, just for a change. People crash their way into a cubicle behind me and start noisily making out. This is probably the place you come for sex. I think I'm actually shaking; probably the excitement. I need to concentrate on Chel for just a few more seconds, to pack her off out of my way. 'I'm not going anywhere,' I say.

'We'd better find Kieran as well as Ras before we can get out of here,' says Chelsea. 'I don't wanna worry anyone.'

'You aren't listening. I said I don't want to leave.'

Chel eyeballs me. 'Cos you wanna snog more strangers?'

'Well, yes, as it happens. I'm just trying to enjoy London.'

Apparently I've got loud, and now the make-up brigade are staring at us, a row of a dozen reflected eyes. Who cares? I'm furious, out of nowhere, because my best friend is, let's face it, *wet*, and right now I need that not to be my problem.

'Look after your*self* for once, Chelsea,' I instruct her. 'You could even, I don't know, have some actual fun. Drop Ras, find someone whose face is less like bubble wrap . . .'

'He don't look like bubble wrap! And d'you think you're looking after *your*self?'

'That's none of your business,' I continue before she can answer. I need to stop my veins burning up from inside, which involves Chel getting out of my way, very soon. 'If you dig yourself a hole I can't magic you out of it, that's all. And if you want to be homophobic about me kissing a girl, just come out and say so.'

'Where the hell d'you get *that* idea from?' Chelsea almost shouts, going red in the face. 'Oh, I know you don't mean it. You're saying it to get rid of me. What's got into you?'

I smirk. Or something smirks, and it appears to be controlling my face.

My best friend looks away, slaps the tiles hard, and stands up.

'Fine. Yeah, you're right about one thing: I need to sort me own stuff out. We can talk about you later. And don't think we won't.'

'Oh, scold me like I'm your little sister, why don't you?' I shoot after her. I want to sound hard. I sound desperate. She doesn't hear.

CHAPTER 18

Eyes follow me, arses bump me, but I don't want just any old body for actual sex. Everyone looks good, but some look better than others, and I deserve the best. I hunt in the sweating dance. *Yan-yan yan-yan* goes the beat of my heart. I don't need Chel. Lights strobe. I need alcohol, touch, heat sinking into my flesh.

There's a dancing fivesome, three girls and two guys. There's a cute probably Japanese girl, but she looks loved up with one of the guys. I think the bigger guy is spare, and he's pretty fine. Pale and thin, but visible muscles on him: lithe-strong, like Rothgern, not a beanstalk. White teeth flashing blue in the lights, blond crewcut, five or six years older than me – but then I look twenty-one. I turn the fivesome into a sixsome. One of the non-loved-up girls seems to mind. Probably because she's minging. Beyoncé comes on. Am I a good dancer? Yes. I'm never going to tire.

'What's your name?' I shout at Crewcut.

'Aaron,' Crewcut shouts back. *Aaron?* Who knows if it's the truth, but oh my God, that's the name of the actor who plays Rothgern. There are some similarities around the arse as well, mmmmm.

'I'm Ruby,' I respond. 'Want a drink?'

Aaron moves away from his friends. I like him. I want

more vodka, which I'm pretty sure was in this latest glass of stuff found on the floor and nicked, only I seem to have downed it in one. I'm invincible. I offer to buy Aaron a drink rather than waiting for him to offer one to me, which I think bucks gender roles, which is a good thing but also financially imprudent . . . Oh, forget it.

'Look, I don't really want a drink. I need a shag,' I say when he conveniently looks unsure. Whoa, I can totally pull off candid and sophisticated! I giggle, in case saying that made me scary. I'm annoyed at myself for giggling.

Aaron narrows his eyes. 'Steady on. Are you a hooker?'

'What? No! I'm just not a shy little flower. Girls get horny too. And asking for what you want's the best way to get it. Right?'

Yes! Now I definitely sound all cool and experienced, and so boldly charming. I love me!

It works. Aaron relaxes a bit. 'Can't argue with that.'

I reach out and tap the tip of his nose like Undercut did to me. Then I pull a condom out of my pocket and wave it enticingly.

'You know, I never met my dad. He's probably a seven-foot pirate captain.' I am not shaking. Or if I am, it's definitely with excitement. Aaron has sparkly, sparkly blue eyes. Pretty, pretty boy. Was what I just said a bit random?

Aaron's grinning. He's playing along. 'I can believe that.' He doesn't think I'm too much. 'I think *you* might be a pirate, Ruby.' We're reverse-flirting. We started with the important bit – now we're establishing enough of a bond that we won't forget what the other one looks like. Suddenly he fills the room. I trace my finger down his hip.

'I'm everything. Looks like you're packing, young sir.'

I can see Aaron glance down at his own crotch, mouthing something like *ahem*, even if he doesn't say it. I am too much, I knew it. To hell with it. To heaven with us!

'Do you know what to do with it?' I prod him further. 'Because, to tell the truth, I really am an innocent flower, and am going to need some guidance.' God, I am a *genius*. I can hide the fact that I maybe am a bit inexperienced behind a game. But we need to get on with this. I don't entirely trust Chel not to call Nurse Mum if she gets in a snivel over Ras and then can't find me.

'I can probably remember,' says Aaron. Then we're on our way to the toilet. I steer us to the cubicle where people were making out earlier – customer-vetted and approved – and I switch to coy. 'Ooh, there's not much room.' Do I sound silly? Yes, but that's the point. Personas for the win. (*Which one is me?*)

I push Aaron into a snog. No faggy foulness this time! His tongue is smooth, and his warm mouth is sharp with vodka, and all the places we lean together, mouth and hips and my breasts against his firm chest, are huge. I pull down his lip, try to bite only gently, but it must be a bit much for him, because he pulls out of the kiss and says, 'Careful,' though he looks apologetic. Sooo vanilla.

Aaron starts kicking his trousers off. 'I'll sit on the seat,' he says. 'Come on.' He pats my hips, indicating where he needs me to stand.

My shorts go down. My bare arse bumps against the almost-cool cubicle wall. I have pubic hair – it just sort of grew, and I've got better things to do than fight it – is that going to gross him out? No, he doesn't seem bothered. And *that is a penis*. It's bent. It's . . . not exactly pretty. But the point isn't to look at it. This is amazing. I'm in a toilet having casual sex! Not lying flat on my back, dreaming about death. Anyway, I don't expect the moon: I've read a lot of fanfic insta-orgasms and watched plenty of American

TV, but I've also read all those rabbithole posts about how a lot of het sex is actually a bit rubbish – double if it's with some random guy and double double if it's in a club toilet. But it's all new, it's all fun!

Concentrate, Yan!

Aaron's hard and he doesn't need my condom – he whips out one of his own. 'I'm not going to make you blow me,' he assures me, like that was on the agenda at all. His body is firm and luscious and I can feel my own nipples tight, tight.

I – I what, *mount* him? That sounds hilarious – and lean my hands on his shoulders, and flex. It maybe burns and stretches a bit, but that's all; this Aaron isn't Rothgern-sized, and I'm wet (though that's mostly Undercut's doing). We slide together. There's a part of another person in me. What else is like that? Ah, the dentist. *No, I am not comparing my first fuck to the dentist.* Keep your thoughts on track, Yan! Because my body does know what it's doing. It clenches and jerks backward and forward. Up and down. It's . . . not a revelation, but at the same time it is because everything is, even the green tiles on the wall are so vivid, and I manage to get my finger in down there so I'm getting plenty out of this exchange too, and there's a dick in me, and all of it is so *real*. I focus on Aaron, who's still good-looking, even in the light. He missed his left lower jaw when shaving though; I want to stroke it. I can't; I'm gripping his shoulder and trying to remember this stuff from the telly. And . . . and the names of the Goth bands scrawled on the cubicle wall are going swimmy in front of my eyes . . . (it's really easy for me to come lately! Yan, *stop thinking*) . . . and here we *gooooo*. The rush. The spinning through me. Long seconds.

I stop jerking. He keeps on, though, more and more . . .

He comes inside me . . . or I hope his face means that, and not that he's having a stroke. I just got off and I'm horny horny horny again. It's the wheeling and burning inside my head, sweeping down through my body but never fixing or peaking. I bet Aaron hasn't guessed it's my first time.

I don't think he's thinking about anything just yet.

After a few moments, he pulls out of me and deals with the condom. There's a *splorp*, and white goo. It's actually endearing. 'That did it for you too? Well, with some help from a finger. I did see that.'

I nod. His manhood doesn't seem to be wounded, which I guess is good. I have a taste of . . . of stars and unicorns, but not even from the sex, it's just what I am now. 'It was amazing. But sex in a toilet, really! I should be growing out of this sort of thing.' Is that overdoing my sophisticated act?

Aaron checks the time on his phone. 'Hey, come home with me, and I'll do even better,' he says.

Wow, I didn't expect that. I really am totally the sophisticate, and there's no reason why I shouldn't go with him . . . except one-on-one it'd be awkward, and I'd have to slow down – and my friends'll go mental. Chel really would call my mum, and worry her.

'It was just a suggestion,' says Aaron, putting his dick away. He looks at me a bit oddly, like he's seen something disconcerting in my face. Whatever.

I get dressed again as well. I'm still utterly hyper, but I've done a thing. Sex with a boy! Now I need to do another thing, and another. And another. Sex with a girl. Kisses. Tell Chelsea everything. I haven't actually properly danced yet! The pressure inside me isn't gone. It's barely diminished. 'I need to get back to my friends,' I explain.

'Yeah, I get it,' says Aaron, studying me some more.

'Ruby . . . thanks for the good time. See you round.'

He half-smiles, and he's off.

I had sseeeeexxxx! And now I am . . . sticky.

Luckily the cubicle hasn't run out of loo roll. I clean myself up as best I can, and attempt to calm down, which involves spinning on the spot and banging my elbow against the cubicle wall. At least there are quite a few cubicles so I'm not causing a queue.

I need to get back out there.

CHAPTER 19

'Well, you didn't come after me,' I point out to Kieran when I locate him, more or less by chance. He's at the bar, again.

'No,' he snaps. Looks like he's had a bit to drink now. 'But whatever. As long as you're alive.'

I shift from foot to foot. Maybe I do feel a tiny bit calmer after the, er, moment of release. Jumpy rather than like my actual head is on actual fire. The posters catch my eye, and it's edifying to discover that I can slow my brain down enough to read them. One of them threatens prosecution for drug dealing, and the other is advertising someone called DJ Hard Alex playing here next Saturday night.

'Has Leah gone as well?' I ask him. It was nice he had a friend.

'Her boyfriend called – they've got an invite to some band's aftershow. I could hardly gate-crash and completely dump you two.'

'You'd like to, though.'

'No shit.' Then Kieran points with the index figure of the hand that's holding his glass. Like he doesn't want anyone else to see he's doing it.

Chel and Ras are standing about three yards away. Or rather, leaning, against a second Hard Alex poster. Not looking at one another. Arms folded, while still holding their drinks.

How did I not notice? (*How?!*)

Anyway. Oh *dear.* The sight is kind of morbidly compelling. Like putting a tin of beans on the hob and waiting for it to explode.

'That looks promising,' I say into Kieran's ear, half-over and half-under the music.

'Yeahhh, well, whatever.' He's sounding a bit slurry. 'I've had enough of being the United Nations.'

I'm sure he has, poor boy. So it's my turn. Because *I* am invincible!

I grin and almost bounce the couple of steps towards Chel, starting to shout as I go. 'Hey, Chel-seeea! I've got a headache! Perhaps we should just all get going.' There, I'm being the BestestFF and doing what she wanted. Might as well, as on reflection we've probably mined all the delights Zippers has to offer by now.

Ras looks a bit startled, Chel relieved – and I think Kieran's relieved too, because he quickly sweeps by, basically scooping us up in his wake. One short trip past security men and through rusty metal doors later, we're in a scrubby area between the rows of warehouses and outlets. Chel abruptly stops walking, plonks her bum on a crumbling wall and takes off her high heels. 'Ugh,' she says, and massages her toes.

I should help in some way, but I keep wanting to laugh. Not even really *at* anything, just *laugh*.

It's Ras who starts speaking. 'Chel, you've got to tell me what's going on here. Is it something I said?'

'No! Well, yes, actually. I just ain't up for moving that fast,' says Chel. 'You said all that about a relationship and – it's just too fast.'

'Why on earth do you think . . . Look, when I said a relationship, I didn't mean I wanted to get married!' He glares at her. 'I'm doing a degree and two jobs!'

'Yeah, you told me that afore. And you know what I thought then? I thought, the guy's trying to persuade himself he wants me that much, even though he hasn't really got time.'

There's a painful pause.

'So what if I was? You should be flattered.'

'But it's stupid, Ras. It's not practical.'

Hm, I should probably speak before they incinerate each other. Kieran's shaking himself as if trying to clear his head of the alcohol fumes.

'Don't mind us,' I tell Ras and Chelsea.

They aren't minding us. He keeps glaring at her. She keeps glaring at him. The situation should *really* be ramping up to explode at this point.

But somehow it isn't.

Ras lets out a long sigh. 'No, it's not really practical, is it?'

'No,' Chel agrees, and sighs too.

'No,' he repeats.

'Yeah. I ain't coming to London for another year,' Chelsea continues, 'and I probably won't get into UCL anyway, and I'm clearly rubbish at clubbing, and I'm . . .' She puts her face in her hands.

Is she going to cry? I don't think so. She's just knackered and pissed. To his credit, Ras is looking a bit ashamed, but in an 'oops' way, not a seized-with-passion-to-beg-forgiveness-of-my-queen way.

'Well, if you do come, we can hang out as friends,' he says.

Chelsea makes a sort of *grarrgh!* noise from behind her

hands. I think it translates as 'yes', but I really need to say something to help.

'I had sex in a toilet!' I announce loudly. And giggle.

Ah. I wasn't quite planning to say *that*, but it burst out somehow, and it's genius. Major distraction! Possibly I've made an idiot of myself, but whatever. 'Wheeee!' I spin around in a circle on the spot.

'You are completely out of it,' Chel says flatly. 'And don't make stuff up.'

'Oh, I'm *not*. I blanged a bo– banged a bloke in a toilet!' I am so funny! 'Don't worry, I'm not pregnant – I know what a condom is! After my dad left I heard Grandma snarking at Mum, "Surely a nurse knows how to use a condom?" Then Grandma looked around and saw me and was completely horrified and grabbed me for a cuddle and promised nothing would ever stop them loving me. I got a bars – a Mars bar out of that, so I thought it was a good deal. Did I ever tell you that?'

And I'm off laughing again. That whole little story came out almost entirely coherent! Everything just seems connected to everything else, though I probably shouldn't say *all* of it. 'I wanna meet my dad . . . Look, how are you *supposed* to feel after your first shag? Huh?'

Chelsea's sitting up straight on the wall now. She and Ras exchange a glance. Have I reunited them? That would be extremely clever of me.

I can't stay still. I start fast-walking towards the main road. A car shoots by and someone leans out of the window and shouts about tits.

I hear quick footsteps behind me. Kieran's voice. 'Jesus, she's snorted something. How'd I miss that?'

Ras replies, 'You're not responsible for everything, mate.'

'I promised Mum,' says Kieran. 'Which makes me an

idiot. Yan, you stupid little . . . Where did you get the stuff?'

And he's grabbing my arm. Whoa, *rude*. I break away and shove him, not hard – but touching his shoulder reminds me of Aaron and the toilet and makes me laugh while I'm still angry. What's going on? Can nobody see? Chel comes up beside Kieran – typical, the Furses banding together – and can't she see anything?

'Get what?' I retort. 'Just because I know how to have fun. Stop being a martyr, Kieran.'

He splutters for a moment, and I carry on before he can actually say anything. 'It was just a funny story! Anyway *I'm not high*!'

'Either she's lying or someone slipped her something,' says Kieran, to Chel. He's got a firmer hold of me now. I almost like it: I can't blow away. 'If we don't even know what it is, we'd better get her to the hospital. Ras, you ever seen anything like this?'

'My dad doesn't bring patients home.'

'Yan, just tell us! What did you take?' demands Chel, sounding panicky now.

Boring!

I can't look at her. The *hospital*? No. No. (Maybe?) Just no. They'll find out . . . What? There's nothing to find out! I need to put a stop to this.

'All right, yes, I bought some, uh, coke.' I almost wish I had – it would at least make sense of things. This is just me now . . . Panic surges. *Hide*. 'I'm coming down already. It was probably mostly flour.'

I hate the look Kieran gives me, like I'm doing this to mess up his night. I know I'm spoiling Chel's week. Ras has a hand over his face. Everything was surreal in the club. Out here there's weeds growing through cracked tarmac and grey clouds glowering out of the night.

'Didn't you do anything interesting when you were seventeen?' I demand of Kieran. 'I suppose you were already saving the planet. Trying to develop a personality so Mummy and Daddy would notice you.'

Kieran relaxes his grip. I'm impressed that he doesn't react all that much, but I can tell I've hit home from the way he clenches his jaw. I hold up my hands like I'm on some TV cop show, showing I've got no weapons. Then I realise I'm balling up my fists. The others are looking at them, and I'm *still* giggling. It's separate from me. I'm looking out past it from deep inside.

I am Isga, rising on her great tail, arms raised, fangs bared.

There's a sick lurch inside my head. I can't . . . can't much of anything. I press my palm to my skull. Is this the booze wearing off? Post-shag crash? It's like my mind has just been wrenched out the side of my head.

'Look – all right – I'm coming down,' I say. *I'm scared.*

The others stare at me.

'I'm coming down,' I repeat. What do they want? Who am I supposed to be? 'Look, I'm sorry,' I continue, because I'm remembering the script. I can keep to the politeness script. I feel my shoulders relaxing just a bit. 'I'll chill.'

I meet Chel's eyes. She thinks I'm being an arsehole, but maybe she also sees that I don't know what the hell is going on. I want to hug her – and hit her – for it.

'Sex. In a toilet,' she says. Her voice is pretty flat, but there's this tiny intonation that says she wants all this to unhappen. She wants me to make it go away.

OK, then I need to do that.

'Nah, I was kidding of course!' I say brightly. Then I

realise brightness is probably as inappropriate as everything else about me right now.

But Chel buys it. She wants to buy it. I notice her sandals are dangling from one hand; she came after me completely barefoot.

'What an hilarious joke,' she says heavily. 'All right. So you didn't have sex, you just snorted some coke and you've gone bananas. That's all. Oh my God, Yan.' She heaves a massive sigh. 'We'd've had a better night in a cow byre.'

'Yep. Yep yep yep,' I agree.

Kieran's speaking to Ras. 'You might as well go, mate. I'll get them home. They're only here till Sunday morning, thank God.'

Ras nods. 'Yeah, sure.' He doesn't seem very sorry about that, but he does sound awkward when he says, 'Uh, Chel, bye.'

Chelsea glances at him in a startled way that suggests she'd forgotten he existed, but is OK with being reminded. 'Yeah, bye. Thanks for – stuff.'

'Drop me a message, then?' he says. 'As a friend?'

'Yeah. Yeah, I will.'

For a moment I think they're actually going to shake hands, but it's not quite that stiff. They just nod at each other, even smile a tiny bit. It's wholesome and strangely charming.

Then Ras walks off. He only spoils the unexpected mellow vibe a bit by turning around to shout, 'Sort yourself out!' at me.

Chapter 20

On the upper deck of the night bus, Chel and I slide into a seat together. Kieran's slumped a couple of metres behind us on the other side of the aisle with his earbuds in. 'Sit there and do not move,' he growled when we got on.

Now I'm watching identical semi-detached houses slide by outside the window. Chel's not speaking.

'No more Ras, then,' I say.

'Yeah. That wasn't meant to be. Guess I *was* trying to be like you.'

'Impulsive and exciting.'

'A bloody idiot, more like.' Suddenly her voice is intense and angry. '*Coke*, Yan?'

'Well, er, yeah, that was a bit stupid.'

'You reckon?'

'Like you don't know anyone who does drugs.'

A low blow there, but Wayne, her eldest brother, is a bit of a wild child. I'm pretty sure he offered her some coke one time last year, and she may have taken it. I don't know.

Her face has gone stony. I'm supposed to be the one person who doesn't carry on like her family's something out of *Shameless*.

'Drugs are for bloody idiots as wants to waste their lives. And that ain't you.'

She's right there. Maybe I should explain I was lying about the drugs after all, but *not* about the sex. No, she'd probably think the sex was even worse. Not because she's a prude but because of the whole toilet, stranger, first time thing. Which was not *entirely* classy, I will now admit.

I whimper. 'I'm sorry.' Wow, some actual tears well up on cue. 'I feel a complete idiot. I won't do it again.'

Chel sighs. She rubs the back of her neck, then her eyelids, so that her eyeshadow's smudged as well as her lippy. 'Well, we're here to find ourselves, ain't we, so we gotta get a bit lost first.'

I sniff. 'Do you forgive me?'

I sound really pathetic now. Surely she'll think I'm faking.

Instead she looks at me sharply and says, 'Yeah, of course,' too quickly. Then. 'No, not tonight. Tomorrow after I've had some sleep.'

'Fair enough,' I say meekly. She's certainly not going to guess the truth, which is that I'm not sure from moment to moment if I'm faking or not.

Now Chel's getting her phone out of her bag. Good for her: when real life gets too much, never fear, fandom is here in your pocket.

Except she's checking the comments on her post about how fanfic is practice and maybe she should write something real next. And, oh dear, judging by her expression that's gone down as well as I could have told her it would. I take a squizz myself.

🌐 21:38 **vikinghusbands:** toes, I'm worried you're being influenced by people who don't take your age into account.

I hope you stay in the Rothskaar shipping community! Remember, I'm here for you.

🏺 21:41 **ships-kitty:** toes, she's right! @vikinghusbands u were SO helpful when I got triggered by that horrible fic last week.

🛡 21:53 **vikinghusbands**: 💕 I think the Archive needs to do much more to ensure young readers don't come across harmful content.

⚔ 21:59 **idris-elbow**: Is this about duskietta's darkfic where Uskaar got kidnapped? I'm pasting over the tags from that fic: *NC-17, Adult content warning, Rape, Sexual assault, Sexual abuse, Dark Rothgern, No happy ending, Don't say I didn't warn you.* So why the hell did you read it?!

🛡 22:05 **vikinghusbands**: Look, I don't need to read it to know what it's like. If a teenager says something makes them uncomfortable, we need to prioritize that. Are you suggesting toes should be reading that kind of thing?

⚔ 22:11 **idris-elbow**: It's up to *her.*

🚢 22:54 **longboat_life**: I think duskietta said she'd been abused herself and wrote that fic partly as a way of dealing. That makes it ok. It's NOT ok to write about abuse just because you want to.

🗝 23:28 **rothgernsleatherpants**: lmao women over 25 in fandom? @idris-elbow and @vikinghusbands, ur both gross. go look after your kids or wash the curtains you old hags.

Oh, this lot is grimly classic. Poor old Chel thought people would talk about her growth as a writer . . . Ha ha, nope.

Luckily the cavalry is here. I check that Chel is too engrossed in writing a new post to notice what I'm doing, and . . .

🔨00:40 **blackm00ds:** @vikinghusbands and her clone crew: So fic is OK as long as it's got no interesting content whatsoever?! If you want purity, stop pestering toes. That'll purify the air here.

🎯00:43 **vikinghusbands:** Do you really want to give teens harmful ideas about what sex is like?

🔨00:44 **blackm00ds:** toes deserves to be able to experiment in her writing without getting gaslit by concern trolls.

🎯00:45 **vikinghusbands:** I deserve to be able to speak up for minors without getting piled on by anonymous cowards.

🔨00:46 **blackm00ds:** If you care so much, where were you when Florence Huang got driven off social media by racists? You fanpols never seem to mind stuff like that.

No response, funnily enough. I'm about to log off, when:

🖤 00:48 **freaksjustkillyrselves:** omg lmao Florence Huang is just fugly. Isga is a slitty-eyed witch who deserves to get tortured to death for what she did to Rothgern.

Shit. I need to respond to that. I need to rip someone's throat out. But Chel's finished her post and is giving me a needy look. I hastily click 'next' and read her post like a good BFF.

tomtartoes-blog.rabbithole.com
Wednesday 00:48

Guys, of course I won't stop writing fanfic! And I want it to be stuff people want to read.

I really understand where everyone is coming from. I think writers should write what they like, but we have to be responsible too. It's sweet of vikinghusbands to want to keep young people safe. I'm not going to write anything really super-dark or dangerous. I just meant something a bit less fluffy, really? More challenging? Like idris-elbow does.

I don't know.

Ugh, I'm really tired, I'm rambling. 😵 Maybe I should have stayed offline completely this week.

By the way, people, I'm NOT blackm00ds, in spite of the anonymous DM I just got, saying so very politely that I am. I honestly don't know who they are.

OK, I'm going to catch up on some fic reading while we chill out on the bus home. @tastyriceballs, I'm diving into your fic RIGHT NOW.

Aaaand she's disabled comments. Sensible. Dull.

She's obviously waiting for my opinion. So much for naughty Yan being in the doghouse. She needs someone to tell her what to think.

'Look, you know appeasing trolls doesn't work.'

I expect Chel to wibble, or say something as feeble as the stuff she just typed, but instead she mutters, 'Why is vikinghusbands after *me?*' Then she jerks her head back as if banging it against a wall that's not actually there. 'I know, I know, it's cos I've got popular. But I don't wanna write things that trigger people!'

She's talking loudly enough that the guy two rows in front of us briefly pauses between bites of his amazingly stinky burger. Chel sees, and actually ducks her head down, and covers her mouth with her hand. 'Poor longboat_life was abused for years by her clarinet teacher. I've seen her talk about it in her journal. But that wasn't because of fic! Anyway, I haven't even read any of the darker stuff they're talking about. I just wanna explore different characterisations, not just fluff all the time. I don't go digging through the Archive looking for weird stuff, like you do.'

'So what *do* you want to write?' It's taking about a hundred and ten per cent of my available concentration to focus on this, but at least it gets the conversation off me.

'I don't even know right now. I'll think of something acceptable.'

'*Acceptable?*'

'Yan, I . . . I can't be doxxed!' Her voice is quiet now, barely audible over the shuddering of the bus, but intense. 'I just can't. My parents finding out what I write. School finding out that the chav–' She breaks off.

'Oh yeah, school finding out the so-called chav is a literary genius, that'd be terrible. And there's no way vikinghusbands has your real-life details.'

'She found oceans'.'

'oceans goes on about being a marine biologist, and about the town they live in. It can't have been hard.' I grab Chel's phone and scroll. 'Look, one of her minions was posting racist shit about Isga.'

Chel takes a moment to read the exchange, then mutters some swearwords and deletes the 'slitty-eyed' comment.

'Thanks,' I say, not all that thankfully, because I was expecting a bit more of a reaction, to be honest. I bet she thinks she'll provoke the rest of that gang if she blocks one of them.

Then Chel says, 'Yan, are you blackm00ds?'

Oops.

'Are you blackm00ds?' she repeats.

'No,' I lie, in a perfectly normal voice, looking at her steadily. Apparently that is a thing I can do now.

Chel sighs. 'Well, I suppose I appreciate blackm00ds' support but stooping to the fanpols' level doesn't help. I wonder if they're that Danish fan as . . .' Chel pauses and waves her phone purposefully. 'Anyway, I gotta read riceballs' fic.'

She hesitates and puts the phone away. 'No. I can't face twenty chapters of Uskaar and Rothgern kissing gently on a beach. It just ain't for me.'

'Good,' I say. 'Good choice.'

Wow, OK. Baby steps. But still steps.

I watch Chel intently from under my hair for a couple of minutes; she just stares out of the bus window.

I yawn and do the same. Some parts of London are not very exciting, and I think I may finally actually be getting a bit tired.

We're almost back at Julie's when Chel looks over at me and says, 'Hey – where did your hat go?'

Chapter 21

This morning we're 'brunching' late in a café near Goldsmiths in South London. Kieran chucked food money at us last night and grunted that he'd meet us at the London Eye, once Chel's seen the college and I've visited Kathy Maynard's studio. I'm not keen on my 'brunch', aka grease, and Chel insisted we get here early of course, so I'm on my phone trying to distract myself from the drip of despair by watching a vlog made by someone who says they'll die if Rothgern and Uskaar don't kiss onscreen in the next season. Not exactly my kind of thing but it's about as intellectual as I can cope with right now.

Chel, wearing her pink strappy top, is sitting cross-legged on her chair, rubbing carefully at a heel blister from last night, and muttering something I can just about hear.

'"UCL is no Oxbridge," he says –' mumble mumble – 'As if Stanfield High –' mumble mumble.

Then she realises I'm listening and says at normal volume, 'Are you feeling better today?'

Last night we tipped into Julie's house and both of us – yes, that includes me! – went right to sleep. This morning Chel had her determined face on from the moment I saw her, and seemed to want to think that the bonkersness of last night was a one-off, and it's all over.

I think it's a Furse family thing, maybe because there's so many of them, that you either forgive and forget stuff all the time, or you drown in grudges. It's handy for me right now. Especially as I'm not up to self-defence.

'Yan,' Chel prompts me.

Oops, I haven't replied yet.

'Yes – I'm feeling mostly better.' Apart from the random despair now roiling around my chest. 'I think I've worked out what the problem was. You know what it says on the label on my antidepressants? "Avoid alcohol". I mean, I've got drunk before, since I've been on the sanity pills, but not as much as last night.'

Chel's mouth forms a relieved O-shape. 'Oh God, of course! You could get some really weird side effects. So you was hyper, and then you . . . ahem.' She stops before she mentions the (non-existent) cocaine.

'Yeah, well, I'm really sorry. I won't drink any more. I certainly won't take anything else.' I wonder if someone did slip something into my drink? I felt so present. Now there's just this blur of static. 'Today I actually . . . I actually feel a bit down.' There, I said it.

Chel looks duly worried, but she says, 'That'll be the hangover. If the depression was coming back, you wouldn't be able to move. You wouldn't want to.'

I squint around the sun-soaked café a bit. In contrast to a few months ago, I don't feel like I'd give my right arm to stop being me and become the pensioner poring slowly over the *Daily Mirror*, or the straggly haired woman behind the counter. I don't want to die. So that's a win, right?

'Yeah, I know what depression's like, and it's not this,' I confirm to Chelsea. I can move. In fact, I *need* to move. My head's full of murky gloop, tossing my thoughts around. My foot jerks under the table.

I consider writing, 'Help' on the table in cold baked bean juice.

'No surrender!' says Chel in a mock-pompous *Nordhelm*y voice. She makes the gesture for *onwards!* in Yrsali's sign language.

'Yeah! We'd better head for Goldsmiths now. We slept late.'

My phone rings.

It can't be the PI. They're going to email.

I yank the phone out of my bag with trembling hands.

It's some robotic recorded crap about how *I heard you were recently involved in a car accident that wasn't your fault . . .*

I end the call.

'Yan!' Chel sounds alarmed.

I swivel my head to her, trying to make my expression blank. What the hell was my face doing this time?

'You looked like you wanted to murder someone,' says Chel. 'I know them recorded messages are annoying, but . . .'

'Oh, yeah, it was just one of those – they are *really* annoying,' I agree. Words come crowding up my throat now: my father, the PI, the credit card, the stolen cash. *I have to tell her.*

Tell her which bit? It's too late. If she finds out I've been hiding all this, she'll never trust me again.

If the PI comes up with some solid information, I'll tell her then.

CHAPTER 22

Goldsmiths College was red, and square, and earnest, and whatever. I don't think Chelsea was really interested – it's way down her list – and I wandered around with my earbuds in, watching cheesy vlogs.

And now we are in Mayfair.

I prod the little silver button by the door of KayEm's boutique. *Buzzzzz.*

All around us are immaculate white buildings and florists blazing out into the summer street, and jewellers with their names carved in shop fronts that look like marble, and expensive-looking people. One man has a terrible puce boater. There are cute girls across the road beyond us and I twitch my arse.

I feel mellow and floaty and secure now: I got this. I'm just fine with the sceptical-looking woman who buzzes us into the shop full of white walls and soft yellow lights and arcing cream and lemon tones setting off blocky pedestals with KayEm's hats and another designer's belts and shoes. Hats on dummies, hats with sprays of net, a hat with a ladybird made of gems, and hats on two yummy mummies who are trying them on under supervision from the visibly uptight old bat.

Said bat is clearly having trouble processing the

existence of Chel, who is gawping and fingering the gold-spiral earrings that she put on and took off twice this morning, while I explained that her nerd-chav fusion look is bold and brilliant and she ignored me.

Fortunately, the bat then clocks the creative genius topping my skull, and when I tell her, 'Kathy's expecting us' we get waved towards the stairs, which have a yellow carpet that's possibly even plusher than Julie's blue version back in Swiss Cottage, if more scuffed. It complements my hat, which is classic Maynard-influenced with a twist. There's an actual slice of (fake) lemon on the brim, and it's reverse peaked in a cocktail style. (The KayEm design I based it on does *not* look like a shoe, whatever *Hat* magazine says.)

The stairs come out at the end of a huge workshop area. On one side is a whole wall of Ascot photographs, with a shelf of fat, smooth spools of thread running above and a row of desks with sewing machines underneath. And on the other, the actual hats.

People – especially people who are my design teacher, who's about ninety and thinks tiles with flowers on are exciting, and is supposed to Encourage the Youth but obviously thinks she should get danger money for dealing with me – say 'Hats?' in a very particular tone.

Well, I say, '*Look.*' Yeah, hardly anyone wears hats any more, but that's the point. They're a deliberate style statement. Unmissable. Great presents, too. And in the end, I just really, really like them. They hold you between the ground and the sky.

Here's a sunhat, trimmed with ruffles, and a flat cap quilted in slick scarlet silk, and an odd topper with delicate lace and festoons of ribbon at the crown. I run down the length of the display, heroically managing not to go,

'EEEAAAH!' – and behind me I hear a voice exclaiming, 'So good of you to come.' Ah, KayEm herself. I think I should acknowledge her.

'This is way bigger than my studio,' I turn around and inform her. 'Mine's a spare bedroom with a damp wall and spiders. Would it be cruel to decorate a hat with a spider?'

KayEm smiles a bit. I hug her, because that's artistic behaviour. I even do the kissy thing! She's got crow's feet under the frizzy tumbledown curls. Over her shoulder I can see her assistant, who's a boy – lots of milliners are men, like TV cooks. 'This is my best friend, Chelsea.'

'Er,' says Chel, and sits on a handy work-stool near one of the half-dozen whirling table fans, pulling her top straight. 'I'm moral support, like. I'll sit out the way.'

'She's creative too. She's going to be a writer,' I explain to KayEm. Because that is so clearly what Chel really wants, deep down, and we need to start being honest.

'Lovely. Do make yourself at home,' she tells Chelsea. 'It's tea-break time. Girls?'

I hate tea. I say yes to it anyway, because I like the word *yes* at the moment. KayEm goes over to a slightly mucky little sink in a corner and gets out mugs. 'Do look around some more,' she suggests.

I practically run around. There's a sack of polystyrene balls beside a table, packaging for posting delicate items I suppose, and I get the urge to kick it – whee! – but I shouldn't do that, so I nobly don't. Here's a table of half-made hats on stands, under the long, bright front window, and each has its own emerging personality. Even the blocks all have different tones and grains of wood. I fixate on an almost-completed red cloche with a black flower that is absolutely my style . . . Could I fold it up and ram it into my bag?

'Yan . . .' says KayEm behind me, in that I-already-said-your-name-once tone Chel keeps using.

'Do you want to have another look at my portfolio?' I demand. First things first.

'Sure,' she agrees. I need to listen to what she says. Maybe she's not going to offer me a job on the spot (not with the male person over there hogging the payroll) but I need input from someone who knows what she's talking about and doesn't peer from behind her cheapo teacher glasses as if my immortal works of creative genius might bite her nose off.

Again, I start to flick through images on my phone. It's odd to hear KayEm using words I've only seen written down. When I say 'beret' with a 't', she quietly corrects 'beh-ray'. That had never occurred to me. Mum pronounces it 'beh-re*t*' – and who else is going to say it in Brockford? How do you make the jump from the outside to the inside of KayEm's world? Well, art college, obviously. I nod along, though I'm having a flash of Mum at home, sitting in the worn green armchair with the coffee stains, tapping away on her laptop, chatting about her favourite authors in her British-Chinese Facebook group or dishing out expert advice on growing roses . . .

How can I possibly be getting distracted right now?!

I show KayEm photos of hats on blocks in my studio, and hats on me, and hats on Chel that go with her round face better than with my long one, and there's my mum in the white felt bowler that I made for her birthday but that's really too delicate to wear . . . Seeing her, it feels like a mosquito nips at my heart. (What's she doing right now, this moment?) Then we go on to Chel's dad in a mostly fedora thing I made, posing a bit stiffly with his I'm-humouring-my-daughter's-best-friend expression.

KayEm has a helpful comment for everything, and about fifty per cent of the time I manage to concentrate. 'Nice. Very adventurous . . .' 'But you need to consider how that cut will look from the back . . .' 'I'd narrow the brim to keep it in proportion with the crown . . .' 'Beautiful fine stitching and imaginative use of the lace trim; awkward join, though.' The only thing she really doesn't like is the woolly hat made to look like an external brain (that was also the one that caused most local distress in Brockford); plus I can tell she thinks Jelly Tots shouldn't be glued to tulle (but art can be of the moment as well as for the ages!). 'Well, you'll get your head around the commercial side at college,' she says, and tells me how she designs for a high-street chain to keep herself in business.

'There's a branch of them in Bristol,' I say. 'They've got hats piled up like plates.'

'Plates sell, my dear,' replies KayEm briskly. 'And money pays for studios in fancy parts of London. But you can afford to be purely creative while you develop your skills and personal style.' (Like I don't already have one of those!) 'You'll be able to work with better-quality materials at college, too.' She gently fingers the fibreglass peak on my lemon hat. 'I like this idea, but the visible seam from the moulding process lets it down.' Huh, so much for eBay's finest bargains. 'Just don't focus too narrowly too early. I did a general degree at London Fashion School. You're hoping to do Fashion Design with Millinery after your Foundation Course, right? Good for you, but you'll need to make sure you work hard on your general subjects as well as specialising.' And now I get tips on how it's 'too often who you know, not what you sew, in this business,' and directions on how to get the most out of my courses 'this autumn'.

OK, a lot of this is useful, and I don't mind looking grateful even for the clichés, but now KayEm's gone and alerted Chel, who was previously in phone-mode, to the fact that I told her I've already got in and I'm starting St Martin's this year. It was only a small lie, to make her take me seriously. It would be weird to un-tell it now.

Chel stares at me. *Look, it's not a big deal* . . . After a bit, she moves on to studying a kind of imploded top hat.

I know KayEm's busy and won't want me here forever, but I need to Maximise the Benefits of our chat. When we're done with my portfolio and she's told me I have lots of promise and should keep her updated on my work (result!), she shows me her own projects in progress, arranged on stands or laid flat on a big table in the light of the long window. I pick up a sea-green panama and gently finger the brim, and it's like the colour could seep into me, and light summer rain spattering on the bright window is a cadence in my head, and I'm expanding and plugged into the world, and *I really need to bloody concentrate* but no, I'm going to cry. Everything is so beautiful; it presses in on my eyes. I want to try on every hat in the place, and learn how each one is made . . .

Tears spurt out of me.

'Oh dear,' says KayEm, looking sympathetic and also a bit baffled, but not as much as I was afraid she would.

'It's just . . . beautiful,' I explain, and remember to put the panama down before first wiping my eyes and then flapping my hand at the whole table. 'The . . . hats.' Is she going to think I'm ridiculous? But she must feel this way too, sometimes.

KayEm sits me down again, and lets me cry for a bit. I know I've lined myself up for more Adult Advice, but when it comes it's not too bad.

'Don't worry about it,' she says after a while. 'Everything feels life and death at your age, but you're not exactly the first artist to ever be a bit high-strung. Drama's *de rigueur* at art college, really, so you've got a few years to get it out of your system. And between ourselves, it's possible I had a cry recently myself, when a certain aristocrat who shall remain nameless said my finished commission looked like a paint tin.'

I nod, and giggle a bit through the snot. It *isn't* just me, then. I'm normal – well, not normal: an artist. Chel'd better remember this next time she fusses.

'This is your first time in London, isn't it? You're from somewhere out west?' KayEm continues. 'I bet you stick out like the proverbial sore thumb.' She actually strokes my hair. 'But you're not the oddest person I've seen even this week, I do promise. You'll fit right in at St Martin's. You'll be in an ethnic majority, too, with the way things are going, if that helps any. The more the fees go up, the fewer Brits study there.'

I both like and don't like that idea. I know art schools are full of rich foreign students, and the St Martin's prospectus has loads of Chinese faces. I want London Chinese friends in my real life, but will real *Chinese* Chinese want to know me? Me with my big Aryan schnozz? Yes; surely they will (even *rich* ones?). I imagine myself hanging out with my fellow students. Creating. Good things will happen. All good things will happen. I'm an artist. KayEm herself says so. I'll stop crying any moment now.

'You all right?' Chel says.

'Yeah. Yeah.'

'She'll be fine,' promises KayEm, and gives me a friendly side-on hug.

Chel's shaking her head. I want to shout at her to back

off. She brings her arm up . . . and knocks a basket of sewing bits off a table. She gasps and flails, but the contents go everywhere.

KayEm bends over to scoot around the floor, and Chel does the same. I probably should too, except . . . snot. I go and wash my hands.

When KayEm stands up and dusts fluff off her palms, the atmosphere's changed a bit. We're now post-cry.

'All better?' she asks, and I nod. 'You're lucky to have fixed goals that you want so much at your age, both of you,' she continues, then looks at her watch. 'I do have to get on with work now, though . . .'

I can take a hint. She's given me almost an hour. I finish my usage of kitchen roll, then give a deep bow. 'Thank you for everything,' I say. 'I shall return. And before that I'll send you updates on my portfolio, yeah. Goodbye!'

'Goodbye,' replies KayEm with a wave like a salute. There's something just a little odd in the way she looks at me, but I haven't got time to bother with that. On to my next achievement.

Chel, on the other hand, is not looking at me at all. She's got a piece of thread stuck to her skirt. As we cross the showroom downstairs to let ourselves out, I reach over to pick it off, and she jumps a bit.

'Chill,' I tell her when we're outside. 'I'm OK now.'

She's not looking at me. 'Yan . . . you burst into tears. About a row of hats.'

'Yes. And . . .? I'm artistic.'

'It can't still be coke in your system twelve hours later.'

'Don't you get it? You're an artist too, in your way –'

Chelsea cuts me off. 'Why do you keep lying?! About having sex, and the weird phone call thing in the café – and now you told KayEm you're starting St Martin's this year. Don't you think she's gonna find out the truth?'

Details! I keep my chin high, breathing in exhaust fumes – though they are surely superior exhaust fumes, as we are in Mayfair. Spikes of light flash off car windows, slicing the air. 'No reason,' I say. 'A bit of exaggeration is how you get on in the fashion world.'

'Are you trying to make yourself more exciting?'

'As if I need to try! That's your mission. Not that it's going very well. You're not even brave enough to write the fics you actually want.'

'What's that got to do with it?'

'Everything. You're a coward. I'm not.'

That was maybe not a good answer. But it was enough to reduce Chel to sullen glowering. Anything to get her off my case.

I'm fine with walking to the Tube in silence. Soon, soon, the weird hole inside me will fill up, and the future will start.

CHAPTER 23

We're early to meet Kieran by the Thames. Apparently Chel still doesn't want to talk to me, and urgently needs to update her blog. Fine. Find a flimsy excuse to ignore me, whatever. I wander around for a bit. And read the post when it's up.

tomtartoes-blog.rabbithole.com
Wednesday 14:09

We're still having a totally amazing time in London.

I took a bit of time to catch up with fandom stuff while bitey was talking to the milliner, and whoa! Look at it all.

Time for more Toes' Recs!

- vikinghusbands did a useful guide about <u>how to write healthy relationships in fic</u>.
- jeebies wrote an absolutely <u>hilarious story</u> about the tomtar getting loose in Rothgern's dungeon. It's definitely naughty but so funny.
- <u>A Guide to Yrsali's Sign Language</u> by yodellingbear. Apparently it's a mix of different national sign languages, some original stuff and quite a lot of rude gestures from

different cultures that presumably the network suits didn't recognise. ☺

• Some super-cute fanart of <u>Pug and the village lad</u> he met last season. The showrunners claim they're only friends, but we know better, right? ☺ Who knew the ship's boy would get so hot?!

I've been bitten by a plot bunny, one I hope you'll all like. How about an alternate universe scenario starting from that flashback scene in 'Humble Origins' where young Uskaar sees Rothgern's entourage ride through his home village? Their eyes meet. Uskaar obviously resents the rich lord showing off his power to the poor foreign peasants, but there's also that 'wow' expression in his eyes . . . Well, you've all seen the ep. What if, after that, instead of becoming a pirate, Uskaar set off for Nordhelm to seek his fortune, and ended up as Rothgern's guard captain? How hot would that be?! They'd both be a bit edgy but they'd practically be equals, so the power dynamics will be balanced.

Huh. She didn't tell me about that idea. It sounds really tame, anyway.

Kieran finally appears, slightly late, and eyes me resentfully. Of course, he still thinks I did coke. And insulted him. That part is kind of true. Oh God, *dull* – but I'd better deal with it.

We're walking across a little concrete plaza towards the huge, bright white struts that hold up the massive Eye. I'm bouncing on and off little concrete benches, almost banging into dads with hunched shoulders and kids with drippy ice creams, but when Kieran smiles briefly at Chel – not at me – I throw up my hands and announce, 'All right, first of all, I didn't actually take any drugs last night. I was just rude. I'm so sorry.'

I don't think he expected that. 'Huh,' he says, and looks back to Chel, who doesn't contradict him. She's gawping at her phone, though she puts it away after a moment. Kieran's legs sticking out of his sensible khaki shorts are hella hairy. Ugh.

'I have to be honest, you *are* a martyr,' I tell him, 'but that'd be all right if you had friends who appreciate you. Which *I* do, honest.' I give him a peck on the cheek. 'And I'm a bit artistic and get overexcited. Sorry.'

Kieran stares at me, not looking as impressed as I'd hoped, and I grin, or rather keep grinning, so hard that I feel like I'm having a fight with my own face. Oh God, I must look like a shark. I feel a weird stab of terror: I can't *not* grin like a shark.

'Artistic?' he says, the word mostly flat but with a weird little wobble at the end.

Chel straightens up. 'Oh yeah, that designer woman said so. Yan cried all over her.' Her tone is neutral too.

'Seriously? What kind of excuse . . .?' He's shaking his head. 'You know what? I don't care. She's just mental. Come on. We've got to queue even to pick up our tickets. I said I'd do this, and I will. Chelsea, you in one piece?'

'You think I might've taken bites out of her?' I protest, then giggle. Isga!

'Yeah, let's have a good time now we're here!' Chel says, too brightly.

All around the base of the Eye are bored people in uniform, and sweaty tourists asking them broken-English questions about *where is Tower of London, pleez*. We shuffle into position and I stare up at the huge wheel. It seems to gradually drag my eyeballs around with it.

'I'm a bit afraid of heights,' says Chel. She always has been – I wondered about that. But it's rather late to bring it up now, isn't it? I suppose she was trying to be brave.

'Dad took my brothers up the Empire State Building before I was born, and Matt pissed himself,' replies Kieran, in a determined faux-normal tone. 'I don't suppose you'll do worse than that.'

'Mm. Ruby were sick on the roller coaster on her Year Five class visit to Thorpe Park,' replies Chelsea. 'All over the teacher. I had to drag her in the next day before she'd believe Mr Davison weren't angry. Else she'd never have gone to school again.'

Oh my God, this is a Furse family conversation if ever I heard one. Except Kieran's lot get to piss and vom in New York.

'Don't barf in here, it'll fry,' I suggest as the capsule creeps into dock in front of us. I step in first – *whoa*, oven. And we're not alone, which for some reason I imagined we would be. The capsule's as big as the kitchen at my house, and a bunch of southern-European-looking students as well as a frizzy ginger woman with two little kids (one crying, of course) follow us in. Then the pod door clunks shut, and up we go.

Kieran and Chel are doing Yan-doesn't-exist body language, which is fine by me. He's telling her about various boring buildings nearby. 'The GLC was abolished by Thatcher in the Eighties,' he tells her, all disapproving, pointing at a place called County Hall. Lefty politics, I guess? I kind of want to be interested. Chel apparently is interested.

But I want to *see*. It's hard to press yourself up to the window properly when there's metal bars in the way, though. I climb up on the bottom one, which is exactly what you're not supposed to do and therefore fun, to see if it helps. The not-grizzling child tries to copy me, and gets told off. The grizzling one cries louder. It's about a hundred degrees in here . . . and also as close as you can get to flying!

'Yan, you ain't supposed to do that,' protests Chel. 'I think I actually would barf if I looked straight down. And what if the glass breaks?'

I know it won't, but I get down because, standing on the rail, the sloped glass by my face was forcing me to look up, not down. I feel like I could reach out and hold London. I squash my nose and my palms against the window. There's the whole city, shining and crawling with beetle-taxis and ladybird-buses and ant-people. Look at the spiky Houses of Parliament, and the straight, long bridges, and the lump of St Paul's way over there, and the Shard like Sauron's tower in *The Lord of the Rings*. The horizon is a hazy line between the intricate people-world and endless blue. I imagine swooping out into the air and just being absorbed into it, and living forever.

Now Chelsea and Kieran are having a deeply inane conversation about how she actually wasn't that into Ras, oh dear isn't that a pity, oh well we can all be friends.

Then I catch my name.

'Yan's just being so weird, even for her,' says Chel. 'She –'

Suddenly the volume from the happy European students hits eleven, and the crying kid gears up to actual screams and I can't hear what Chel's on about, or what Kieran replies, though he looks like he doesn't want to get into it. Sensible of him. Except that kid's voice is piercing; like it's physically inside my head. I bang the side of my skull and then the heel of my hand into the window;

sensations, hard and real! Intensity inside, intensity outside. Everything feels good. I kiss the window and stare and stare, down and around. The Thames below is huge, slow, unstoppable, majestic. Two little boats cut tiny wakes through it, and I touch them through the glass. The sun wraps around us when we get to the top, and the students are ranged along the other side of the capsule in silence now, and there's nothing but the metal oval we're standing on, and my friends, and the squalling brat. I whip my head around.

'Can't you control him?' I demand of his mother.

She shrinks back a bit. She's got bad hair and tired eyes, and she's so busy dealing with her kids that she's barely been looking out at the city. That's how you end up if you play by the rules: a sad little life in Brockford or wherever, and if you're lucky you'll escape once a year, for a week in London or on some crowded beach.

And what are the consequences of not playing by the rules? Nothing worse than a few lectures. I am *queen*. I also feel weirdly sick and awful, but that must just be the stuffy air and sweat between my breasts, and clothes sticking to me . . . I shut off these sensations in one corner of my mind.

Suddenly Kieran grabs me by the arm. He did that last night, when maybe there was a reason, but now there clearly isn't and I don't like it at all. I yank myself away, and obviously he's not going to start a row in here, so he lets me go, though I can sense the glowering. He thinks I'm the weird one for pointing out that some selfish woman is spoiling the ride.

'Calm – *the hell* – down,' he growls.

'No, you calm down! What if I *can't*?' Of course I could, if I truly wanted; I just somehow don't.

'Bollocks you can't. Stop screwing things up for Chel. Artistic? Please! Just listen to yourself.'

'Look, you don't want to be here, so you could just bugger off home.' I'm grinning again so he must know I don't actually mean to be rude. Do I mean it? My voice is harsh. How is it even my voice? 'Why haven't you?'

'Because, God help me, I promised Mum I'd look after you. I'm surprised Chel hasn't chucked you in the river.'

'Like you care what your mum thinks. No –' I look him up and down, as far as I can in the tight little space – 'actually you do; that's what all the eco tat is about, isn't it?' I reach around and tug at the handle of his backpack. 'You do really believe in the politics, but the tat's about annoying Mummy and Daddy.' I grin wider. As well as being happy recently I've got so damn exquisitely smart.

He's narrowing his eyes at me. Like I've hit home but also like he's honest enough to admit that about himself and not get in a pretend snit. Good lad. 'I respect you believing in something,' I say. 'But you need to live a little. Why don't *you* try coke?'

OK, now he's opening his mouth to snark at me, but I forestall him by blurting, 'I was clinically depressed all spring.'

'Yeah?' He does soften just a tiny bit. 'I'm very sorry. Well, now you're overcompensating.'

'All right, beard-brain. I'll try to be boring.' The capsule's starting downwards, plus the child's stopped wailing, like he knows he's ruined the ride and his job is therefore done.

I turn away and press against the window again. There's this thing called *l'appel du vide*, which is French, and means you want to jump off high places, though you wouldn't actually do it, and there's no way out of here anyway. Only what if the glass *did* somehow melt, and the world fused, and I stepped into the air and twisted and blurred into the sunshine? I would crush and smash onto stone, and it's not like I actually want to die any more but it would be beautiful . . . I know you hit the ground splat and you split open and there's internal organs everywhere and nobody's smiling, I do know that, but right now it's *all* beautiful. I stretch my arms out in spite of Kieran, and the force of the blue of the sky is a punch in the heart. 'Look, everything's wonderful!'

Kieran doesn't respond. Has he given me up as a bad job? Good. *Help.*

'Come on, Chel, take a look,' he says. 'The glass isn't going to break.'

She gets up to stand beside him.

'Everything's always beautiful,' I say.

I do not want the capsule to go down. But I do need my so-called friends to get off my back, and I don't actually want them to be miserable, which when I see Chel's face reflected for a moment she clearly is . . .

They're muttering together. I can't make out every word, but he's telling her I'm selfish and she should stand up to me. She says she sometimes does, but today is different. He says he doesn't see how it's different. Whatever.

The angle of everything is changing as we go down; people switch from tiny dots of hair and sunhats into bodies, then faces. They're turning normal. I'm not. What goes up does not come down.

CHAPTER 24

Chel doesn't sulk very often, but when she does, it's epic. You just have to roll with it if you don't want her to spray acid like a Kaltstrom sea-serpent. She's scuffing along, actually limping now, until she eventually takes her left sandal off and carries it, which makes her limp more. 'Damn thing,' she mutters.

'Well, we're going home now,' replies Kieran, who's gone kind of wooden, like he's given us the benefit of his wisdom and it's our lookout if we don't listen. 'I suppose.' (He doesn't sound keen, even though he clearly wants to get away from me: what's that about?)

'All right,' says Chel to him in the too-bright voice. Then, to me, under her breath. 'Kieran thinks you're just being selfish and there's nothing wrong with you. He thinks I need to stand up to you.'

'Well, you can if you want.' I can take it: I'm tough. 'But there *is* nothing wrong with me. If there was, you wouldn't be talking to me about it – you'd be calling the men in white coats. There probably *are* some in London.' Unlike back home, where they shut down the adolescent mental health unit and sent everyone to a place miles away with a two-year waiting list, and I was too depressed to go anyway, and super-denial Mum certainly wasn't going to push the issue . . . and who cares?! I want an ice cream. And I want to feast on the finest imaginable cuisine with a prominent journalist and an eminent lawyer, as will come to pass this evening. My appetite's returning. I'll conclusively persuade the olds to let Chel live with them.

'Who the hell else can I talk to but Kieran?' Chel says, almost to herself. 'I can't call Mum and Dad – they'll think it proves we should never have set foot outside Brockford!'

'And what would you tell them anyway?' I demand. 'That I got excited about hats? That I wish I was getting out of the village and going to uni this year instead of next? Well, that's really big news.' Chel eyes me in silence, so I go on. 'Come on. Everyone knows I'm weird. I *am* weird, compared to them. That's why you like me.'

Chel stops dead. I'm wondering if the problem is me or blisters when she goes on, quietly but really intensely. 'Yan, I ain't up to this. It's supposed to be an adventure, but I just messed up with some guy, and I'm kidding myself I can cope with London and, even if I could, oh my God I'll be seventy-five thousand in debt!'

Oh dear, a meltdown. 'It could be worse,' I point out. 'oceans says they'll have to sell their kidneys to pay off their student loans, and I'm not sure they're joking.'

Chel babbles on. '. . . and I'll just hide in a library anyway because can you see me, like, networking? You'll be at fashion school, making a million friends and – I should just go back to Brockford right now!'

OK. She's really upset. I care about that. I don't feel it, but I know intellectually that I care. So I work out what to say, and the tone to say it in. I can do this.

'Chel, you *can't* go home. You just don't want to be

alone in London – and you won't be. You can live in a library for three years if you want, I'll bring you . . .' God, I can see the image in my mind but I can't think of the word. 'Thingies . . . I mean, sandwiches.'

'Get real. You won't need me,' Chel says.

'I will! I do! Yeah, you're worrying about me for no reason but it's bollocks to say you can't . . .' I've lost another word. '. . . can't cope.'

Kieran's got ahead of us – and stopped walking, kicking his heels until we catch up. 'Tell her she's going to love university,' I instruct him.

Peace-boy common sense to the rescue time? No, apparently not.

'University,' he says slowly. 'You have a homing instinct for the worst possible subject.'

'Er, what?' I say. But then I remember something he mentioned in passing last night and realise *he got his second-year exam results today.*

Aha! Poor bastard. He's forging on, though, like the trooper he is. 'Chel, I guarantee you're going to love university,' he says. 'Two minutes talking to you is enough to tell that.'

'Maybe Aunty Sharon was right,' frets Chel obliviously. 'Maybe everyone else is humouring me. Maybe Mum just let me come here so I'd realise I can't cope.'

Kieran continues undaunted. 'You've got about a hundred people supporting you, including your best friend, even if she is a total bitch –'

'Hey, I'm only a bitch sometimes,' I protest at the same moment as Chel says, 'Yan ain't a bitch.'

He throws up his hands at that. 'What do you want me to say? Yes, you could stay in the dump you came from. It's up to you.'

'Dump?' Chel retorts sharply. He's earned himself a good glare from both of us. Brockford is ours to judge.

I get a brief flash of home: trees against the stars and owls hooting; my mother in the garden, sinking her roots into the soil, performing mysterious rites on the future ingredients of stir fries and taking breaks to post on the British-Chinese forums on her soil-stained laptop. Or more likely, at this time of day, wielding a tongue depressor or poking boils. My little studio will be waiting for me, with its row of hat blocks and sewing machine and ribbons and felt and silk scraps that Grandma sent me . . .

Suddenly, Chel kicks off.

'Look, mate, whether you knows it or not, you got everything. We ain't got money, we don't go to a posh school. Yan ain't even got a dad.' She's got her hand on her hip, sandal dangling from her fingers. 'Back home, we get, "What's that book, Chel-pee Furse, can you Furses actually read?" and "Chinky's got a barf bucket on her head again, hur-hur." Then it's, "Oh, maybe you can get the grades, but are you sure you'd feel *comfortable* at UCL?" And that's from the bloody teachers!'

Kieran shakes his head, incredulous. 'How's that my fault?'

'Well, you happen to be right in front of us,' I explain to him helpfully. 'Chel's usually calm but when she goes off, she really goes off.' And he's a nice guy, so it's safe for her to vent at him. God, I'm an emotional genius. I should be an agony aunt. 'You could move to Brockford,' I suggest to him. 'I can just see you selling overpriced organic coffee to the tourists.' Chel's anger-scrunched eyes widen a bit at that, because I am so totally right. 'Yes – you should move to Brockford, and Chel could move in with your parents,' I say. 'Suggest that to them.'

Kieran looks like he's about to bite me, then he checks himself and lets out a little laugh, definitely a bit hysterical. 'Actually, that might even work! Dump the disappointing, hopelessly naive, idealistic son for the earnest, studious little genius.' He pauses again, shaking his head.

I know when I'm onto a winner. 'Julie's working in her home office today. You don't want to go home and tell her about your exam results. What college do you even go to? It's some crappy fifth-rate job, isn't it?' I stab a finger at him. 'I bet your parents pushed you to do loads of stuff at school and you were rubbish at all of it, and got rubbish A-levels. But it's OK, Kieran! If everyone was smart there wouldn't be space at UCL.'

I'm being cruel now. But I can't stop reeling this stuff out of him, and I can't stop throwing it back at him, because I can't *stop*.

Whoa, he's balling his fists up. Might he hit me? 'Yes, Yan,' he almost snarls. 'I'm at Gregg College, doing Politics because I thought that might at least be useful for Eco Focus, and I'm failing because apparently I'm stupid, all right? A Peterson who's thick as two short planks, as Mum says whenever she forgets she's posh now. You want to swap places with me, Chel? What're your politics? I'm pretty sure Mum would swap me for a sack of potatoes if it was *realistic*.'

Chel's been listening to the rant in silence, looking increasingly stricken. 'Kieran, you ain't thick,' she protests. 'You just ain't academic.'

'I'm only there because they insisted,' Kieran informs us, 'and I don't think I'm going back in the autumn. There's a guy at Eco Focus HQ with a spare room I can stay in if Dad kicks me out.'

Poor sod! It's going to be morbidly fascinating hanging

out with Julie and Mark tonight now we know all this stuff.

'You'd . . . drop out?' Chel breathes. To her, that's like chucking a diamond in the Thames.

Kieran just stares at his foot. Hey, I think he's crying . . . No, not quite. He runs his hand down his face and kind of crams the expression back inside. (People are starting to stare at us. I stick my tongue out.)

'I'm sorry, Kieran,' says Chel. 'We're both sorry. I'm hot and knackered and Yan's – Yan is God knows what at the moment. I'm sorry.'

Now Kieran's checking his phone so we can't see his face. 'You know what, there's an Eco meeting tonight, and why the fuck *should* I go home? I was supposed to go to the concert with you, but screw that. You can have my parents to yourselves. Hell, ask them to let you move in next Monday, if you want.'

'Absolutely you should!' I agree, and nudge Chel.

'Oh, Kieran, I'm sure your parents ain't really . . .' she begins, then exclaims, 'Ow, my *foot*!'

Looks like she's stepped on a pebble.

'Wait a moment,' I cry. 'I'll get you some shoes!'

Not far away there's a stripey booth thing, like you get on the beach, and it's got pairs of really cheap flip-flops dangling down one side of the counter. I run off to buy Chel a pair.

When I get back, she accepts them like she doesn't know what else to do, and puts them on in silence. Kieran's disappeared – a bit rude of him, but he probably wanted to go off and be upset somewhere. There's a lot of that about.

'Not got anything to say?' I prod Chel.

'Of course I ain't!' she snaps. 'What the fuck?'

Ooh, sweary Chel! That question is ridiculously vague, so I don't answer it.

We start walking again. Chel's ignoring me and possibly crying a bit.

Eh, she does that sometimes now, I suppose. I decide to go online and let off a bit of energy as blackm00ds. Cos – ooh, surprise! – Chel's latest post has already got a load of idiot comments that barely relate to the original post at all.

⚔ **14:22 idris-elbow:** Sounds excellent. I'd love to read an alternate universe created by you.

🛡 14:40 **vikinghusbands:** toes, this has all gone too far, and if you don't check yourself I'm worried it won't end well. The scene you're talking about in 'Humble Origins'? Uskaar is FOURTEEN. And he was attracted to a 21-year-old, and you're suggesting the 21-year-old was attracted to him too? There's a word for that. A nasty word.

⚰ **14:43 longboat_life:** Yeah, the thought of Uskaar going to the castle when he's still 14 and meeting Rothgern is really triggery. 😔

⚔ **14:44 idris-elbow:** WHAT FRESH HELL IS THIS. Y'all have finally LOST YOUR MINDS. You think because one guy saw the other before he was of age it's pedophilia?

🛡 14:46 **vikinghusbands:** Yes, that's the word here. And toes should not be saying that Pug is 'hot'. He's the ship's boy. He's 15.

🗿 14:47 **yunia:** @vikinghusbands: I'm 14. and Pug is hottttt.

~ 193 ~

🌀14:49 **vikinghusbands:** @yunia I'm worried someone has made you think you need to sexualise yourself when you aren't ready. DM me and I'll help.

⚔ 14:50 **idris-elbow:** @vikinghusbands: you know telling girls it's wrong to be sexual is textbook misogyny?

🌀14:53 **vikinghusbands:** You people can defend rape, incest, child abuse, whatever you like, but you have to understand it does actual harm.

⚔ 14:54 **idris-elbow:** INCEST?!

🌀14:55 **vikinghusbands:** toes just recced a fic of tomtar in a dungeon. They all look identical and they have very large families. If they all, ahem 'have a go', well, some of it has got to be.

⚔ 14:57 **idris-elbow:** Well, bless your heart, @vikinghusbands, I just don't have any reply to that logic. Congratulations.

🎭14:58 **ships-kitty:** @vikinghusbands, OMG, I never thought of that but you're so right. I can't believe I thought I enjoyed that fic. 😮

⛵14:59 **longboat_life:** That seems a bit of a stretch @vikinghusbands . . .?

⚔ 15:00 **idris-elbow:** YESSS. Kid, purity cults are not the way to go.

🌀15:03 **vikinghusbands:** Look, @idris-elbow, maybe you're a good person deep down. But you ship Yrsali with Isga. An 18-year-old girl with a 300-year-old murderess who once tied Rothgern up and obviously meant to do worse.

🗡 15:03 **idris-elbow**: @vikinghusbands, God, I'm so TIRED of this. Finding stupid reasons to call queer relationships abusive and queer people predators is EXACTLY the same bullshit we had in the 80s. Exactly the same. Yet Rothgern and Yrsali kiss in the actual show!

✊ 15:06 **freaksjustkillyrselves**: ur THAT old??? lmao.

🔘 15:10 **vikinghusbands**: Yes, @idris-elbow, Rothgern is 14 years older than Yrsali, so that's wrong too. But it's the show. We can't get at the showrunners. We can save fandom from people like you and far-oceans. Who's too scared to turn up today, I note. And by the way, the word 'queer' is a slur.

🗡 15:11 **idris-elbow**: So was 'gay'. Go learn some goddamn history.

Oh my God, oh my God, this is the most hilarious thing I've ever seen.

Well, sort of. Objectively it's terrible, but it's hilariously terrible. Everything's hilarious.

It's still pretty early in the US, and this is unrolling before my eyes. I wouldn't be surprised if vikinghusbands actually DMs her minions to summon them when they're needed.

Time to post some truth bombs.

🎵 15:11 **isga-bites-u**: @longboat_life, toes is not responsible for how you deal with your trauma. @ships-kitty, there's not much point talking to you because you have a bully-worshipping turd instead of a brain. @freaksjustkillyrselves (classy name!) how about you take your own advice? And @vikinghusbands, you can join her. You call ME a coward? You're a hypocritical fuck who deserves to eat my shit.

Ah, crap, I can't think of anything really clever and keep up with Chel at the same time. And we're almost at the Tube station. I press 'post'.

CHAPTER 25

I kick a guy in the arse on the Tube – only a light tap, really. But the bastard shoves past me, and he does not need to touch me where he does, so I think, *Right!*, and go for it. He can't get me back because I timed it perfectly – the doors are closing. This is the most fun I've had in ever. Chel's constantly watching me, except for a minute or so spent flicking through pictures of her family on her phone. Seems she misses them after all. The other people in the carriage are pretending not to look at us but I know they are. I'm kind of floating above everything in a pinkish fog.

Chel freaks out when we get home to the Cream Suite. She flumps down on her bed, opens her mouth like it's time to make a mighty speech, and goes for it.

'You're out of control, Yan,' she accuses me, then bites her cuticle. 'Like, scary out of control. With KayEm, you was . . . I don't even know!'

'Huh? We went through that. People cry sometimes. You cried that time you got a C in English.'

'Your reactions are totally out of proportion! I want you to be OK and you just ain't. You attacked someone.'

'One kick is not a –' *find the word; Chel just said it!* – 'an attack. That guy deserved it. And I feel fine.' I bounce on the bed. I could reach the ceiling!

'You're telling bonkers lies for no reason. And – are you waiting for some kind of phone call? I thought we didn't keep secrets from each other.'

Suddenly the *Nordhelm* theme tune surges out of Chel's pocket.

A voice call. I assume Chel turned the ringtone on by accident, but it seems not, as she grabs the phone eagerly.

'Ras?' she demands.

Ras?!

And apparently it is, because she goes on, 'Yeah, yeah, thanks for calling. Look, your parents are doctors, right? And you studied Medicine . . .? I know it was just three months, but I don't know what to do-ooo.'

Can a person projectile sob? Chel's suddenly having a go. The snot flies.

'There's no one else I can talk to,' she continues. 'Kieran weren't interested . . . and I can't blame him. I think she actually *is* mental, and what am I supposed to do?! She had a crying fit at this designer woman's place, and she attacked a guy on the Tube – kicked him. She were depressed earlier this year, medical depression, but ordinary like. Now she's telling weird lies all the time and she's got this *smirk* on her face . . .'

'Hey, that Tube guy was an arsehole,' I point out loudly.

But Chel's obviously determined to embarrass herself as she keeps spewing our business to her sort-of-ex. 'If I tell my parents this stuff they'll say it's what happens if I leave Brockford. Julie'll think it's what happens when she lets plebs in the house. Yan were an absolute cow to Kieran . . . Yes, again today. God, this makes no sense. Shit shit *shit*.' Chel covers her face with her free hand. 'Maybe she bought more coke last night and had some today?' she suggests through her fingers.

'I swear on Rothgern's taxed – Rothgern's waxed torso, I am not on drugs,' I say, even more loudly this time. And while Chel's busy squashing her own nose in, I grab the phone. Ras's tinny voice is burbling out of it.

Chel reacts faster than I expected, glaring at me and wrenching it back. But instead of ramming it to her ear again, she puts it on speaker, still keeping a tight hold.

'. . . a cardiologist, not a psychiatrist,' Ras is saying. 'But obviously he did rotations when he was training, and there's a psych ward at the hospital where he works now. There's this one long-term patient there who has to come to cardiology sometimes and he tells us about her. Dad says half the time she's completely hyper and can't stop talking, and she thinks it's funny to insult people. Or she tells everyone she's Halsey and she's here to give the patients a free concert. She's delusional. And she gets these brutal depressions as well.'

Pause.

I can hear birds outside the window.

I can hear atoms betraying one another.

I can hear –

'So I wonder if Yan's bipolar like her,' continues Ras's disembodied voice. 'What they used to call manic depressive. She should get to a psychiatrist as soon as –'

I've heard enough.

I go to grab the phone again. Chel stuffs it behind her so I kind of end up shouting at her hip. 'Cardiologist, Ras?! Your dad's a cleaner!'

Ras says, 'Hang on. The boss is coming.' There's a surge of noise like stools scraping and someone talking about crates of beer in the background; he must be at his bar job, revving up for the evening. Muffled conversation. I don't look at Chel and Chel doesn't look at me.

Half a minute later, speakerphone-Ras starts again. 'He was a cleaner when we first came to England, Yan. It took a long time to jump through the hoops and register his qualifications with –'

'I do not care!' I shout over him. God, I am not going to claw at Chel's arse to get hold of the phone, because part of me is so aware that this is ridiculous, and yet –

'You'd better hope you're bipolar,' continues Ras, ''cos if this is just your natural personality Chelsea's not going to be your friend for much longer.'

Chel is eyeballing me, with a sort of blank defiance, like she's daring me to say it isn't true. Expecting me to deal with the scariness so it's easier for her. Nothing new, then.

I sit back on my heels on the bed. 'All right, Ras, so, *bipolar,*' I say as calmly as I can. 'Like some woman who thinks she's Halsey and is basically completely insane.' I am not insane. I'm right here, watching Chel's mint-green miniskirt ripple slightly in the breeze from the window as it dangles from a hanger on the wardrobe door, and it's beautiful. I'm not insane. 'Do I look like a tragic case, Ras? Have you seen me pissing myself and begging outside Tesco with a can of Special Brew?'

As I'm speaking, the image swims up into my mind: a youngish guy with matted hair and his stuff in plastic bags who used to come into my grandparents' takeaway, waving a tinny and saying the Pope had told him he was entitled to free chips. He could've gone to the English chippie down the road, except the Pope also wanted him to convert the heathen with kindness. He spoke to me one time outside the shop – I was terrified – but Grandpa sometimes gave him food when it was quiet, and even nodded politely along to the ramblings about Christianity. 'One of those manic depressives,' he explained to Grandma, shaking his head pityingly. 'He can't help it.'

He can't help it I can't help it he can't I can–

Speakerphone-Ras just said something else but I've no idea what.

'Didn't hear you, you're breaking up,' I say.

'I said, not everyone with mental health difficulties ends up like that,' he repeats. 'Look, I'm not an expert, I just bought a psych textbook for uni and read about ten per cent of it. I think lithium works for bipolar? The important thing is to get checked out, as soon as you can.'

'Yeah, Yan, listen,' says Chelsea feebly. I won't slap her. I won't. But if I ever see Ras again, I'm going to punch him in the face.

Because *lithium?!* That's for hardcore nutters!

'Oh, I should get it checked out?' I snarl. 'Well, *that'll be easy*. The NHS just falls over itself to help. Or rather the NHS just plain falls over cos the local Tory MP nods through any cuts the dickwad he made Chief Executive comes up with. If your dad's a doctor, you should know how it is.'

I lean forward and cut the call off.

'No,' I say to Chel. 'Just no. I don't care what your ex says – and what kind of loser gets an ex basically before they've had a relationship with the guy, by the way –'

'Yan, just shut *up!*' She's coming to life again. 'Insulting me is not gonna help.'

'Chelsea, you know *nothing* about how I feel.'

Because I cannot, will not, go back down into hell. And anyway, being mad, not depressed, but mad like *bipolar* is a white thing; if you're Chinese it just doesn't happen, or if it does they put you away, and that's the end.

'I reckon it's time you called your mum,' says Chel

tentatively. 'I know she weren't that great about the depression, but she came round. You can't deny that you're twitching and grinning and talking double speed. And kicking people. Do you really think that's all right?'

'Yeah, brilliant idea, Mum was so supportive of my depression.' My foot is waggling madly against sprigs of yellow blossom on cream arranged in repeating swirls on the duvet, going on and on and . . . Why should I hide it? My brain feels like it's turning inside out; the world is a dense, burning, glittering transparency. The curtains behind Chel are as rich and gentle as plant fronds underwater. Bloody Chel . . . She's just embarrassed about messing up with Ras, and she's making stuff up to take me down. She's envied me her whole life . . .

And now she looks like she's working out a plan. She's googling on her phone. I scoot around beside her, like we're about to read a fic together. How I wish we were.

Instead, she scrolls the Wikipedia entry for bipolar. There's a list of symptoms: *twitching* (but everyone gets restless!), *lying* (yes, when I need to!), *shoplifting* (once!), *arrogance* (well, screw you!), *driving too fast* (I haven't had a single lesson!), *drinking too much* (also once!), *hypersexuality* (hardly a good description for one quick shag in a toilet!), *aggression* (yes, brand the Chinese girl as aggressive for having opinions, nothing gross about that), *overspending* (as if either of us would ever!) and *laughing*.

There you have it, ladies and gentlemen: laughing means you're mad.

Chel pauses in her scrolling and looks at me expectantly. I scootch away so I'm lying on my back, raised on my elbows. I've given up on controlling my feet; they can do their own thing, sticking out past Chel's bum over the space between the two beds. 'So what it basically says is that anyone more interesting than a cortoise in . . . I mean, a *tortoise* in a coma, is mentally ill.'

'Aggression's on the list,' she says flatly. '*Are* you blackm00ds?'

I'm not dignifying that with a reply.

Chel's nostrils flare. 'My God. You are. All right. Fine. Least now I know.' She keeps scrolling. 'It also says . . . there's no cure.' Her voice is flat. 'It says, *manic patients can be resistant to understanding they aren't well*. And – oh! There's this thing called *hypomania*, which is like mania but you ain't completely out of it. Instead you're – well, like you are, Yan. You don't have to be completely delusional to be hypomanic.'

Her eyes widen a bit as she looks at me. They're still puffy, but she's not crying any more. I guess that's good. And it's most kind of her to concede that I'm not delusional.

'Ugh!' I throw myself dramatically backward, so that now my head tips off the edge of the bed and I see everything upside down. Downside up. The colours stab at my eyes. I am not mental. But I need to hide, or they'll get me. All of them. Chel and the Brockford spider-web. Whatever posters they put up in the school hall about how you should ask for help if you feel an ickle bit sad, I do not think we are allowed to be bipolar.

'I'll talk to your mum, if you want me to,' says Chel. 'You're right, I'm the one as got her to see the problem when you was depressed. And . . . I think I need to tell Aunt Julie now.'

I sit up again. 'Don't you dare.' She can't. She absolutely can't. I'm not putting up with this. 'You'll spoil everything! Our trip!'

'What else can we do? You think we can just go out to dinner like it's all normal?'

'We totally can. I mean, what do you think you're going to say to Julie? Yan got a bit excited when she met someone doing her dream job, and kicked a guy when he groped her? And told her loser son some home truths? As if.' *This must not happen. They must not see me.* 'Anyway, tonight's not about me, it's about you. I'll just load up on posh curry while you build family bridges.' Then I have the most excellent, obvious idea for keeping Chelsea on side – in fact it was rather clever of me to keep this information back so I can use it now!

'I know I'm wound up. It's because . . .' I say, leaning towards her, confidential. Then I make myself go all hesitant. 'Because . . . I . . . I'm waiting for a report from a private investigation company. They're looking for my dad. That's why I'm anxious about phone calls, see?'

Aha, yes! That does the job! Chel freezes in place. Her eyes go wide again. 'You – what? Oh my goodness, Yan, why on earth didn't you tell me? This ain't – this ain't your imagination, is it?'

OK, I'm going to hold on to my temper. I think this will go best if I do that, and guilt her. I get out my phone and show her the thread with Kirby Investigations.

'I'm telling you now, like I omised pearli – promised earlier. And I wanted to before, but this is *so* personal, even you might not understand. You with your great-big-warm-loving family.' I look sad. I even manage not to twitch. 'And . . . I haven't told my mum.'

'*What?*' Now she's totally hooked.

'I just borrowed her credit card, you see.' No need to go into the cash/PI office dodge I had to pull the other morning. 'We did talk about it once a few months ago, but she said –' I imitate Nurse Mum's stern-but-fair routine – '*I understand you want to know your father, but I'm not having that man get inside your head. Wait until you're eighteen*. Well, that's not long now, so it doesn't make much difference, does it?'

I can practically see the gears turning in Chel's mind. 'Well . . . I . . . Your mum does have a bit of a complex about your dad, which ain't surprising. But yeah. You deserve to at least know where he is. You've got enough sense to decide for yourself . . .'

Then she gets an expression that suggests she's revising her assessment of whether I have any sense, so I press on. 'I'm almost certain he's in London. Mum's as good as said so a couple of times.'

'Ah. Yeah, my dad says he always used to be on about that, back in the day,' Chel agrees, picking unconsciously at the blister on her heel and rocking a little in cross-legged position.

'All right,' I say. 'All right.' I need to focus and get this stuff clear and coherent so she'll actually listen. I try to speak slowly. 'It was your family who helped me understand all that wasn't my fault, remember? When we were little and my mum wouldn't say Dad's name, your mum let me babble about him. Remember when your dad said my dad was an arsehole and I was so shocked a grown-up said a naughty word that I stopped crying? I hent wome . . .' I pause for a breath. *Keep talking slowly. Sanely.* 'I went home and told Mum that your dad had said "arsehole" and I thought she'd be angry but she actually burst into laughter and said maybe some men are all right. After that things bot a git . . . got a bit better. Did I ever tell you that?' I'm quite sure I did, but I'm piling on the persuasion.

'Depression made me a bit of a cow, I know that. And . . .' Time to play the ace, because I didn't want to upset her, but that was before she pulled this crap on me, and I am thinking clearly now. So clearly . . . So clearly I just about keep my thread. 'Uh – yes – I almost died of depression. I thought a lot about milling . . . about killing myself. And I thought about my dad, and what if he has depression too, and what if he's . . . dead?'

Bloody hell, it's hard to act tragic when your foot's trying to shake off the end of your leg and hit the ceiling. Now *that's* an interesting mental image. 'I've got to know. Or this bipolar crap, if he's got that, well, I'll look into it for me as well.' As if! 'But really, if I've been too much, then, well, everyone always says I'm too much, except you.' A nice bit of extra guilt there! 'It's just be meing . . . me being me, slightly more than usual.' If I do find my dad and he'll talk to me, I'll tell her what he says, everything. 'Unless you think he's dangerous? Do you think mentally ill people are all dangerous?'

Hm, am I pushing too hard? What am I even trying to achieve? I just need her to back the hell off. Leave me alone. I wish I was somewhere dark and silent where I could fucking *rest*. We have to go out tonight and make Julie and Mark fall utterly in love with Chel! Whoa, that speech I just gave was so convincing, wasn't I convincing?!

'Of course I don't think you're dangerous,' Chel says. The gears are turning in her head again. 'And if you're really gonna hear about your dad tomorrow, I understand that you want to put off looking into . . . *this* until after that.'

'Yep,' I agree happily.

Chel says, 'It's a bit like in "Arctopus", when Uskaar's long-lost mentor turns up, and reveals that he . . . er . . .' She trails off.

'This isn't quite like that,' I reply. It'll suck if I meet my dad only for him to get eaten by a mutant octopus five minutes before the end credits. 'Maybe a bit, though, just with a etter ben – a better ending.'

'But if you *are* bipolar . . .'

'Then I'll keep it together for just another day. Evening. If I know what's supposed to be wrong with me, I can watch for it, right?'

Chel looks completely and utterly out of her depth. My heart aches.

I almost snicker. Time to press the winning point. Slow and clear, Yan, slow and clear.

'I need to know my father hasn't committed suicide. I *really* need to know that. It's nothing to do with Mum.'

Yep, there, I said the stupid word. *Suicide.*

It has its effect. Chelsea swallows. She really doesn't want me to die, which is very sweet. 'Yeah, obviously, I see that.'

'So just leave me alone for tonight, OK?' I lean forward. Am I being threatening? That's unwise. I lean back. Now I probably look like a drunk sea-serpent.

'But what if –' Chel starts.

'One night! Think about it: it'll be less cruel to Mum to ell . . . tell her about Dad once I've actually heard, no?'

And by tomorrow I'll be fine. I mean, there's nothing actually wrong with me *now*. Apart from my foot wanting to hit the ceiling, yo.

Chel rubs a hand down her face again. 'I dunno,' she says. 'I dunno. I dunno. I dunno.' She repeats it a few more times. Presumably it's giving her some sort of comfort. 'Oh, all right! When you was really depressed you managed to pull yourself together for a short while sometimes, right?'

'Yes.' Mostly on the phone to my grandparents, who'd have freaked out. 'Well, that's all settled, then. I'm going to get some fresh air.'

Cos otherwise I'm going to burst out laughing, and Chel will get all weird again.

I go out into Julie's fancy back garden and march round and round a bush. Lucky there's a tree between me and the house, so nobody can look out of a window and wonder what I'm doing.

I check my phone occasionally as well. Chel's posted something brief, probably reccing a picture of Uskaar and Rothgern in pink wedding dresses getting married on a romantic beach. Though actually, come to think of it, that might be worth seeing.

Except . . . wait . . .

What?

There's quite a lot of replies to my last blackm00ds comment, the one where I told half the fandom to eat my shit. Except . . . apparently I didn't post as blackm00ds. I was still logged in as isga-bites-u.

Oops.

tomtartoes-blog.rabbithole.com
Wednesday 16:57

I'm having . . . a really hard time at the moment. I don't know what to do. I wish I could tell some of you what's going on, but it's too personal.

And then the replies to my last post. I just don't know what to say. Maybe I'm a pervert, I'm sorry. I had no idea about bitey being blackm00ds, and there's worse stuff going on now. I can't even say. I'm really sorry.

🖉 **17:19 idris-elbow:** Yeah, it looks like bitey meant to switch to blackm00ds to make that comment on your last post, but forgot to change her login. Y'all need to talk. This isn't cool.

🔸17:27 **anonymous:** lol @isga-bites-u is such a retard

🔘17:20 **vikinghusbands:** Oh dear, toes. Your 'best friend' is blackm00ds, and you really never knew? At least you have the grace to say sorry, but how can we be sure you're being sincere? 😏

👑17:23 **tastyriceballs:** @vikinghusbands thank you for being the only adult brave enough to stand up for us. @tomtartoes, I've been collecting links to all the shitty things your 'best friend' said to vikinghusbands and me and other people and I'll do a master post of them tonight. I'm not doing this out of spite, but to warn people that it's not safe to be around her. I guess it looks like it's not safe to be around you either. 😔

👑17:31 **longboat_life:** This is messed up. But I guess a lot of people are horrible in fandom at the moment, and bitey was trying to defend you? I actually wish I had someone like that. And I actually do hope you guys make up.

🔘17:32 **vikinghusbands:** @longboat_life, I'm here for any young fans who need me.

👑17:35 **longboat_life:** Thanks.

🔸17:39 **anonymous:** Aw dammit, does this mean no more blackm00ds smackdowns? I'd just bought an industrial-sized sack of popcorn.

💂17:40 **freaksjustkillyrselves:** theres an 8-YEAR age gap between Uskaar and Rothgern, shithead shipping them is GROSSSS

What a stupid mistake I made. This sucks donkey bananas! Bad, bad Yan.

I should care. I definitely care.

But everything I said to those losers was true!

And Chel is being so pathetic.

I'm sick of the sight of this bush.

I keep marching around it, though.

I really don't care. I can't even be bothered to blast these sad wankers, either as blackm00ds or isga-bites-u. Looking at it ethically, it would be wrong not to let Chel deal with all the stuff on her blog herself, because she has to learn. We're all on our own, aren't we, in the end?

Where's far-oceans? They keep vanishing.

I wander off to bash the back of my head hard against a tree trunk.

Bang bang bark bark boing boing.

This will not stop why will this not stop?

A reply appears under the first comment. It's from Chel. Then another appears, super-fast, on vikinghusbands's comment, and so on all the way down, apart from the one-line 'lol, retard'-type ones. Chel must be copying and pasting, because they're all the same.

📝 **17:40 tomtartoes:** I really didn't know that bitey was blackm00ds until now. I'm REALLY SORRY.

CHAPTER 26

I check the mounting sum on the little digital fare meter in the driver's cab as another light turns green and the taxi takes off again. We've passed Lord's cricket ground, signs for the zoo, and a huge mosque with the evening sunshine pinging off it, and the Sherlock Holmes Museum, and Baker Street station, and here we are in Marylebone, with lights and rush and babble and a man pulling down the shutter of his café – *crash* – and a pub with hanging flowers in a thousand colours. A huge lorry splashes us with shadow, then rumbles on by. Julie's place is like a mountain base camp – every time I leave I get higher.

I keep sneaking glances at Chel. She's pulled herself together; good for her. I'm gonna support her by being the best of bestest BFFs *ever* tonight.

'Twelve pounds and ten pence!' I exclaim, reading the meter again.

'I take it that's a lot of money to you girls?' Mark asks now. He's crouching on a fold-down taxi seat too narrow for his bum, juggling a phone and a load of papers about some natural-gas company and some African government.

'*Duh*. Twelve quid is a lot to most people.'

Kieran did come home, just before we left, but he stormed upstairs with an impressive amount of *stampy-*

thud-thud, then refused to emerge from his bedroom even when his father knocked on the door and Spoke Sternly through it, so me and Chel have the elder Petersons to ourselves tonight. She's in conversation with Julie. After unwisely asking me what music I like – as a result, she now knows more about K-pop than she could ever have imagined, and the nuclear earworm of 'Sorry, Sorry' by Super Junior is bouncing madly round my head – Julie winkled out of Chel that she 'used to like a lot of chart' but is 'looking forward to exploring new musical avenues this evening'. But eventually Chel got going with the intelligent questions and now Julie's telling her some of the cultural events in London that are cheap enough for students, or free.

When we get to our destination and climb out of the taxi, I goggle, as does Chelsea. I reach over and gently push her hanging jaw closed, which makes her jump and shoot me a momentary almost panicked glance.

This restaurant is located about five minutes from the Houses of Parliament, and it's so posh it doesn't even advertise itself. There's just an arched door leading into a lobby and then a kind of hall, that's actually a wood-panelled old library with two storeys of books and a balcony and bottles on some of the shelves.

'Rather nice, isn't it? Reminds me of school,' says Mark to both Chel and me. I'm really not sure if he's sending himself up or not. Chel nods woodenly. I get the impression he's studying us both.

Never mind that for a moment. I'm Instagramming everything for the benefit of Tash and the others back in Brockford. Suck up my luxury lifestyle, plebs! There's a *crest* on the cloth napkin I shake grandly across my lap. I refuse to be intimidated. The olds are consulting the menu. Everything is extremely fine: the lofty ceiling, the rich dark wood, the snowy tablecloth. Fine and refined.

Mark leans back in his chair to order something I've never heard of, but that's probably a drink that costs two hundred pounds, from a waiter behind him. Julie's selecting alcohol for me and Chel as well as herself ('You must try this; it's heavenly – do tell me if you like it.' Does she think we've got much experience with cocktails?). Then we're ordering food. Julie gets some exotic variation on salad, but even if I haven't had much appetite lately, I'm not missing the chance to dine upon chicken *à la* stupidly expensive.

I can feel the plush seat under my sweaty thighs, drying out now in the air con: it's sleek-sticky-smooth with a little lip on the edge. Ha! Sexual innuendo. I remember the softness of Undercut's breasts . . .

After telling Julie how each member of her family is doing, Chel's clammed up again, eyeing some weird carved bit on the ceiling. Time for some Yanity. I lean over and ask Julie, 'So how exactly did *you* escape from Brockford?' Get 'em to talk about themselves, adults love that.

'Oh, that!' she says dismissively, before forging on. 'Well. It wasn't easy. Mum and Dad couldn't imagine why anyone would want to move away from the family at all, let alone to London. I had to insist the school order some prospectuses – it was all done by post then of course – and study in the garden shed for some peace and quiet when the village library wasn't open.'

Chel nods along earnestly. She doesn't have to resort to the shed, though that may only be because my room is available to her.

'Then I was posting off applications and so forth myself,' Julie continues. 'Mr Porter in the post office declared . . .' She pauses as a crisp-shirt-sleeved arm inserts itself between her and Chel and deposits poppadoms. 'Mr Porter declared London was a pit of drugs and degenerates. Which it is, a bit, I suppose.' Julie waves her glass of wine, which is already getting low.

'Mr Porter?' replies Chel. 'The bloke as complains to the police every time someone drops a chocolate wrapper? He's still there.'

Julie puts her elbow on the table. A Brocky accent nudges into her voice. 'Really? He must be well over seventy.'

'At least! He ain't too bad, though. He led the campaign to save the library, as much good as that did.'

'Save the library? In Market Street? It's closing?'

'Not quite. It's run by volunteers. Two days a week. You ain't – haven't – been back in a long time, have you?'

'No, no, I haven't,' says Julie, posh again. 'Oh my goodness . . .' She stares over my shoulder. 'Closing the library. That is not good.'

'Don't vote Tory, then,' I mutter, but I manage to keep my voice low. Julie's moving on to give Chelsea Networking 101, and I certainly don't want to interrupt that.

I turn to the food. It is fanc-*aaaay*.

Handling her plate and spoon like they belong to the queen, and Her Maj might arrive at any moment to object to their being pawed by proles, Chel dabs a glob of mango chutney onto a poppadom. I stare at it as it gloops slowly from the spoon . . . shiny, so shiny. I grab one of the giant crisps myself and manage to crush the side of it by banging it into my glass on the way to my plate. Oops.

'And what about you, Yan?' says Mark suddenly.

I jump. Then shove crumbled poppadom into my face so I've a moment to orient myself. *Chomp chomp chompety chomp.*

'We haven't had much time to talk,' Mark continues.

'What do you want us to talk about?' I counter.

Before Mark can respond, more food arrives. There's some green stuff in a dish, that probably isn't mushy peas. Puree? Of spinach? Spinach *à la* goo, yeah. I don't like spinach. But I want to try everything.

'This looks like a cow's been standing on it,' I say.

Mark snorts a laugh.

'After digesting it twice,' I add.

He laughs again. 'You've got a strong personality.'

I hesitate. I'm getting a mental image of sticking a fork through my eye and into my brain. Why?! For one thing I don't actually want to do it, and for another the fork might bounce.

Where was I? 'Talk to Chel, talk to Chel, she's the interesting one,' I say, flapping my hand.

He stares at me.

For a moment I have a strange sensation of a powerful mind brushing against my own. Then it's gone, and I feel something is lost. But the Petersons *have* to focus on Chel. Fall in love with her.

Bugger, I've dropped green goo in my cleavage. I fish it out. That ensures Mark's attention stays off me – a bit of basic decency there, then, good – and Chel is now holding forth about the reasons for Liberal Democrat popularity in the South West, though here I think she's quoting my mum.

At any rate, she is continuing to impress the rich relatives as the curry comes, a fancy boat-shaped thing full of creamy-orangey chicken korma, and a hill of rice, and we all dig in. Except me, because my stomach already feels like it'll burst. I play with my food, trying to hide the fact that I'm not eating. Occasionally I smile encouragingly at Chelsea, though the brief looks she shoots my way suggest that she's not finding my expression helpful. What's the problem? Surely getting cross-examined by a lawyer and an investigative journalist is scarier than me.

Although nothing is scarier than me. I should know, I have to be me. Urgency is building in my throat. Why? Because I care so much about Chel. She has to pull this off. She has to stop acting like she's just having a polite conversation. Now she's even saying that she'll miss Brockford a bit. That's not in the plan. She's supposed to be praising London. She doesn't understand the urgency. She doesn't understand I'm –

BANG! I lean forward and my plate rams into the boat of curry, slopping some over the side, because I'm mal-coordinated as hell. The surge of rage is actually kind of wonderful. I'm like a peach balanced on a razorblade; any moment the skin will split and –

'Yan!' Chel hisses, staring at me like I'm now so far off-piste I'm on a sunbed. 'Just . . .'

Yeah? Just what?

There's a moment's silence, or rather a moment when the background of polite laughter and cutlery noises drifts across the table.

Chel was supposed to do this for herself, but she won't, and it has to be done, so I will do it.

'Look,' I say to the Petersons. 'You can't stand your youngest son, the other three have eared coff – cleared off, I mean – already, you're softer than you look or you wouldn't have your grandkids' drawings on your study doors, and you don't have a daughter.' I pause for a deep breath. 'You should let Chel live with you during uni.'

Now all three of them are staring at me stupidly. Chicken falls off Julie's fork.

'You know it makes sense,' I urge the Petersons.

What don't they understand about this extremely simple suggestion?!

'Er . . .' says Julie, and glances at her husband. (I like the way these two look at each other. Posh passion. Torrid Tory true love.) 'Well, that is an idea, you know,' she says.

Mark rubs his bald patch. 'Mm, I suppose it is,' he replies, waggling his caterpillar eyebrows. 'But . . .'

YESS!

'Excellent,' I cut him off, then add for good measure, 'You could pay her fees as well.'

Mark chokes a bit – at the same time as looking slightly impressed. 'Steady on, girl. Julie had to make her own way.'

'Yeah, when there were grants –' I start.

Chelsea interrupts me. 'That would be absolutely wonderful, Aunt Julie,' she says earnestly, leaning over the table so her tits are almost in her curry; we're both so elegant. 'Just somewhere to live, of course, I wouldn't expect anything else. I mean, I wouldn't expect even that . . .' Fortunately she manages to shut herself up before she talks them out of it completely.

Julie nods. She looks like the idea is passing some kind of initial test in her head. 'Well, we'd have to think. There are some practical issues to consider, but in principle it might be doable.'

'Definitely,' I say. Imagine it, Chelsea: three years of marble bathrooms, triple-pile carpets and not having to pay hundreds a month to live in a rabbit hutch crossed with a pigsty.

'It's true we won't support Kieran if he continues to be unrealistic.' Julie sounds a little sad. 'So it'll be just the two of us rattling around that house,'

Mark gives a wry quirk of the lips at the mention of his

fourth son, who is merely a kind, caring person and not an award-winning dentist or a banker. Then he says, 'It's up to you, Jules. I don't get involved in your family.'

'I, er . . .' says Chel.

'We'll have to talk to your mother,' says Julie, then glances at me at the same time as saying, 'It seems like this was Yan's idea.'

The dream is coming true. I am the bestest best friend ever. I am going to explode. The plainly starkly obvious thing to say next occurs to me: I need to tell the Petersons I'll come and live at their mansion, to keep Chel company. I need her.

Chelsea is grinning in a dazed sort of way as she reassures Julie that yes, this was my idea but she is up for it. I open my mouth and try to arrange the words before I speak them so that they don't come out as nonsense.

Then I spot him, over Chelsea's shoulder. The enemy.

Colin Carston, MP.

Colic.

CHAPTER 27

Once upon a time, not very long ago at all, there was an adolescent mental health clinic not far from Brockford. It was purpose-built, in consultation with teenagers, all that stuff. So of course just before the Blip the local NHS Trust decided to close it down.

I know it's not actually that simple: sometimes NHS Foundation Trusts go into 'special measures' because of whatever issues. And sometimes the authorities sort this out, and other times they send in a nice shiny right-wing chief suit who concludes the answer is cuts, cuts, cuts. And your local Tory MP refuses to meet with the smelly juvenile yokels who gather at a local town hall to protest, and supports the powers that be to wave the cuts through.

Chief suit: one Gregory Marsh.

Tory MP: one Colin Carston.

And here they are, with three other suits, sitting around a nearby table, chatting and reading their menus. I've seen Colic a thousand times on the TV, often just before or after Julie. He's got a smirk like you stomped on a worm and smushed it into his face to make lips.

There are surely deaths on these bastards' hands. And here they are to piss money up the fancy walls.

I'm not enraged; I *am* rage. I jerk my chair back, and

I'm over there in half a dozen strides.

'Hello, Colic. Gonna ignore me like you did those protestors in January?'

He looks up. The smirk doesn't falter but his eyes turn stony.

'Terribly sorry, but I'm in a meeting,' he says, and gestures at his crop of cronies.

'Well, I expect you get so many protestors you don't know which ones I mean. The adolescent mental health unit you –' I poke a finger towards Marsh, who's stock-still and watchful, paused halfway through tucking his napkin in – 'SHUT DOWN. Are you lot utterly out of touch, or just evil?'

Marsh grits his teeth, and finishes with the napkin, but it's not him I'm most interested in, he's just a drone. Colic's a Tory MP.

'How much medicine could you buy with the amount this costs?' I demand, pointing at their table . . . where there isn't actually any food yet. Details.

'I don't think you quite have a grasp on economics,' says Colic. He's obviously registered my accent, and a 'Future voter!' warning has pinged into his lizard brain, but he can't keep the condescension out of his voice.

'And I don't think you grasp your job, which is to represent the cood – the good of the people in your constituency.'

Out of the corner of my eye, I can see some waiters approaching rapidly yet without appearing to hurry. I haven't got much time. I want to hurt this man. Hurt all these fancy people who know nothing about anything real. *I* am real.

I lean over and snarl.

Colic looks terrified. One of his balding clones snaps

his menu shut and pushes his chair back.

A pink, manicured hand clamps down hard on my shoulder, then another one lands more gently on Colic's. Julie's reached us before the waiters.

'Colin, how lovely!' she says.

'Oh . . . Julie Peterson, isn't it?' he replies. The two of them switch focus to each other, like that'll stop me existing. Julie trills some inane response.

And now there's a chunky brown hand on my arm. A waiter.

I am not going to be led meekly away.

I kick Colic on the shin as hard as I can.

He howls. I might only be wearing canvas shoes, plus I hurt my own toes, but I got him right on the bone. It's petty, but it's highly satisfying.

That's it: I get grabbed. But not before Colic almost falls out of his seat, flailing at Julie as he goes. Why can't they put things like this on the nightly news? It'd be great for the ratings.

Now Mark and Chel close in around me, Mark firmly edging out one of the grabby waiters. 'All right, all right, I'm most terribly sorry, please bring the bill.' He's talking to a whole clump of hostile Indian faces now. (Oh, come on: you guys spend all day serving rich scumbags, were none of you cheering me on?) Oops, I've created a public scene . . . I grin around the hundred faces in the huge room, under the glittering chandeliers. It was so worth it. We all know who's in the right here. And sure enough, one waitress, standing with a group of others, winks at me. *Yessss!*

I get hustled to the door and out into the street. Mark ostentatiously pulls his wallet from his jacket. Julie's still inside, presumably kissing poor Colic's ego better. I catch her voice trilling upwards through the general racket –

oh, and rumours are spreading around the room; I hear someone ask, 'She punched him in the face?' Ooh, I *wish* I had.

Now Mark's having a go at me, in his deep old lawyery voice.

'You silly child! You could have got arrested . . . Wait . . . Oh, for . . .' He wavers, groping inside his jacket. I think he's left his phone behind on the table. Can't have that! He heads for the door, but they won't let him back in.

Chel's hiding behind me, or from me; she actually moves with me when I turn around. I stop trying to catch her and hop up and down, peering, trying to see what's going on inside the restaurant.

Before long, Julie comes out. She's carrying Mark's phone . . . and trying not to giggle. She motions for us all to cross the road away from the restaurant, and then she actually dissolves into laughter. (Aha! Am I a boon to humanity, or what?)

'Oh my God, Mark, oh my *God*.' Julie's practically cackling. 'She kicked that Carston man in the shin. Yan *kicked him in the shin*! Do you know how many people want to do that? I wish I'd had a camera crew. Oh, Chelsea, don't look so shocked. You should hear the rumours about him . . .' The giggles take over completely.

'Yes, I'm sure it'd be hilarious for us all to get arrested,' growls Mark.

Julie waves dismissively. 'I don't think Carston wants me or anyone else reporting that little scene. He was pretty keen for me to scram. Yan, we've obviously got you drunk. I didn't think you'd had that much – but I suppose you don't get a lot of practice.'

Mark sighs. 'I know young people tend to be impatient, but assault is not the way to challenge government policy.'

'Are you sure?' I demand. 'I mean, you probably want to kick pots of loliticians. Not Tories of course, the decent ones. And it was funny.'

Mark looks down at the pavement.

'IT WAS FUNNY,' I persist.

Then I remember: the great plan. The greatest of great plans which I, bestest of best friends, just brought to fruition. Though I didn't get around to telling the Petersons I'd come to live with them too; maybe I'll wait just a little for that. And I'd better not do anything to undermine the achievement so far.

Mark is now giving me a positively harassed look. I giggle. Julie is glancing back towards the restaurant; I rather think she's snickering again.

'Uncle Mark . . .' says a timid voice.

It's Chelsea.

She visibly takes a deep breath, giving the old folk time to turn around and stare at her. 'I think . . . I really should have said this afore, but I just didn't – don't – know what to do. I . . . I think Yan's not well. Like really not well. In . . . in the head.'

Oh my God. She goddamn said it.

BITCH!

TRAITOR!

I'm suddenly so furious I could lunge at Chelsea, standing there with Quiet yet Sternly Tragic Resolve glued to her po face the way the bloody smirk's glued to mine. The muscles in my cheeks are starting to hurt. Chel thinks I'm insane. She's telling these old fools I'm insane. After everything I've done for her.

'I'm a bit drunk,' I retort through gritted teeth. 'Like Julie said.'

Julie's finally calmed down, and is looking at me

speculatively. 'Yes. And that is partly our fault. Are you going to throw up?'

I shake my head, because if I open my mouth the cramming words will gout out, flooding downstream like a timber clatter rattle river rush . . .

'I really don't think that's the problem, Aunt Julie!' Chel persists. 'Or not the only problem.'

Why oh why does Chelsea have to learn to assert herself *now*? She said she'd wait until tomorrow to talk about this! We *have* to wait until tomorrow. For some reason . . . to do with my dad? *Why is my head full of liquid fur?*

'No more alcohol for you.' Julie's peering at me. 'I think you got away with that little performance, and you probably wouldn't believe me if I said I didn't enjoy it just a little, but the joke's over.' She makes a calm-down gesture, holding both hands out with her palms towards the ground.

Mark's shaking his head over his phone. 'Really, this all just makes me glad I'm not seventeen any more. Come on then, girls, enough drama. We should . . .' Then he pulls an exaggerated worry face. 'Crikey, Jules! I got the start time of the concert wrong. If we hadn't left now, we'd be late.'

'Well, then!' I announce. This is vindication!

Mark and Julie hurry off to nab a taxi that's just dropping people outside the restaurant. Perhaps they think Chel and I need a moment.

Which we do.

It's a bit rich that Chel's calling me a scary nutter, because she's the one clenching and unclenching her fists now, and breathing hard.

'Chust – just chill, Chel,' I urge her. *Chill, Chel, chill, ill . . .* 'I'm fine. I mean, how much did Colic deserve that? Did you see his *face*? Did you notice I got you three years of free accommodation?!'

Chel's going a bit grey. 'Yes. Thank you for that,' she snaps, staring at books in a nearby darkened shop window. 'Honestly, thank you. Seriously. But you *are not fine*. This can't just be about – what you're waiting for tomorrow. You're ill. I've tried to help, but I was right, they won't listen!' She stares into my eyes. Hers are full of tears. 'Why did I think my rich aunt would listen?'

'She won't listen cos it's not true, duh,' I inform her airily. The smirk's back, so I probably look like Colic, and *I hate myself and I can't stop.*

Chel continues, 'All right. I didn't just grind to a halt when you was flat on your back, and I can't now. Just – don't you screw my life up, *please*. They ain't exactly adopting me; I reckon I'll be more like some kind of pet. Maybe that ain't fair, but you know what I mean. But I need it if I'm gonna afford uni, yeah. And they could still change their minds. So just *shut up*. For the next few hours, *shut up*.'

'You could be a bit more grateful. But all right.'

She turns on her heel and heads for the taxi that Julie and Mark just stopped.

'Huh,' I mutter, following. Throw the Blip in my face, why don't you, Chel? Julie was totally into me kicking Colic. Ten thousand out of ten, would absolutely recommend putting the boot into evil old gits.

Mark and Julie are already inside the taxi and I shove Chel in after them, hard, before she can say anything else. It's genuinely nice she wants to help me; so nice that it's almost a shame there isn't actually a problem.

In the taxi, it's all normal again – if rich, glamorous London is your normal. Julie, who is clearly not the type to waste time, starts on about possible practical arrangements for Chel living with them, which is probably the one thing that could effectively distract my BFF right now. Mark's glued to his phone, wild tufts of hair sticking up around his bald patch. I resist the temptation to tug on them. I watch the little digital red meter tick up, up, up beside the driver's head (it's like watching money burn) and bounce around in my seat. I get the impression it's been collectively decided that for now I don't exist, which I can get behind, because I just want my own thoughts. That's all I'll ever need now. My thoughts are surfing over muddy depths and it's *good good good*. It's all falling into place. Falling, falling. Apart, over, into place, down; falling.

Mark suddenly looks up from his industrious lawyering. That fierce attention catches at me.

He asks, 'Yan, what *are* you so happy about?'

It's an honest question, not snarkage, so I answer.

'I'm happy you're giving Chelsea somewhere to live.'

Of course that's not a lie, but this old buzzard is smart. He knows it's not the full truth either. Again, I get that sense of a probing mind, seeking a point of connection.

I wish there was one, really I do. But I'm out of reach.

CHAPTER 28

We tip out on a back street next to a giant lump of concrete. A sign says this is the Royal Festival Hall. Julie's talking about tonight's programme, which consists mostly of some randos called the Belsey Singers, doing stuff called 'Virtue' and something like 'Song for a Theeny'. Hordes of grey and expensively dull-looking people are shuffling in the same direction as us.

I'm hoping for monks and censers and stuff at a choral concert, but when the show gets underway there's instruments to start with, and we get half an hour (an hour? a century?) of what sounds like basic classical (don't ask me; Mum learned violin to Grade Seven then dumped it when she left home, and never let me near a stringed thing). I consider the question of London Fashion School instead. I'm going there tomorrow, for a proper open afternoon, and I need to think of what to say. The course I'll apply for . . . I can't remember the name of the particular course. Wtf, wtf, wtf? Ftw, twf, fwt . . .

In the interval I go to the toilet. It's better than dealing with the Fursing and Petersoning, and I can grin to myself and twitch if I need to, and attend to something else, too. I've got thirty-six rabbithole messages, probably abuse about blackm00ds, but that can wait until I've grounded myself with a read of Chel's finest ficlet, the one that's sufficiently daring that she had a wibble about whether it was acceptable and private-locked it; but I have her login.

'Filthy pirate,' snapped Rothgern. 'Answer me, or be clapped in irons . . .'

It doesn't take long to get off. Twice. I come so hard I bang my head against the wall, and that's so silly it makes me laugh, and I'm laughing and riding and almost fall off the bog seat . . . Oh, it's all so inappropriate! I have got to develop some class before this toilet thing turns into a habit. My ears are ringing . . . no, it's not that, it's the interval bell. How've I spent so long in here? There's no time left to check messages. I have to go back to my seat.

'Where did you go?' demands Julie as I settle down.

'Toilet,' I explain. 'I mean, that curry!'

That shuts her up.

The show restarts. I am buzz buzz buzzing as a reedy slow voice starts up out of a prim little man who's standing in front of the rest onstage. My leg is shaking. I force the movement to stay in my right thigh, which is next to some random aristo-lady, not next to Chel.

London Fashion School . . . I'm distracted by the way a particular footlight winks from visible to invisible when the man in front of me makes the tiniest movement of his head. More singers join in.

My hat, which I took off like a docile citizen, is getting sweaty in my fingers. Chel slaps me when I stretch forward like I'm going to put it on the person seated in front of me. Not pokes, slaps. Without taking her eyes off the stage.

Everyone's singing now. Is this Latin? I can't make it out, or I can only make out a bit of it: 'Hallelujah, hallelujah' – the Christian usual. Yet something catches at me. A twist in the harmony pierces my brain and hooks my heart, which bursts like a ripe fruit. All sound is language; rich with connections, connotations, communications . . . The music is enveloping, rising, threads of voice weaving the universe, weaving the static buzzing poison into order and beauty, and I am carried up with them. I inhale and exhale music. The top of my head is coming off. *Hallelujah*. I'm rising from my seat. I don't believe in angels, but if I did, they'd sing like this. The music is golden curves in the air. The refrain drags me up to the sky, and I am here in my body, witnessing. I am up – and Chel physically holds me down. The music's making her cry too. Chel, I understand that angels don't exist, *of course*. Duh.

This is so, so right.

CHAPTER 29

'Wasn't that heavenly?' says Julie on the way out.

Chel *mmm*s. I'm avoiding her eyes because I don't need the downer, and the olds are avoiding my eyes for whatever stupid reason of their own. We're like one big dysfunctional family.

Then Julie again. 'Oh, dratted new heels.' She takes one shoe off and rubs the side of her foot.

'Carry regular shoes around with you,' I advise her. 'I've seen office workers do that. Or just wear them all the time if you prefer. Up to you, wenihay.' Dammit, I can't be arsed to correct that to *anyway*. Instead, I ululate (another splendid word; splendid splendid!). Only for a few seconds, but enough to make everyone in the lobby look around. And what a fine lobby it is, so many angles and stairs and carpets.

Chel looks terrified. Of *me*! When I try to grab her hand she pulls away. I laugh, and want want want to hit her. Except of course I don't want that: ridiculous. I spin; I almost fall over. I laugh laugh laugh.

Now Julie's staring. Everyone's staring. Maybe the top of my head really did come off.

Chel points to me. How rude! 'Aunt Julie, please, just look at her!'

'My God,' Julie says flatly. 'All right. Yan, what is this?'

Suddenly Mark sets off marching fast towards the outer doors. We all scurry after him, even me.

Once we're outside and away from the flow of people, Mark stops, rubbing his caterpillar eyebrows. 'Enough. Jules, we have to get real. It's twenty minutes spent in the toilets, that's what it is. And the money that went missing? I don't think it was Kieran's dreadful friends after all.'

Oh crap, I'd forgotten about stealing that cash. There's a big, hairy, smelly silence, only spoiled a bit by a busker launching into some Hendrix ten feet away. But the drugs thing *again*? It's not my generation, it's their lot who're obsessed!

'For the last time, I'm not on coke!' I shout, and twirl around. 'I'm high on life! Check my pupils!' I stick my face into Julie's. She looks away and shrinks back, doing a demure little wave thing. Screw you, then.

'You're high as a damn kite. You were trying to stand up in your seat!' Mark informs me, like I might have forgotten. Which I kind of did, actually. There are blurs. All that counts is here and now! 'Our eldest had his idiot moments with cocaine. That's bankers for you. But while you're staying under our roof –'

'Uncle Mark, she's telling the truth!' bursts out Chel. 'It's not drugs. It's – it's bipolar disorder. Manic depression. I'm sure of it. We googled it, and this is mania . . . What do we do?'

Oh dear. How exquisitely dull. Chelsea's a coward. She can't cope with me, she can't even cope with owning her own writing . . . but because I am magnificent and munificent, I will finally sort that out. Shortly. I'll tell her parents about her fic if she won't. Just not now. What exactly to do just now is an interesting question. What I want is to fly away and become one with the Earth and Sky. I can't, though. Physics and stuff.

I keep walking instead. This place is a warren. There's bridges and stairs and doorways and dark and light. I stride along, ride along, rush, rush faster. Chel grabs me and shouts something about how stealing is a symptom . . . but oh no, I've had enough lectures. I shove her backward into the side of a bench. People scatter and fuss. Music took me higher, higher, far from Brockford, far from everyone, even from London; so so so much higher. I start to run, dodging Chel. Behind me, Julie's phone rings.

Mark's in his sixties and overweight, Julie and Chel are in heels, and I'm in canvas flats. It's easy to disappear into the crowd. It's all so easy, when you don't care any more. I just need to wait out the night, and the PI will call, and I will finally know – something. For now: I will pierce the heart of life. Even if I don't yet know where or how. Well, I just have to keep moving.

CHAPTER 30

A million options spin through my head.

I am in Waterloo station, a giant hangar of rushing and rattling and light flashing on metal and tannoy boom. What I need is to find the centre of things. I bleep my bright blue Oyster card against the bright yellow circular reader and get the brown Bakerloo (most London name ever) Tube line and pop out of the ground at deep blue Piccadilly Circus (second most London name ever) station into rush and buses and the huge advertising screens, digital eyes a storey high, staring at me.

Hello! I'm so alive! My fist won't unclench. I run alongside a white limo with a blond girl leaning out of the window, waving and shrieking; it pulls ahead and I'm in front of a bus that brakes hard. 'Stupid cow!' shouts someone. I've lost my hat (again!) – I'll make a thousand more. In Chinatown, a boy with black gelled spikes follows me, but I can't stop even here. Chinatown blurs into Soho and back. My phone is ringing and ringing: *Isga's Theme*. I should turn it off to save battery, but it's my soundtrack. But *come on*, people. There's a dozen messages and nine actual voicemails, all about the same thing. Chel: 'Where are you going?' 'This is serious. Call me.' 'Don't do this to me! I'm scared.' 'Are you going back to Julie's?' 'Just

CALL.' The messages keep racking up in my fandom inboxes, too.

People are itching in my head. I can't be bothered with them now: I have to get things done. I have to *be*. But right, let's do this. I lean against the window of some chain gambling place and get methodical with emails and messages.

1. To Chel: 'Like I said I'll find out about Dad tomorrow and I just need my own headspace till then. Chill. ilu.'
2. To Julie: 'This isn't Chel's fault and if you decide not to give her free accommodation because of it then you are made of shit.'
3. To Ras: 'I will let you be her friend, but if you mess it up I will kill you.'
4. To Kieran, because I'm being thorough: a bullet-point list of how to be less drippy.
5. To everyone in Chel's Brockford family: links to her fics, because I get it: we're both sick of hiding. If *I* tell people, she won't have to be terrified of vikinghusbands doing it any more.

No fear of anything any more.

Right, onto fandom messages. There's one from far-oceans, who's been AWOL for a while.

18:46 far-oceans: Sorry I'm not on rabbithole much at the moment but if you want to message me I might be able to reply. Your friends are worried about you.

Nah, oceans, you'd just ask sensible questions. I don't need questions! Plus I just used all my available focus on the latest truth bombs, oops.

Let's look at some more DMs. Should be good for a laugh!

17:49 ships-kitty: Screw you.

18:05 vikinghusbands: You need to explain yourself and give a full apology to toes and everyone you've bullied.

18:56 anonymous: Ur blackm00ds? Then ur funny but what a cowerd.

19:19 jaarv-pecs: Ugh, I never got why tomtartoes is best friends with you. Did you threaten to boil her cat?

20:41 anonymous2: YOU HYPOCRITE.

. . . aaand quite a few more in the same vein. Enough. I can't be bothered to reply. I'm never going to care what anyone says ever again.

I delete the blackm00ds account. Easy: I want to purify and destroy. What else . . . I've still got a bit of awful poetry on my phone, in a document entitled 'Never EVER share', so I wipe that too. I am light and clean. I need to get higher, purer. Static in my head is getting in the way of transmogrification (great word! Sounds like I should turn into a cat). I'll delete isga-bites-u and be done with it all.

If I do that, I'll lose all far-oceans' messages.

I wonder what oceans is doing now. Giving a squid an IQ test, or drawing Yrsali winning a swordfight or just hanging out with Hannah and Pixie. Their partners. Who love them.

My finger hovers over 'delete account' but I don't do it. I'll think about it later.

Another message, on a different app.

00:14 **Mum:** Where are you?? Chel says you've run away!

NO. I'm not talking to her. She understands nothing.

00:16 **Me:** Having a night out, don't worry. Big day tomorrow.

Tomorrow. London Fashion School, *meeting my dad.* Why am I certain it will happen? Because I can command the universe, that's why. *Is he like me? What will it mean if I find he's like me?*

I have a dozen photos of my dad. I flick through them on my phone. Mum looked so happy with him sometimes – here they've got their arms around each other on Torquay beach, Dad's chin almost on Mum's head. He was lovely at first, she said. Working as a market porter when she came to the village. Went down on one knee and presented her with a bunch of spring onions. They made it to about six months before the rows started. I can imagine it. 'Get off your backside, Jim, and get a proper job!' vs 'Chill out, Biyu, I'll have a stint at the garden centre when they get busy for spring.' It had reached crockery-smashing levels by the time I remember. Him doing the smashing, not her. There are no photos of that. But here's a photo from just before he left, with the Yanlet standing between her mummy and daddy, holding their hands, a roller coaster in the background. I don't remember it. But it happened.

Now I am happening.

Soho is a warren of small streets, taxis stuck in treacly jams. Closed coffee shops alternate with open bars and sex shops. Rainbow flags. Men are hand in hand; straight girls in gangs. There is too much in my head. My phone is on about three per cent. It shuts down. Oh well. Was I waiting for an email? Can't remember.

I'm on about three per cent, come to think of it.

Oh fuck I'm broken I want to hide.

In a tiny alley, there's a gap between two piles of crates in a niche between two buildings. I crawl in there, and drag half a disintegrating cardboard box across to cover the gap. Grit pokes into my arse cheeks and it's stuffy and I don't want to lose the tiny light that filters through the cracks, but I clasp my arms around my knees as if I could press myself in till I disappear.

I doze. The smooth river inside has become clattering rapids, pounding my mind through thick, sweet, fiery darkness.

tomtartoes-blog.rabbithole.com
Thursday 01:17

Right. I don't know if I should blog about this, but honestly at this point I'll try anything.

There's something wrong with bitey. I don't just mean the blackm00ds stuff. Something's really wrong. We went out to a restaurant and a concert with my aunt and uncle and she was just . . . totally out of control. She kicked a man. And then she ran off, just off into London. She was ranting, and I talked to the guy we made friends with earlier this week and his dad's a doctor and he thinks bitey might be bipolar.

It's almost a relief, actually, because I knew something like this was coming, and I've googled bipolar and . . . it fits. I feel terrible about saying that. Terrible about everything. We've called her mum of course and she's coming here on the first train. I just . . . it's just possible that there's someone out there she MIGHT have told where she's going? @far-oceans, I don't want to hassle you but if you're reading this, if bitey's told you where she's going, PLEASE DM me. Her mum's going up the wall. This is all such a disaster.

01:40 **lyssapeeps:** Oh no, bipolar can be bad. I've started a #findbitey tag.

01:59 **vikinghusbands:** Oh, toes, I'm so sorry. This does explain a lot, even though it's not an excuse. Try not to worry. She's not worth it. It's kind of you to defend her but you need to look after yourself as well. I say this as a friend. Bipolar people are just trouble, unfortunately. 🙁

02:26 **dora_theroarer:** I just started sketching this fanart of Isga, so I'm going to finish it and put it in the #findbitey tag. Maybe it'll summon her back!

02:37 **freaksjustkillyrselves:** Here's a link to a great fic that'll cheer your friend up. 🙂 Uskaar kills Isga and becomes king of the nixxi.

03:00 **anonymous:** LMAAOOOOOO BIPOLAR!!! FUCK THAT BITCH! She should just kill herself.

03:07 **anonymous2:** Yup, I'm getting that sack of popcorn back out.

🐱03:59 **minidarthvader:** Nordhelm is just appropriation of Scandinavian culture anyway.

⚓04:29 **far-oceans:** toes, I don't know where bitey is. Ill answer your DM soon. Bad timing. I'm just really busy with my own shot and shouldn't even be typping this. Doesn't mean I don't live you and boaty

CHAPTER 31

I shoot up into the light. Zero to a hundred and ten per cent awake in three seconds. It's early but the sun's up. I *slept*! My body's stiff, but I force it to hurtle (hurtle! hurts!); I have so much energy that I am energy. The future is a blank slate plate in my head. What's going on, again? Oh yes, last night sucked. Today: finding my dad! Finding me! Doing . . . stuff. Transformative, excellent, excelling, dynamic, definitively glorious *stuff*.

'Eh, eh!' a voice grunts.

Oh. I've hurtled *into* someone. A guy dossing with his legs in a torn blue sleeping bag stretched out into the alley. He stands up, and he's got huge muscles and dirty grey hair round a shiny patch and is tattooed and rough-looking. He's got three tinnies of Special Brew on the go or scattered around. He's between me and the way out of this little square of closed shops. Did I mention he's big?

Uh, this is how you get raped and murdered, right? Well, actually, the best way is to move in with a man, which I think is the biggest statistical risk for women, but right now I just kicked a homeless guy in the shin (yeah, it's developing as a good signature move, but this time it was an accident) and, uh . . . I back away.

'It was you dossing down there?' he asks in an Irish

accent, pointing vaguely at my former box-nest. He has lager-breath.

'I'm not homeless, I'm, er . . .' I press a hand to my forehead. *Chelsea says I am insane.*

Tinny-man isn't at all fazed. 'Yeah? There's a lot of that about,' he says conversationally. 'I can still satisfy a woman, you know.'

A heartbeat. Two. This guy is as good at logically connected speech as I am.

Also, this is bad on a stick, isn't it? I need to slip past him. Instead I go back up to him and say, in much the same tone, but with the full force of my shiny Yan-ness, 'Hey, don't say stuff like that to teenage girls. It freaks us out.'

I am heroic. And I have no filter whatsofuckingever.

Tinny-man considers, then nods; he's conceding my point. 'All right. I can, mind you,' he says, and he tilts his chin like he's challenging me to argue, at the same time as stepping back so I can pass.

Pride flashes in his eyes.

He's not going to hurt me. He just wants someone to see he's not dead yet.

'I believe you,' I say. 'And I – I'm Yan.'

The homeless guy reaches down for a tinny. He picks it up, and toasts. 'Mickey.'

We look at each other. He belches. I run.

CHAPTER 32

At an early opening kiosk on Oxford Street, you can charge your mobile for a quid. I sit on an upturned plastic flower bucket, jiggling my leg, amused as the kiosk guy keeps failing to not ogle me. Seems I ran around so much last night the rim of my canvas shoe rubbed quite a lot of skin off; oops, I should probably have noticed that. Ha, the guy offers me a plaster! I grin. A lot.

Messages flood in. Around the time the phone hits thirty per cent, the screen lights up. *Isga's Theme*, the Water vs Fire version, plays – Chel calling yet again. Oh for goodness' sake, all this panic about nothing! Screw everyone and everything: I am euphoric. I say it aloud a few times, 'Euphoric, euphoric, *yu-for-ic*'. I spread my arms out to embrace the city, the world. I'm so happy, I just want to share it, and not a single person understands!

All right, all right, I'll answer the bloody phone.

'Yan? Oh my God.' There's a noise in the background, and Chel shouts away from the phone, 'No, Julie! It's her. Yan, are you all right? Where've you been?'

'Will you stop with the drama? I'm fine. I . . . I slept on some seats at Waterloo station. It was really comfortable. Not wanting to waste time hanging out in Swiss Cheese doesn't mean I've "gone missing".' OK, she probably can't see me making air quotes. Or almost dropping the phone. 'What the hell have you told my mum?'

'The truth! She's coming to London on the first train. It gets in at eight-fifteen. Come on, we can –'

'What?' Oh my God, I could punch Chel sometimes. 'Send out police search parties, why don't you?'

'If you don't come back right now, then yeah, that's the plan. You're technically a minor where this kind of thing is concerned and you ain't of sound mind.'

I do not believe this . . . My foot hurts now I've noticed it, and there's blood on the back of my shoe, which fortunately is red, but not an identical shade. I take the shoe off and chew at it to see if I can work the blood out that way. This makes the kiosk man look at me funny (funnier), but I seriously doubt I'm the oddest thing in central London.

'YAN!' My phone is shouting at me again. 'I know you're still there.'

Oh, for . . . 'Look, I'll meet you for a few minutes if you're so worried.' I can't hear from the PI before nine-thirty, and this way I'll be able to head off the incoming Nurse Mum. 'Um . . . um . . .' Fuckety fuckety fuckety I can't think of the name of a single place. Where even am I? I can't stay still any longer; early crowds are building up shuffling zombie hordes and I launch myself into them, invent the sport of pavement slalom and dodge into the road, slip between shoulders, faster, faster, faster . . .

'Trafalgar Square!' I shout into my phone. 'Lions!'

Yay, I remembered! And I like those big, black, lump-stone lions. I like everything except the things I hate intensely and look, there's a waffle-stand, a woman, a boy, a Tube sign, thing, thing, things. Some lads shout at me. Everyone admires me. I shall be the Van Gogh of headgear. If I quit losing my prize creations. So embarrassing: I really must get it together! Or I might end up in hospital . . . Nah, where did that thought come from?!

Chapter 33

Chel seems to have got here first. Did I get lost? Well, it means I can sneak up on her, around the lion statue.

'All right, here I am,' I say, and flap my arms before she can hug me, because if I am touched I will explode. 'I haven't died and I don't believe I'm on a mission from the Pope.' The Pope's a loser, anyway. 'See? Not mental. Can I go?'

'Oh!' Chel's hugging me anyway. I'm all sweaty.

Someone in the crowd of boiled-lobster tourist faces shouts, '*Ben! No!*' in a tone like they want to commit murder.

'Oh, Yan, where have you been?' demands Chel.

'God, I'm really gross right now.' The hug practically made a squelching noise; how embarrassing. 'Have you got a wet wipe?' Chelsea always has a wet wipe. She gives me a wet wipe. I mop my armpits. 'Hi. I'm gross!'

I stand on one leg and shake the other, then stand on the other and shake the other. I shake each other!

'Right,' Chel says. 'Your mum's almost here. We can all get the next train back. Or Julie'll pay for you to see a doctor privately right away.'

She's using the voice that older members of her family use to extract obedience from younger ones. But me, sit still in some doctor's office?

'What? Look, let's just have a coffee –' Except we don't do that sort of thing; it's a waste of money. Money really *should* just materialise in my pocket if I wish hard enough; it's a rather poor show that it doesn't. 'Then you can go look at that college like you were going to this morning –' see, I remembered: a college! I'm a good friend. Can't remember exactly *which* college – 'and I'll go see London Fashion School.'

Chel's breathing hard. 'OK. I get that you can't help this, but just *try*. You did when you was depressed. You're in no state to look round London Fashion School! You reckon you're gonna find out if your dad is in London and I respect that, and more to the point I can't actually stop you cos when it comes to it you're bigger than me, but afterwards . . .'

She's got her hand on her hip; I want to smack it away. Does nothing faze her? 'Haven't you got anything else to worry about?' I demand.

Chel grits her teeth and for a moment her eyes flash like she's as mental as I am, which is intriguing! 'As a matter of fact, yeah, vikinghusbands doxxed me. Now of all times. I s'pose she's gonna do it to you at any moment. I don't know how she got my details, but if she's got mine she'll probably be able to get yours. But we are not worrying about that now.'

'No indeed,' I agree. This is hilarious! She assumes it was vikinghusbands who emailed her fics to her parents! Well, of course, she probably didn't have a relaxed chat with them about the *Nordhelm* username of the sender. And she's clearly not going to appreciate right now that I did it for her sake, so she can finally be brave. I'll explain later.

'Yan,' she blethers on, 'you started kicking people, dancing in the street. Stealing money! You ain't been eating.

If your dad's in London, maybe we could go see him together? Ras sent me some links his dad found, about bipolar –'

'Oh, if Ras is involved it must be the truth then ultimate.' My words are coming out the wrong way round now. Oops. 'So you are getting back with him?'

'What are you on about? Couldn't me and you go together, though? To see your dad?'

'NO.' You wouldn't get it, you can't get it, fucking standing there chill and self-contained as a fridge. This is for me; it's my father; it's my sickness; I need what he will say to me, even if it's death. You cannot judge us. 'He probably won't be in London anyway. If I find out he isn't, I'll come back to Brockford with you.' Ha ha I doubt it, but it's worth a try to shut her up.

'You better.' The drippy fucking determination dimple appears. Puh-lease.

The best form of defence is attack.

'All right. Go on, then, Chelsea, tell everyone I've gone mental, whip up as much drama as you can. Sorry to inconvenience you when you're busy with your UCLs and fancy relatives and Rases and fandom groupies who think everything you write is fantastic as long as it stays inside the tame little corner you're cramming yourself into because you're scared. *I'm* not scared!'

Now she's pulling a tight little face. 'Yan, you needn't worry; you're all anyone's thinking about right now.'

Huh. Chel's so pretty, always has been, but now she's looking undeniably tasty. It's the pale curve of her shoulder, I think, swooping down under a thin pink crop top. I stare at it. I probably should not be ogling my best friend. That's like bad, Baddy-McBad level. I have things to say, though. Erudite dynamite! 'It's not my fault I don't fit.'

'Neither of us fits! I been called a chav and a nerd for

seventeen years. And I'll suck up to the fancy relatives *so I can afford go to university*, and don't think I don't know how lucky I am to have rich relatives to suck up to. Plenty of people ain't got that. But some of us ain't only children who get all the money spent on them, neither.'

'You're saying I'm rich?!' All right, so Uncle Liko helped us get a mortgage when Dad left. It was the only time Mum accepted his help, for my sake, she said. I know I'm loved. It was me being born that brought my grandparents round to their wayward daughter because who could resist the flailing fists and dandelion hair and advanced dribbling skills of the cute little Yanlet . . . but now the Yanlet's got big, and ugly and mad . . .

Chel is banging on. ' – trying my best, while you just run around –'

'I CAN'T HELP IT!'

I press my hands to my temples, but only briefly, because I am not going to show insane. Black energy is flooding out of me. Your big brain isn't on toxic fire, Chelsea. You couldn't hack this.

'Can you ever help it?' Chel demands. 'Yan the mouth, Yan the attitude, Yan the artist, Yan the only yellow girl in the village, Yan the tragically afflicted. Yan who thinks being offensive is funny even when she's not mental. Yan the literal manic pixie dream girl who has to have all the attention or . . .' She clutches her head with one hand like she's the bonkers one. 'I'm sorry! I know that ain't fair, but what am *I* supposed to do?'

'Not pack me off to the loony bin, I'll tell you that!'

'That's not what's happening!'

I stick out my tongue, which maybe detracts from the dignity of my argument. Oh, hell, she's crying. Fuck her. Fuck *me*.

'Yan, you need treatment.' It's a male voice, familiar, weary and exasperated but with a soupçon of fear – Kieran. Where the hell did he come from?

Nowhere. He's been standing there all along, but bits of the world are falling away, they don't cohere, and I registered him but didn't connect.

Chel's crying more now. 'Do it for your mum, if not for me.'

'If you touch me this time, I'll scream *rape*,' I inform Kieran. The statement goes plunk on the ground, like a dropped ice cream. A woman passes, in a dress so bright it could be made of spun emeralds.

I start walking; I have to walk so I don't explode. Everywhere there's crowds going at half the speed of a snail – shuffling zombie hordes of foreign teenagers with harassed teachers; old couples wandering hand in hand; tourist families stopping to peer at guidebooks and wave selfie sticks or just gape at everything around them. *Get out of my fucking way.* I don't need this, I am heading for the future. And right now, I'm heading for the edge of the square, getting out of here. My so-called friends want to fix me, infect me with blandness. It's like the episode where some dumb love-interest-of-the-week slips magic herbs into Yrsali's drink in an attempt to 'fix' her speech impediment.

And she is furious about it.

Now Kieran and Chelsea actually flank me, guard-style, not just walking on either side. It's almost funny! Meanwhile, over (around) my head, they're having one of those What to Do About Yan conversations like people had when I was depressed.

'I'm not deaf,' I remind them, dodging with exquisite skill around a patch of dried sick. (So many textures and colours!) 'And I'm not mental.' I'm going forward, not back. If I bash myself on the ear to try to knock the burning treacle out of my head, will I look mental?

'Yan, we just can't let you go,' says Kieran. 'One in five bipolar people commit suicide.'

Great. This is what I get for mentioning that subject to Chelsea.

'I don't want to kill myself!'

I wonder if it's possible to get to the top of Nelson's Column? Man, I'm being so random today.

'I just feel it would be a fun option,' I explain, 'like thinking you could take up tennis but you're not sure if you'll get around to it. When I was depressed I wanted to kill myself all the time, but I just didn't have the energy.' I'm probably not helping myself by burbling about this, but while it's not like my control centre has shut down, it's sort of stupefied, stupid-ised, while the rest of me clatters along, snort-giggling. 'I mean, I'm not an idiot, clearly suicide is not a fun option, except, you know . . .' Now my foot is kind of sliding around stickily in my shoe: yuck. 'You want me to be bipolar, so I can get depressed again? Well, yank – thank you sovery much.'

Chel and Kieran aren't saying anything. Chel's gone kind of grey. With mottled bits of red from the heat. Not a good look. *Help.* I stop and turn around. The terror's sealed away, deep beyond reach, and I'm a sludgy, glittery, grinning flame-lit bubble, hanging in emptiness. What am I doing to my friends?

Something smacks hard into my thigh.

I stagger. When I right myself, Kieran is crouching over a little girl who's sprawled flat on the ground and starting to wail. He picks her up and carefully dusts her off as her father rushes up and apologises.

'Hey, it's OK,' says Kieran gently, and the child slows down mid-sob to stare at him, breaking into a smile.

The kid is very cute, with stubby little horizontal bunches. A delightfully clumsy little fucker, her father is drivelling at me, Kieran's so kind, she ripped a bead out of my skirt – I'll go kick the mini-bitch out of K-boy's arms and she'll sail over the fountain and splatify against a big black statue and slide down. *Thunk!*

I am brilliant, hilarious, omnipotent. I'm practically Isga.

I want to hurt a child. I'm gloating over the idea of hurting a child.

My thoughts are obscene. My own thoughts humiliate me.

Help.

The little girl glances my way.

She's afraid of me.

Fair enough.

Chel's looking at me. I'm in a tiny clamshell boat and she is on the shore getting farther away and the grey northern waves are rising and the gulls are crying.

We are right here.

'I'm coming back later,' I say. I probably am. I mean, I haven't got anywhere else to go unless my dad turns out to live in a convenient palace. And it'll be winter at some point. Cold. 'I am honestly not suicidal. I mean, *me?*'

Hm. But I'm getting weird brain flashes of dead me hanging from a nearby tree. My brain is swimming in battery acid. (Whee!)

Think.

'Now I seen you, I know you're in no state to go anywhere,' says Chel. 'Never mind your dad. You come with us, I'm calling the police right now.'

So. Here we finally are.

But I know Chel is trying to help. Her voice has a treacly echo in my head, it's sinister at the edges, I ignore her words and just listen to the crackle and spit. Kieran comes up beside Chel and says something I wish I could understand; the words 'be all right' are in there, I think.

'I really like you, Kieran!' I beam. 'You deserve *the best*.' That is very important. 'I'm sorry I'm me.'

My phone is somehow in my hand. I look at it.

There's an email from the PI. I guess their working hours aren't necessarily limited to their opening hours.

I don't know if I can speak.

So I read.

And it's happened.

There's an address.

I look it up on the map.

Then I've got words again. A few, for Chelsea.

'My dad lives in a flat near sueston – Euston station. No, I'm not telling you exactly where, cos you'll follow me. Though you can't run as fast as I can right now, I assure you.'

Chel's eyes widen.

'Your dad . . .?' says Kieran, bewildered.

Chelsea's silent. I feel very clear.

'If he's bi-fucking-polar he'll know how to help me,' I point out.

Will he? I have no evidence for this. He might not even want to tell me, or see me. But my argument has emotional weight and romantic power.

Just give me a few more hours of this breaking bliss.

Fuck sense!

Is my argument working? Chel's nodding, if as stiffly as a marionette. God, people are stupid. What am I hoping for? *Nothing.* Keep moving.

Perhaps my father is healthy, and the sight of him will jolt me to sanity. Perhaps he is broken and I can scorn him, and in that lies sanity.

I allowed myself depression; I cannot allow myself this.

'All right, all right,' Chel says. 'Yes, this is super important to you, Yan, and really personal. I get it. But when you've seen him your mum'll be here, and she can take you back?'

Now I'm the idiot nodding. Because yeah, right, home where there's rope in the shed, a river at the bottom of the garden . . . Sounds good, though, sounds like a rest from this.

I need to meet my father.

I back away from Chelsea.

'Think you can catch me, do you? When I'm like this?'

She's shouting as I start running. I take care not to hear.

tomtartoes-blog.rabbithole.com
Thursday 09:31

Well, we just saw bitey. And she went off again.

I didn't want to let her, but there's something she needs to do, and anyway she basically ran away. Me and K can't keep up with her. It's like she's possessed.

I don't know if I should have posted about this at all, but I did. Am. Thanks for the stuff in the #findbitey tag. Especially the screencap edit with Isga at the top of a mast doing lookout!

And now I'm practically hallucinating with tiredness so la la la dee dee dee my best friend's gone mental and doesn't want me. And hardly any of you are reading because it's night in the whole US now.

OK that's all I can manage. Thanks, everyone. Except whoever emailed all my fics to my family. God, it tells you what a state things are in that I actually forgot to mention that. What the hell, guys. I have no words. What the hell.

10:24 **vikinghusbands:** I was very sad to wake up to this, but honestly, maybe it's better if you don't find her. And somebody doxxed you? I'm so sorry.

  10:33 **idris-elbow:** Like you aren't the one who did it.

  10:34 **vikinghusbands:** ME?

    10:35 **idris-elbow:** You do it to people who won't join your gang. People you think are vulnerable.

    10:36 **vikinghusbands:** IT WASN'T ME. It was probably far-oceans.

     10:37 **idris-elbow:** Why the hell would they doxx one of their fandom BFFs?

     10:39 **vikinghusbands:** I've told people before: she's clearly unstable.

      10:40 **idris-elbow:** Nobody asked you. And oceans' pronoun is THEY.

      10:44 **vikinghusbands:** How nice for her.

10:43 **freaksjustkillyrselves:** people hate isga cuz she's a bitch and messes things up between uskaar and rothgern not cuz she's asian female.

  10:46 **vikinghusbands:** I don't care about her ethnicity, she's a bad person and people who are shipping her are messed up. 'bitey' was disturbed and couldn't see that.

  10:47 **freakskillyrselves:** Yeah, these pedos will say

anything to make it sound like we're the ones in the wrong.

   🗡 10:50 **idris-elbow:** How is the PEDO bullshit a fit for this situation?

     🪑 10:53 **freakskillyrselves:** Duh you and that blackm00ds bitch ship Isga and Yrsali. 300 years old and 18 years old!! I bet you think Pug is hot. 😫

       🗡 11:01 **idris-elbow:** I'M A LESBIAN. I can see Pug is cute, because the show makes him up to look that way. IRL teenage boys are about the least attractive thing to me, I promise.

        🪑 11:02 **freaksjustkillyrselves:** Old hags admit they're attracted to Pug! omg I just threw up a little in my mouth. Electric chair time. 😫 😫 😫

🎰 11:01 **lyssapeeps:** #findbitey!

◎ 11:10 **vikinghusbands:** Oh no!! Look what I found on nordhelmer.com. This is so sad. <u>Nixxi Queen Isga to be killed off in next season, actress Florence Huang reveals</u>

CHAPTER 34

I found the place on the map, but it still takes me over an hour to get there because of the thing where my brain is in bits.

My father, my father.

He'll probably have gone to work by now. Or it could be the wrong guy after all (with the same name, born on the same day).

I'm *here*.

It's a big, long, dark red building, the kind you call mansion flats. (Is he rich? They don't look like 'mansions'.) In order to ring the bell, I have to stop walking. My feet hurt. I wheel and halt at the door. A double door with rows of buzzers; 'Jim Harris' says one.

I need to ring the bell . . . But then some guy comes out, going to work, and gives me a funny look but lets me slip through the door. Whatever – you know I'm sweet and harmless, fucker. Yeah. Might as well get some use out of the stereotypes.

I'm in. It's a bit like a council block only nicer, with trees and stuff in a courtyard, and outside stairs. Concrete walkways. Red and grey and sun. Me shaking. I have such longing; for what, what for?

The door I knock on is opened within seconds, by a

white man who looks like me.

Oh.

He's real.

I shouldn't really be surprised.

He's older than the photos – also not surprising – and less skinny, and paler, so his freckles stand out more, and his red-brown hair is thinning and sticking up – I think I woke him – and he's real, and everything is perfect. I am meshed into sweet, sharp moments of meaning: it's all come together so I can meet my father, who is me because there is so much of me that does not fit, and neither did he. The frosted glass of his door flashes shards of light; there's a cobweb in the top corner . . . This is my dad.

'Ohh,' he says. '*Yan?*'

'Uh-huh. Dad.' When it comes to noses, I'm looking in the mirror. 'Are you going to work?'

'No.' He pushes the door wide open. There's a slightly sour but homey smell and – a pink plastic tricycle under the coat rack. Another child? Why didn't I think of that?

'Not mine,' he says, seeing my stare. 'This is a flatshare. Kofi's kid visits. He's out, by the way. Do you want some tea?' There's still some Brocky in his accent. He stifles a yawn, but his eyes are on me.

'Yes, please.' We're following a script. I hate scripts, but right now I need this one. I trail my dad into a kitchen that's pretty manky but contains an actual teapot, as well as loads of ingredients – good quality brands. I remember Dad could cook. As he gets milk from the fridge, I glimpse broccoli and pak choi and beansprouts. He makes tea. It really is a comfort, even in hot weather. My father was at school with Chel's dad's younger sister. Broke her heart, the family story goes.

Dad asks, 'Milk and sugar?'

'MILK.' I'm shouting. One arm goes flapping.

He studies me quietly.

I could just ask him: *Are you . . .?*

I can't get it out. Wouldn't be polite to start with that, anyway. What does one ask one's long-lost father?

Bile and fire.

There's no room to pace in here, so I start tapping hard – banging – on the table, which is probably rude. My dad has a football tattoo. As he stirs milk in, I see: on the inside of his forearm is a foot-long scar, stretched along the vein like a fat, twisted worm. The kind of scar you only get one way.

'How are you?' he asks.

'Fine. Fine fine fine fine fine FINE FINE.'

Shut up shut up *shut up*. I need to talk, not get stuck on one word like a . . . like a . . .

My dad smiles at me, just a bit painfully. His eyes are very blue. Well, everything's very very at the moment, but I can see the charm. Ripped, too. Is it gross to notice that about your own dad? He's got dimples. Boyish. Waves of intensity immensity crush and crash inside me.

'So how come you're here?'

'Wantedtomeetyou! You'remydad . . .'

'I've wanted to meet you too.' The charming, lopsided smile again. I see why she liked him. 'How's your mother?' Pause. 'Did she send you?'

'No. I got youraddress offaPI.' Slow down, slow down slow DOWN. Have a grown-up conversation. 'Didn't even tell her at first. I think she's going to be angry.'

'Very likely. I knew she'd never chase some loser guy – not Biyu.' My father shakes his head a little. 'But you wanted to meet me? I must admit, I'm pleased. And fidget away, Yan, it's all right. I can see you're hypomanic.'

Pause.

He continues, 'I did wonder if you'd inherit it.'

Longer pause. That's his reaction?

He hands me a mug of tea; our fingers don't touch. He sits at the table. I thump it. He quirks a half-smile at my fist. *He must see this.*

A father. An answer?

I point at the scar. 'What's that?'

'That's history,' he says, unruffled. And it does look old. (Is it my future?)

NO.

Tell me how to make it not be.

My heel hurts. I don't have to hide now. I start to say something and it comes out garbled and then I forget what it was . . . *Try again.* 'Have you got a job?'

'Yeah, I'm home today because I'm on shift at the weekend. I'm a foreman at a building site in . . .' I stop listening. He's a functional adult; good. I want a hug. His scar matches his hair. The precision, clarity and speed of my thoughts! The . . . where the hell was I? My brain's spun ninety degrees to the world.

I keep talking while I work out what to say.

'I kicked Colin Carston,' I say. I think that's good? (Oh God, I wanted to kick a child . . . Don't think about that. Dial the sun down.)

My dad's eyebrows shoot up. 'The MP? For real?'

'Yesforreal. I am not hallucinating! We're staying with Chel's rich relatives; they took us to a posh restaurant. He was there with a crunch – bunch of cronies. Chelsea, that's Chelsea Furse, is my best friend.' Yes, I must talk about normal stuff. I don't want him to think I'm always like this. 'I'm about to start Year 13.'

Dad's looking amused. Settled, even. (Settled, can he be?)

'The Furses!' he replies, reminiscent. 'I never got on with Terry, though I suppose he's basically all right, if you can actually get him to speak. They're from the wrong end of town, mind. It was someone from up their way as scrawled "Chinks go home" on the door and smashed the living-room window, not long after you were born. I lost a few friends over that. Well, when I say lost, I mean I thumped Gary Barker into the middle of next week when he did a little speech about how he didn't condone it, but what did people expect, a woman like her moving to a place . . .' Dad breaks off, looking grim.

I can't process all this. Someone broke our window? 'Mumnevertoldme.' She doesn't always, about things like that. Wants to protect me. 'She doesn't like fuss.' (People scrawled 'Chinks go home' on our door? And my dad punched one of them out . . . *And then left her?*)

He comes back from the past, focuses on me again.

Dad, can you help me?

'Look, you're not . . . expecting me to come back, are you?' he asks.

'Huh?'

'I know I owe Biyu an apology. I was a kid, full of myself, thinking I was in love. But in those days, back in Brockford, she was coming, and I was going, you might say. I couldn't have stuck it forever, even without the depression. I'm guessing you know that feeling, at this point, since you're here in London. I wish I could put you up, but you see how it is here.' He gestures around. He's watching me, like I might stick a flag saying 'Colonised by Yan' in the table or something.

'I didn'tcome tomakedemands ofyou!'

'OK . . . good, good.'

He's getting me wrong. Also, he's dissing Brockford,

which makes me think of the quiet in the fields behind Chel's estate – or rather the different kind of noise. Peace. Oh God, imagine peace. And cows that don't judge you. (Cows! So big, so solid, so still.) And roadkill. OK, forget the roadkill. 'Ijust wantedto meetyou. I haven't run off! OK . . . Ihave. Temporarily . . . ily ily. I'm going back.' Am I? 'Can I have a plaster for my heel?'

Might he say he'll look at my bleeding foot, if not my bleeding mind? But he's not a nurse, of course. He waves me towards the bathroom, where I poke at my damaged skin. There's a number of blisters but only one thing that qualifies as a cut. The plaster the phone-kiosk guy gave me has rubbed off so I put a little bandage on even though my shoe will shred it. I stand in the middle of the tiny room and spin and flap my hands.

I boing back out into the kitchen. My father is clearing away cold tea. Was I a while? A silence has set in. And the words spin all through me.

Help exalt hold me.

He sees I'm unwell *exalt hold me need.*

'Youcould havecontacted me *once*!' I accuse. 'To warn me I might get like this.'

There.

My dad puts a mug down too hard; *thunk*. 'You're not wrong,' he says, and blows out air. 'But I wrote to you on your birthday one year, remember? Biyu got in one of her strops, of course . . .' He scowls at the past again. Comes back to the present. 'You turned out pretty, like her. Have you got green fingers? She could grow a sunflower in a thimble.'

Ha ha. 'Plants die when they seeme coming. I'm notlikeher . . .'

I'm not plants, soil or sunshine. I'm not mild measured hopeful. I . . .

'Anyway, I want to know you now,' says my dad. 'Like Biyu said, it would be your choice to contact me when you were eighteen, and I guess you are.' Then his smile gets a bit sly. 'Only, you know you're a walking trigger? I guess you're not having much fun now – but wow, the run-up you must have had. I'm a little envious. I get mostly depressions.'

'Iwasdepressedallspring. You you you –' My brain's tripping over my mouth. A trigger? *'HOW DO YOU DEAL? I WANT A FUTURE THAT'S NOT IN A LOONY BIN OR SPLATTERED ON A PAVEMENT.'* Shouting again. Well, it's kind of important. I don't want to die. 'Aretheremeds that really help? Lithium?' I swallow. I'm not banging the table. I'm not. Hurrah for me . . . *BANG BANG.* 'Sedatives?'

My father sucks his teeth. Preparing to answer?

'Oh, Yan, it really does break my heart this is happening to you. Anyway – well, yeah, my mate Charlie swears by lithium, but he's an accountant so how would you tell if his personality's been squashed? When I got diagnosed bipolar, about ten years ago now, the doctor put me on it. The stuff made me calm all right, but it turned my brain to cotton wool and I couldn't get off my arse till mid-afternoon. For me, it's been about diet, exercise and positive thinking. Those tackle the depressions, without –' he smiles – 'squashing the highs.'

I look around. I don't think the positive thinking is entirely fuelled by pak choi. There's whisky bottles by the spice rack. My father's fingers are nicotine yellow . . . and everything's blurring, tears, brain-fire, *make it stop, make it last forever,* I will happily mainline vegetables if that helps, but *'WHATDOIDORIGHTNOW?'*

My father is coming around the table, and *he hugs me.*

It's clumsy. We don't know how to fit each other, and he smells of cigs. His hands are callused. I'm shaking with . . . with mental mental mental, and now there's a lot of tears and *you're my dad. I can feel the warped skin of your arm through my top. Where* am *I*?

'Being creative helps,' he says. 'Come on, have a look.'

At what? When Dad pulls away, I follow him into what must be the living room. There's shelves of kung-fu and action DVDs, rock music CDs and adult-education textbooks. (What's his, and what's his flatmate's?) He points to the mantelpiece over an old, stopped-up fire. There's a row of little carvings.

'Here,' he says, picking up a swallow and handing it to me. 'See? Nothing like creativity for getting focus. And get whatever treatment works for you, but don't let anything damage that.'

He stands back. I *fucking concentrate*, and examine the little bird. It's accurate, with beautiful, outstretched wings. I imagine it perching on the apple tree at the bottom of our garden. 'It's lovely,' I say. 'I make hats!'

'Hats?' He's unsure.

'Yes!' I'll tell him. Prove myself. Swimming out of depression I took a bolt of red silk in my hands and thought of it falling in waves from a dark felt crown. Colour came back. And kept coming coming coming, and burns me up now. 'I'm applying to . . . to . . .' I can't remember the name of the place. 'Art college. I like beautiful things, and they sort of contain you, and if people are going to think you're weird, well, you might as well be weird. Weirder than they dare be. Make what they can't. Screw it. A person animates an outfit from inside, and I am real, all over. There's a lot of me.' If I made Grandma a hat, would she wear it? I forgot to send her a postcard. 'And sometimes you just like doing a thing, you know? It's from you, and not from anything or anyone else? Do you get it? Do you?'

'Of course.'

Hats, carving, kung-fu movies, *Nordhelm*!

He's studying me. The air thickens between us: tea and pain. Force but no direction, an answer not answering. Jackie Chan's on top of a pile of DVDs, looking so alive he might chop my kneecap. There's too much (cheap) furniture in here; ashtrays, a worn blanket tipping off the back of the sofa. The monster in me is named now.

'How do you think I can help you?' my dad says, a bit sadly.

'YOU'RE SUPPOSED TO TELL ME!'

I hurt Chelsea. I'm chewed up with terror, sick with glory, **I BANG MYSELF ON THE SIDE OF THE HEAD I'M SODDING MENTAL OK.**

Crack.

I've clenched my sweaty hand and broken the carving. Jagged edges jab my palm. 'Oops.'

My father retrieves the bits, cig-stained fingertips brushing my skin.

'God, s-sorry,' I say.

'It happens.' I've annoyed him. Well, I'm tired tired on fire, and dirt's ground into the walls here like exhaustion, and I am here for one thing . . .

'TELL ME HOW TO OUTTHINK MYSELF!'

His forehead creases. He sounds exhausted as he says, 'Kid, no one can do that.'

'NOT GOOD ENOUGH.'

My father shrugs apologetically. Self-containedly.

He said he envies me.

O danger and glory.

I rip away from Earth. Get up, get away. Where am I, anyway? Some dump.

'I have to go,' I inform him.

'Oh. Already?'

Yeah, easy. Ten steps and I swim, bask out into my sunshine.

The man follows me onto the walkway. 'Hey, keep in touch!'

But touch merges. As I emerge, the sun is a throb. Its blue bed is transformed: seas of white sparks swim through it, dancing, and I will not stop, I will fly forever, not looking down at my settling corpse.

CHAPTER 35

tomtartoes-blog.rabbithole.com
Thursday: 10:14

I do not believe this. I am sick of people using the comments section of this blog to have their stupid fights just because you think I'm too nice to start deleting stuff and blocking people. I know bitey/blackm00ds said some terrible things but cut her some slack, she's obviously seriously ill and she's my best friend and she's gone missing. How about NOBODY tells ANYBODY to kill themselves?! BECAUSE HOW BIG AND CLEVER DO YOU THINK THAT SOUNDS RIGHT NOW? 😵

That article about how they're killing Isga off though. God, the timing is appalling.

And Mum and Dad if you're reading this, then OK, whatever, you'll find all my fic listed on the sticky post on the front page. Enjoy. And to the person who doxxed me (as if I can't guess who you are) – also *whatever.* Honestly, I've got bigger things on my mind.

📖10:58 **longboat_life:** I have issues with bitey but this is obviously really bad. Bipolar isn't anyone's fault. I hope she's OK. Seriously.

🔘 11:02 **vikinghusbands:** toes, I understand why you're lashing out. But it's deeply hurtful to be accused of doxxing you.

    🔳 11:19 **ships-kitty:** You're the best, @vikinghusbands. 💕 So understanding. 😌

🔷 11:05 **anonymous:** Oh boy, I'm ordering a whole crate of popcorn.

🏆 11:14 **rubyshoes2:** Sis, I don't know what to say! I'm talking to mum and dad about the fanfiction. I think mum will get her head around it. Can't wait for you to get home so I can give you a big hug. 🥺

🎵 11:29 **isga-bites-u:** I just met my fatheer and logged in here case words help but I saw that article. THEY ARE KILLING ISGA. So they can get a wider audence. They are fckig KILLING HER so what is the point?

🔘 11:29 **vikinghusbands:** All right. I feel passionately about building this fandom community and defending its members from problematic content, and I know some people don't like me because of that. But I know this: if you want your friend back, toes, you've got to be firm with her. You said you just let her run off? If she needs help, if she's not rational, indulging her isn't going to do her any good. Find some adults who can help. She'll thank you eventually.

I've ended up in a park, a square. There's waving, wavering green green leaves above me, and randos wander with coffee. Nothing is wrong; my mere breath washes everything clean.

I just read that they are killing Isga.

Fresh shards of bottle glint on the ground beside a bin. I pick up the base – revelation, reflection – an intact, ragged circle like a flower-face – and prick my finger gently. A tiny pain, sharp and delicious, shifted sideways from what pain usually is . . . There's the spines of a broken umbrella; I could stick them into my jugular, except I don't know where that is.

Thoughts tumble and blur like bike spokes, twirl, whirl, skirl (is that a word?) the world. I wish Chel could see it. I left her behind . . . Can't go home because it won't be there; home's no longer home when you're no longer you. Plath clacks in my head, *a million filaments* . . . I'd like to lie down in the snow and dissolve. Not very practical, in August.

My father said he envies me.

I will be hypomanic forever. Beyond any knowing I've known. Beyond mortal pleasure.

I will never let go. It's what I have.

One of Chel's hundred messages said I'm selfish. My phone flashes: 'Come home, Yan,' from Mum; Tash from school is having a party; new art by longboat_life – for me! Isga rising over the Thames, scaly tail wrapping the city, fangs dripping; tagged #findbitey. If only.

That woman is eating a little packet of sultanas and raisins. A bus crawls by and the movie mega-macho-man on the poster smiles with eyes as real as my heartbeat: for me, for me. I might die, but my soul is a page of a book that would float away into the sun; words spooling out, eternity, birds, breezes; the green green wavering waving, and above it blue aching with shards of light. I kicked Colic. A woman is staring; fuck you but no it's a statue, a head and shoulders and third time lucky I decipher the words: Noor Inayat Khan, a war hero – her last word was 'liberty'. I lean on her. All my words unravel in fire. The father I found won't help me.

They're murdering Isga. The article said how it will be. Florence Huang leaked it because she's so angry.

---

nordhelmer.com

. . . The showrunners have previously spoken about wanting to up the stakes in Season 4, to attract a wider audience. With a whole fleet of longboats arriving to support the Jaarv in the final episode of Season 3, it's clear that more and bigger battles are on the way.

According to actress Florence Huang, in the mid-season 4 climax, the united forces of humans are pressed back to the coast, where Isga and her nixxi watch them being butchered by a new 'air race' who attack from above. At the last moment, the nixxi decide to intervene, but Isga is wounded. She professes her love for Rothgern and dies in his arms.

In Season 3 she had him bound in kelp and taken to her quarters . . . then fade to black. Season 4, fade to later, and always we die. The different die, the fearsome yellow and brown queer-bodied queer-minded ones.

I am in terrible danger.

I have to decide what to do about it.

My forehead rests against stone.

Facts don't fit now.

Danger whispers the last of me, down deep, encircled by bloody flames.

I can't walk without shaking.

Danger. Where are the people I love?

I can't make a phone call.

Danger. Where the fuck is *me*?

Sinking with Isga.

My people live in my phone. Perhaps they can clear my head.

I have over sixty message notifications. And far-oceans is finally online. Has been for a while, it looks like.

07:51 far-oceans: BITEY YOU IDIOT.

Well, that's straightforward. So short I can read it. And even respond.

11:16 isga-bites-u: it's middle of night where you are when you sent that
11:18 far-oceans: Yeah, well, they're still adjusting my meds.
11:19 isga-bites-u: Meds?
11:22 far-oceans: I'm bipolar. Just had a rough couple of days. I haven't really got the spoons for a conversation now but I see you need it.

Oh. I seem to have stopped marching around in favour of sitting on the ground.

11:23 isga-bites-u: ??
11:25 far-oceans: Yup I'm bipolar type I. I think you may have type II.
11:26 far-oceans: Have you looked up the differences? I won't go into it now but basically bipolar I makes you madder, and bipolar II makes you sadder. I once spent

a week thinking I was invisible, which wasn't the best, but I don't get depressed that often.

11:30 far-oceans: You're clearly still there, I can see your status. I'm just gonna keep typing. This can be OK, but you need to go to the ER right now.

11:31 far-oceans: All right, we can talk about other stuff if that helps you. I saw vikinghusbands doxxed tomtartoes.

far-oceans is typing . . .

NO. I interrupt.

11:32 isga-bites-u: I did that
11:32 far-oceans: Did what?
11:33 isga-bites-u: doxx
11:34 far-oceans: Okaaaay . . . I didn't expect that. Can I ask WHY?

It's too much. I log out. I don't need this. I needed Chel open. Like me. Undefended. So what if she hates me? My blood brain bone hate me.

far-oceans is bipolar!

Isga is going to die.

I cannot even find the gate of this 'garden square'. So unimpressive. Unresponsive. Inactive unconnected detached defective . . .

I must rise beyond it.

On a church nearby, a stone god is tortured. Who could surrender this rapture?

Disease encroaches.

oceans is bipolar.

The flowers are scalded in sunlight.

I will message my mother.

Sweet, impervious danger. I send Tash and Chloe a picture of the square, saying how nice it looks.

I will message Chelsea.

Isga coils on her rock and sings, 'Sunshine girl, come to me . . .' but I cannot mark my way in the waves.

I think I'd better go to A&E.

Chapter 36

Please, sir, can I have some sanity?

In A&E: about thirty people. Wandering or coughing or hunched up, holding miserable children. Standing fans do nothing for the heat. The desk woman sits behind glass that goes up to the ceiling – sealing – she has a queue. I'll have to walk up to it, stand in it, tell her I'm mental, and wait.

Bright yellow signs 'Administration Blood Donors Exit' bore into me. I flinch, I blink. I can't –

'Oh, Yan. Thank God!'

It's Chel. Here before me. Well, I got lost. A few times.

'I only got here a minute ago. Sit down,' she says, and pulls me to a corner. Sit? It sounds as feasible, as reasonable, as climbing into an iron maiden . . . I do it, though, because it is what you do.

'Desk-k . . .' I say. 'Shouldn't we queue?'

Chel shakes her head. 'Your mum's coming any moment. She'll look after you.' She gives me a hug. I want prescription drugs. I think.

'HI, Chel!' I shake my foot manically, maniacally. My foot shakes me. I tuck it beneath the other. All-over vibratatatation. People stare. HIIII! I'm high.

'I met my father! He's really bipolar! And said nothing useful.'

A revelation sensation! Or maybe not. 'Thank God you're safe,' says Chel. 'What *did* he say . . .? No, I can't start that now.' She rubs a hand down her face. She's knackered. I did that. Oops.

'SORRY! Sorry sorry.' Isn't it funny how an ordinary word sounds strange if you say it over and over? I'm letting Chel down again. Father not helping. I'm doing little dance moves in my seat.

'Oh, Yan,' says Chel. Her voice is strange, too. 'We seem to keep on doing this.'

'Yes, dramatic reunions! I'm going to get pills, though. You've got free accommodation for uni!'

'Mm, maybe.' Chel seems lukewarm, which displeases me. 'Mum had a shout at Julie down the phone for not looking after us properly. Then Julie went off at Kieran and he said, fine, I'm gonna live with my mate right away, and marched out. It were quite fraught, actually,' she mutters, then seems to come back to the present. 'But that ain't the priority right now.'

'Wow!' I punch the air. 'Good for him. HELL YEAH! Even better for you!' People are drawing back all around us. I'd rather think about Chel than about myself. 'What a night. And you reckon vikinghusbands doxxed you?'

'Yeah . . . But right now ain't the time . . .'

'IT WAS ME DID THAT!'

'Did what . . .?'

'Yeah!'

The desk lady's staring. I think she's phoning someone. I just grin at Chel.

'Wait – *you* doxxed me?' She boggles. That got her!

'Well, only a little. Just to your parents. No one else, don't worry. You just need to be braver.'

Chel draws a big breath. I suppose she'll start shouting.

~ 274 ~

I knew it was coming.

'Why did you do that?' she says very quietly, as if she's wondering to herself rather than asking me.

'TO STOP YOU HIDING! YOU WANTED THE ATTENTION! COS *I* CAN'T HIDE, CAN I?!' That's why I've come here. To see what I can have seen and see.

'I didn't exactly want . . . No, we ain't talking about this now, neither. I can't take it in.' Chel's sadness makes me sad. 'I know you can't help Yanning two thousand per cent at the moment.'

'INDEED NOT!' I like the word *indeed*. So crisp and formal and full of *eeeee*. 'I LOVE YOU!'

There is a *slight* pause. 'And I love you too. But I reckon I'll love you more when you've got this sorted.'

'FAIR ENOUGH, CAPTAIN!'

Chel nods, a bit wobbly and dazed-looking. 'I have *got* to sleep.'

'WAIT! YOU'RE GOING TO LEAVE ME?'

'Well – for now, yeah, when your mum comes. You're in the right place. All this is just a bit beyond me.'

I nod. Nod nod nod nod. 'IT'S BEYOND ME AS WELL!'

Chel snorts with laughter, then presses the back of her hand to her mouth when she gets her share of the wary looks around us. 'That shouldn't be funny. Why's that funny?'

'WELL, WHY NOT FUNNY?' I point out. 'IT'S ALL RIGHT! GO BACK TO YOUR FAMILY!'

Chel puts a hand on my shoulder, which absorbs just a little of the shaking. 'You're family,' she says. 'Oh – here's your mum!'

She waves towards the glass doors at a half-running blue dress.

It is indeed my mother, coming for me in A&E. Crying. Black, grey-shot hair swinging, lip wobbling. I want to protect her; how strange. But *that's what I'm doing.* So I don't go dying. Don't go sideways like Dad. oceans said, *It can be* OK.

'Oh, *Yan!*' Mum catches me up in a fierce hug. The top of her head presses into my cheek; I hug back. Relief. She will help. Won't she?

'HI, MUM!' (Still verrrrry happy!)

Mum hugs Chel too, briefly, then says, 'Thank you so much, Chelsea. It's all right, I'll take her now.'

'HEY, I'M TAKING MYSELF,' I say. 'I got myself here! But go forth, o Chelsea, to academic glory!' Some fine *Nordhelm* cheese-speak, there. If slightly adapted. She's off to sleep then to bond further with her adopted poshnobs, and I'm on on on ON cos my off-switch broke.

'She'll be all right, won't she?' Chel asks my mum.

Mum hesitates slightly. Looks me up and down, suddenly all nurse-y. 'I'm not an expert in psych,' she says. 'But someone here will be.'

'OK,' says Chel. 'I understand it's gonna take a while.'

'UNFORTUNATELY!' I am much nodding.

'Bye, Yan,' says Chel sadly.

'DON'T WORRY!' I assure her. 'I'M GOING TO UN-BREAK NOW, SOMEHOW.'

Chel gives me a hug. A few more of my mad shakes are absorbed into her body.

'BYE-BYE, CHELSEA!'

She's gone.

'OK, we need to get you fast-tracked through here,' says Mum.

I believe the staff apprehend that too. A bloke in scrubs is hovering, eyeing me carefully.

I practically shout at him, 'Aha! Ahaha! Pleasegiveme sanitypillsnow PLEASEPLEASEPLEASE?'

tomtartoes-blog.rabbithole.com
Thursday 13:20

OK: the news in brief. bitey got herself to A&E, and her mum's there too. I wouldn't exactly say she's OK, but I guess they're assessing her, and there'll be news later. Just wanted to tell people that. She's physically all right. I think she understands that she's hypomanic and that she needs to do something about it, even if she is having a great time in a way that makes as much sense as that vittra who gets obsessed with shoes in the musical ep, but is clearly real.

I just got 'home' to my aunt's. And I am going to bed!

✏ 13:40 **idris-elbow:** Really glad to hear this. Tell us more when you can, and if you want to.

🏰14:19 **lyssapeeps:** 💞 💞 💞

⛴16:26 **far-oceans:** Sleep rules. I hope you're faaast asleep as I write this. I'm sorry I'm not around much. I might be able to DM tomorrow.

CHAPTER 37

My mother is here, in her blue dress. I am here, more or less.

We sit in a corridor, alcove, opposite blue curtains. Can't really talk here, with all the doctors and real patients coming by. I'm taken to wee in a cup. Mum holds my hand, but I shake her off. Sorry. Too busy vibratatating. Sitting is . . . challenging.

'Chelsea told me everything,' she says quietly. 'You . . . saw your father?'

'YES!' She's asked about him! So I can tell her. 'He lives in a flat near Euston. He's charming, I get why you . . . er, liked him. He's a building site foreman . . . scars, carvings, a fridge of veg. He's . . .' It's somehow still hard to say this. '. . . diagnosed bipolar.'

Mum sighs. 'Is he, now.'

'Yes. What, is that a problem?' It means we know what's wrong with me!'

Another sigh. 'If that man's wangled a psychiatric diagnosis, he'll see it as a get-out-of-jail-free card.' She shakes her head, as if clearing it. I know that feeling. But she can't know his, our feeling!

She continues, 'He saw you in this state and packed you off to A&E *on your own*?'

'I think he was jealous.' Cue weird close awkward moment with Mum. 'I mean, this *is* really fun.'

She draws back a little: oops. Hey, it was my idea to come.

My idea, me, responsibility. Listen to me all coherent! (While boiling and bleeding, jammed into red sky, sealed in caramel, breath by breath by willpower *not exploding*.)

'Don't let him get to you,' she says.

'Yeah, well. I don't think he wants to.'

Mum leans forward and hugs me. Smooth arms on my back. I sneakily bite my finger behind her, I need the sensation, I need intervention. It's been half an hour . . . An admissions doc's finally coming!

'Hello, Jan,' he says, old, white and smiling. 'I hear you're feeling agitated?'

'UH,' I say. Cos I can yak drivel, but I am ocean and that question was thimble.

'What do you think is wrong?'

Mum comes to my rescue. 'I'm her mother. I'm a nurse. She was depressed in spring, and –'

'And they put me on ANTIDEPRESSANTS! Hahaha really clever!' I tell him the brand of the pills, and the dosage. 'I'm here looking round unis withmybestfriend Chelsea and I got abitveryexcited . . . CANYOUMAKEITGOAWAY?'

He's unruffled. 'Well, your urine tested clear for street drugs, but it's possible your current medication isn't right for you.' NO SHIT, SHERLOCK. 'OK, you'll need to see the psychiatrist, and she's with someone at the moment, but a milligram of lorazepam is standard, to take the edge off. And there's a place you can wait. All right?'

Mum looks uncertain. 'Drug her?'

'YES PLEASE.' He said *standard*. I've got a real,

treatable illness? 'WANT SANITY PLEASE NOW.'

I am not all that father.

Nor am I currently me.

A smaller room. Blank white walls and one high window. A bench and a battered-looking table, both bolted down. Well, hell, I fell . . . an almost-cell. I'm pulsing with meaning, but I can keep the lid on for one more minute, till pills.

A not-mum nurse comes with a polystyrene cup. I take this pill and it will take my edge off.

I take this. My edge cuts through my brain which is ramming at right angles into reality in an almost-cell that's stale stuffy and sunless.

My mother is here. On the bench beside me. Hands clasped in her lap.

There's something I want to ask. I ram words into order.

'Mum, the Pope chips man.'

'Huh?' She's startled.

'At the takeaway! When we lived there, after Dad left.' Has she forgotten? 'Am I like him?'

Mum's face clears. 'Oh, *that* poor man. Whatever made you think of him?'

I don't know what to tell her. Perhaps it's the fact that I'm mental?

'Well . . .' she continues, recalling. 'He got better. He came in one day just before we left, and said he'd gone on lithium. He gave your grandfather a twenty for all the chips.' She even smiles slightly.

I like this story. *He got better.*

(I am manic. I'm slipping down rapids of acid static. Crying lava tears.) 'I need lithium.'

Mum scowls. 'Don't be ridiculous. That's a serious medication, with serious side effects.'

Oh.

I am not serious. I'm just too much. I'm too loud weird white Asian dramatic sexy fucked arrogant Yannic.

I seem to be standing up. I seem to have crushed the polystyrene cup. I let the shards fall. I lean on the smooth white wall, and I slap it once. My mother looks, sharply. I seem to be waving my bloodied foot, oops. She looks away. *I'm sorry.*

'I understand you're scared,' she says. 'But this isn't like in films. They're not going to label you and drug you up.'

'THE MEN IN WHITE COATS WON'T TAKE ME AWAY?'

'No! Of course not. They might take you overnight for observation. But as you're calming down, and it can't just be the lorazepam in such a short time, they might let me take you home. I can probably get you an emergency appointment with Dr Pawley.'

Pawley – the Bath clinic. Attempted discretion, as she did with my depression. Hide hide hide. Why not, we did it before.

'I should never have let you come to this wretched place. As for Jim . . .' She sighs. 'You are almost eighteen. You have the right to know him. But him telling you you're bipolar . . .!'

She gets up, comes over, puts her hand on my arm. I will not flinch from the overwhelming shriek of sensation.

'I've seen bipolar patients,' Mum continues. 'And if you were acutely manic, you couldn't have made it here. You'd be out of control, trying to scrape ants off your skin, maybe violent. It gets ugly.'

'YOU DON'T BELIEVE ME.' I haven't totally checked out of my head, so I must be pretending? 'THERE'S BIPOLAR II. A SHITSTORM OF SHIT BUT YOU STAY

SANE ENOUGH TO WATCH IT.'

And Mum finally looks uncertain. 'Oh, Yan, psych isn't my area. Maybe bipolar onset can look like this, I don't know. This stuff's not cut and dried. Just explain calmly to the psychiatrist how you feel and we can go home.'

She's back to watching me, all wan and wary. Steps towards me, her blue dress a flag flaming at me far down my glittery sludge pit. I am too mad to be normal and too sane to be mad. The ants scamper through me, though I know they can't. Words splash into lava and incohere with fear.

'You do want to go home?' Mum demands.

I actually get out my phone. It's that or explode.

Message from Chel: 'Thinking of you.'

far-oceans' final message after I signed off: 'I'm telling you to go home and get help. It can be OK.'

Yes and no. What will home be? You build it from scratch, build it out of your mind.

'Yan!' persists my mum sharply. 'Why are you on that damn phone now? Just try to calm down.'

'I cam – I am calm. I have friends.'

'Oh, the *fandom*.' Mild and derisive, weary.

'And I don't give up! You taught me that!' Though I can't nice away all the ugly right now. I am standing still, and it shreds me. The awful sun bangs through the window, it burrows into me. Angels slam through my temples. Oh joyful day, *make this go away*.

The psychiatrist comes.

Street clothes, name badge. Dr Muhammad.

'Hello,' she says.

I reply, 'NO.'

Mum's lips go thin.

But one side of Dr Muhammad's mouth quirks up. A sense of humour!

'Bad day, then?' she says. 'But it's nice to meet you, Yan. Can you tell me what's going on?'

What's. Going. On?

My mother, as ever, is brow-raising, hopeful. Prompting me: don't let the side down. Come back now, and hide. Back down there *where I will die*.

No.

I start screaming.

The sound flays the poison air. Four days in London, crashing and crushing my best friend, Kieran, Aunt Julie and stranger. And now my poor mother: I'm pushing her off as she tries to hug me, but – rather unfortunately – *this is me*, surging converging weeping hammering the wall to see if I break, riding the rapids far from my torn roots, with the sunshine over. Gone nova, and loud pushy stubborn weird arrogant Yan is currently BATSHIT and will waste no more time fudging it. Take me away, then. Any shame, any hope of peace is worth it to stop this.

The psychiatrist watches me. And holy crap, there's a security guard in the doorway. She motions him to wait, though.

I cross the room, stride past Mum and Dr Muhammad, slap the opposite wall, shriek briefly. My mother is crying. I'd rather be dead. Death is burning my head!

Dr Muhammad is cool, rational, curious. Asks, 'Can you slow down a bit so we can talk?'

'NO. Andyou knowthat!' Stopping's what takes the energy: upside-down logic. The pressure and stress of my mother's distress receding back down the glitter sludge tunnel. They are killing Isga. I focus on Dr Muhammad: 'AmI completelyinsane?'

'Insanity is relative. You're engaging with me, for example.'

'So you think I'm pretending too.' I lean back on the

wall, slap the wall, so I face her.

'That would be a strange way to spend a summer afternoon.'

NO KIDDING.

'Do you know who you are and where you are?'

'I am Yan Harris.' And I can't help it. 'This is a London hospital. I norget the – *forget* the *name* cos I'm mental.'

I am here, where I feared to go. Through hell marching. Everyone far behind me.

'OK, Yan, good. And can you tell me how you're feeling?'

FEELING?

Ache hat art father. Fear cheer mother inferior. And the sanest thing is revealing it all. Uncramping my soul.

'Actually I'm *bored*, doctor.'

'That's an interesting take.'

'Oh, is it? You try being like this.' I sweep my arm round the almost-cell, the general hell, my horrified mother, the short, wary security guard who just wants to go home to his wife unthumped by nutjobs. 'How dare this happen to me?' And I'm up in her face. 'I WANT MY LIFE AGAIN.'

Dr Muhammad steps back, a little. Smiles at me.

'And what does that entail?'

She asks such strange questions, far off in sane-land.

Well. Once there was world, and I dragged through it illness. It scooped out my mind and replaced it with faeces. Then fire burned the shit, and the shell of me landed in this nightmare farce.

'IT ENTAILS FUCKING TREATMENT! THE RIGHT FUCKING TREATMENT! I'M SO SORRY I'M SCARY.' I am sorry, truly. 'I DON'T KNOW HOW TO DO THIS ANY BETTER THAN YOU DO, MUM, OK?'

I want to make hats again, one day. 'I'M HERE TO GET THIS SORTED! ANY IDEAS, DOCTOR?'

Rage-pain, pacing again, flame in a hurricane, sick and murky; hello, my friend the wall, I could slap you again.

'Certainly a course of treatment is likely to be helpful, if we can determine which one,' says the doctor.

Mum's gone all teary. 'Yan, I promise I'll make sure you get whatever you need.'

'WELL . . . GOOD!' I announce, not all that incisively. London has flooded me. I want Chelsea. I think something is achieved.

At my request, they usher out Mother. The doctor asks 'routine' questions. I answer: no, I don't sleep much; no, I'm not being abused. Yes, I have a support system: Chelsea and 'my other friends': my mer-loving pirate queer-minded ones, though I don't name your truth here.

I mention making hats.

The doctor feigns interest in that.

'Unusual hobby,' she says.

'UNUSUAL PERSON,' I stress. What I care about is, 'CAN YOU TREAT THIS?'

'Most likely. We'll try.'

'I'M BIPOLAR.'

'That looks like one possibility.'

I want better promise than that, bitch. I came here to fix my life, but I know Chelsea is right and this is bipolar which is never over and I will never be stable and certain, there's only my mother crying outside, and the doctor scrying me round and round in this furnace of white I am turning and I burn like the endless righteous ocean and I –

oh, wait –

I

   am
        easing

to partial relief.

       Slowing
           down.
             Lorazepam
               kicking
                 in.
I   *It's*
   give   *taken*
      this   *from*
        up   *me*

?

Chapter 38

I am heir to peculiar horizons. A handful of bullshit, a handful of diamonds.

For now, the doctors send me home.

tomtartoes-blog.rabbithole.com
Sunday 11:15

Sorry I haven't updated in a couple of days. Especially sorry I haven't written more about bitey, because I know some of you do really care. 😊

But I've had a lot to think about. And I wanted to wait till I could definitely give some good news. I'm on the train home now.

The A&E doctors checked bitey out, but sent her home rather than admitting her. Her mum is a bit shell-shocked – more than bitey, I think, *facepalm* – but she's going to make sure there's proper follow-up this time. Of course, nobody's actually committing to saying it's bipolar at this point, but that's the working assumption.

bitey's mum says she's spending a lot of time sleeping. Please keep sending your good thoughts (and kinky fics and headcanons and pics of Isga, obvs).

On to fandom.

I owe @vikinghusbands an apology because this is wild, but it was actually bitey who doxxed me to my family. She thought I needed to be more open and honest about who I am, and that was really not her decision to make, but what's done is done and the interesting thing is, while I *am* angry with her it's just not as big a thing, overall, as I thought it would be. So . . . hi again, Mum and Dad.

@vikinghusbands, I'm sorry I accused you. That advice you gave about how to act with bitey was obviously genuine, and I've thought about it. In some ways you're right.

HOWEVER. I'm not having you say that bipolar people are 'just trouble' and 'not worth it'. bitey is my best friend and she's worth everything.

AND: I am not joining your stupid little purity cult. There's no right or wrong way to write a couple of TV characters shagging. I am not going to start flinging hate at people just because they make art I don't like. Rothskaar is not the only pure pairing and everyone and everything else is not 'problematic'. Or if it is, then life is problematic! And the show flirts with dark stuff all the time, so how is it different when ficcers do it?

Yes, I'm only 17 but I live in a three-bedroom house and I've got three older brothers. I knew what a dick was before I discovered fanfiction.

On that note, @tastyriceballs, I just don't happen to be into your style of writing, OK? It's nothing personal.

Anyone who posts racist shit in here is going to get deleted and blocked. I might not be able to make you less of a dickhead, but my bff doesn't have to see your hate.

OK. So.

As for my own writing, I want to keep growing, and that

means trying different stuff. I've started planning a new fic I definitely want to write. In the show, Uskaar's afraid of people finding out his granddad was a vittra, and Rothgern has despised vittra ever since one killed his wife. Usually fic has them healing each other once they get together.

But what if they get together but Rothgern keeps saying Uskaar's a monster; and Uskaar thinks he has to serve Rothgern to work through his self-loathing? Unhealthy, yep. But also real. I want to start exploring stuff that feels real, and see where it takes me.

It's really bad that Isga's getting fridged. It's obviously because the showrunners think she scares the ~~white cishet male~~, sorry, the wider audience, and it's the last thing bitey needs. I do sort of feel I should stop being a fan, for bitey, but I guess you love what you love. Let's see what else Season 4 has to offer.

Phew, London was intense but I'm so glad to be home. I want to sit and read for a bit. I'll do some Toes' Recs tomorrow.

🏢11:51 **lyssapeeps:** Anything you write is sure to be great!

🏺 11:59 **tastyriceballs:** ok toes at least you're honest but I'm really hurt. 🙁

🚢12:08 **far-oceans:** I got zero spoons right now, but you go, tomtartoes!

◉12:39 **vikinghusbands:** Thank you for the apology but I'm afraid for you, toes. What if you write something sick and someone at your school finds out about it?

🧦 12:58 **isga-bites-u:** Wow @vikinghusbands . . . you just never change.

🖊 13:10 **idris-elbow:** bitey!! *glomps*

🧦 13:12 **isga-bites-u:** Yeah well I'm not exactly myself but I'm alive.

🍶 13:20 **tastyriceballs:** OMG bitey. I'm blocking you. I stand against bullying.

🖊 12:45 **idris-elbow:** I'm excited your writing is progressing.

🍶 12:50 **tastyriceballs:** @idris-elbow, I'm afraid patriarchy has seriously got to you if you think encouraging people to write gross kinks is progressive. I'm blocking you. @tomtartoes I'm sorry but I'm blocking you too, to protect my mental health ☹

CHAPTER 39

A few days after I return from London, Chelsea and I are sitting on the knee-high wall that divides the end of our garden from the little River Brock. It's evening. The stream is at its late-summer low. Butterflies flit around. My mother's inside putting her feet up after a day at the clinic, but she'll be out here soon. The beans need watering. I told her I'd do it but haven't had the energy. I haven't the energy for much, and I don't really care.

I got emergency zonk pills from the GP right after we came home. At least that means I'm in no state to damage anything. And I'm on some kind of fast track that means I only have to wait two months for a psychiatrist. 'We'll see what he comes up with,' said Mum, who has a new post-London look when it comes to my buggy brain. A bit freaked out, a bit glazed over, but mostly Action Mode.

I wish I could bring the sunshine girl back. But it'll be a while.

Yesterday Chel and I had The Conversation about me doxxing her, and blackm00ds, and all the rest. She said it wasn't OK, which I knew, but perhaps it will be. Fortunately her family seems to have decided fic is just one more weird thing about their beloved genius. Of course, after the brilliant roasting Chel gave her on Sunday, vikinghusbands will probably be hunting down her details to out her at school, but I think post-London Chelsea is less afraid than she was.

Now she's telling me what she's heard from Kieran. He's settling into his mate's spare room, and it's all good. As for Ras, she's doing some kind of mutual writing critique with him. I'm glad about these things, I think. It's a bit hard to tell from the bottom of my current sludge pit, which is not a glittery one.

I get the impression she has something else to tell me too. She pulls at a blade of grass dangling over the edge of the wall we're sitting on. 'Er,' she says.

'Next time in London will be better,' I promise. I still like the dream: Yan and Chel storm the capital. Or rather I remember that I like it. That future is still in my mind, but it seems stiff and fragile, like a cardboard skyline. 'You should visit your aunt and uncle before you move there.'

'Yeah.' Chel doesn't sound very enthusiastic. I want to ask what's wrong, but I can guess. It's just as well I'm too zonked to feel how terrible all this is. But I brought it on myself.

'Look, it's OK,' I say. 'I'm not going to turn up on Aunt Julie's doorstep and embarrass you. It's really nice of them to, um, not want to follow up about the – about the money. And I'm not going to go shoplifting. Or running around randomly. Or kicking people.' Unless I see any especially evil Tories.

'Aye,' says Chel with some feeling, and a glare. But there's clearly something even bigger on her mind. She continues in a rush . . . 'All right, I suppose I should just say this straight out . . . I don't wanna move to London. One week were enough for me.'

'Oh,' I say. 'Oh.'

I need to think.

Think!

See Yan think. See Yan process information at the speed of a slug chewing lettuce. I need to react. I think I am reacting. 'Oh,' I say.

'You're my best friend forever, and you'll get better. You'll be accepted into St Martin's and do great,' she says. 'But I had a couple of days on my own with Julie and Mark after you come back here, and then I been on the phone to Julie, and it's all actually been a bit much, you know? Visiting them were one thing. *But . . .*'

'Uh-huh?' I'm not really up to asking for details, but I think I can guess. Hypomanic Yan might have been a disaster area, but I did draw off some of the olds' scrutiny.

'Mark and Julie's kindness is a wonderful opportunity,' continues Chel very carefully. 'I'm lucky to have relatives to help me out. I appreciate that. But I ain't a project. And I ain't a big city girl. Should've known that.' Another blade of grass gets ripped out of the bed. 'I don't wanna get out of our house just to move to somewhere else that's as mad in another way.'

'But you're not forgetting uni and staying in this dump?!' That thought is enough to rouse me, and I half-turn towards her, actually poking her with a bit of wilted grass. If she doesn't go to uni, it'll be partly my fault.

'Nah, nothing like that!' she says, and it's her slightly indignant tone that reassures me most. 'I don't mind normal towns, or if I do a bit it'll be worth it. I just wanna go somewhere I can hear myself think.'

'Well, uni applications don't close until January, so you've got time to choose,' I say. The slug I'm calling a brain is trying to get a wriggle on, and managing a wobble. My best friend won't be with me in London. It's selfish to be sad about that. As if, in this state, I'll get into any college anyway.

Chel cocks her head and looks at me, narrowing her eyes in the sunlight. 'Some of 'em close in October.'

'Huh?' The brain-slug struggles to dig up a memory of the school 'advice' sessions. 'Only . . .'

'. . . Oxford and Cambridge,' Chel finishes for me. Then she's off, whacking her mini-skirted thigh with a fist. 'Well, Oxford, for me. I looked it all up and there's outreach and funding programmes if you ain't rich. I'm smart, and I'm proud of it, and if my family don't always get me they love me. And no, I ain't applying cos of what Mark said about it.' I may have been giving her a questioning look, there. 'It's cos of who I am. And who I wanna be.'

'That's great.' I don't have much to add. Because it is great, and I kind of knew deep down this was coming. I kind of helped it.

I need a better response, because Chel's eyes have gone really big and she's looking at me defiantly, as if I might stand in her way. But I can't really bridge gaps in conversation at the moment. I have to wait for people to come to me, bringing whatever they bring.

And Chelsea's brought something big this time. *Get it together, Yan.*

'Of course you should apply!' I stick my arm out in an attempt to hug her, except I'm still mal-coordinated, and it hits her in the shoulder. But she moves easily so we can snuggle together, rather sweaty though we are. 'And you're sure to get in! It'd be nice if we went to London together but how likely am I to get there in this state anyway and – yeah.'

All right. That's all the braining and wording I can manage right now. There's a lump in my throat. Not that the pills will let me cry, but it's there.

'Oh, you will!' says Chel stubbornly. There's a quiver in her voice too. The sun is sparkling on the purple wings of a butterfly. The stream is burbling. My mum's coming out of the back door with her gardening gloves, but she's not looking our way. She's going out with Dr Jones tonight, and I know I'm happy for her, and I'm happy for Chel.

My concentration is still pants.

'Yeah,' I make myself say.

'If you can smash bipolar disorder, wowing some fashionista applications board should be no problem,' Chel urges.

'Well, maybe.' I want to point out, *And if you can cope with hypo me you can certainly face down an Oxford interviewer*, but that subject's too fresh to safely touch. 'The smashing is a work in progress. I can't send St Martin's a portfolio that doesn't exist. They specify quite a few particular things I haven't done yet.'

I'm in no state to design anything. I can't do this, I can't do that. I'm waiting, without even knowing what for.

Chel doesn't reply. One of the many reasons I love her is that if there's nothing to say, she doesn't say it.

'You gonna keep watching *Nordhelm*?' she asks.

'Yeah, probably, though you can watch the episode where they –' I wave my hand so I don't have to say, *kill Isga* – 'and give me a summary. If they "fix" Yrsali's speech impediment and marry her off to Rothgern, though, I'm noping out completely.'

'At that rate, I might an' all.' Chel sighs. Then she suggests, 'Wanna come for tea at ours? You ain't been round for ages. Mum's asking about you.'

I consider it. I think of people peering at us through their windows as we walk through the village – I don't even know what they'll have heard about me – and then all the cheerful racket at Chel's house, and at the same time her mum and Ruby sympathetically Not Saying Things to me and about me and around me. 'No,' I say. Then I amend it to, 'Not yet. Soon, though. I'm tired today.'

Chel stands up. 'Yeah, I get it. Soon.'

She's taking me at my word. Of course that's what I wanted, and yet . . .

Before she can walk off, I grab her hand and peer up at her in what has to be the most pathetic way . . . And really, bugger this. I know who I am. I *will* get back to being who I am.

I let go of Chel, and solemnly fall backward off the wall onto the bank of the stream, before sticking my legs up in the air and blowing a raspberry.

'DEADED!' I declare. 'WHY IS YAN DEADED?! YAN WANTS TO LIIIIVVVEEE!'

I hear Chel laughing. Then her face appears between me and the blue sky. Her features are in shadow but I can make out her smile. 'You're *temporarily* deaded cos you're recovering from a serious illness. But you better get up! You'll get grass stains on your blouse.'

'Blegh,' I say, then hook my knees over the top of the wall as if settling in. Though the rough stone is digging into my thighs.

'All right, well I s'pose you're comfortable there,' says Chel.

Another of those purple butterflies – Mum would know what they're called – appears beside her, dancing in the air.

It could give me ideas for a hat. I know the concepts are there, sitting just out of reach. Let me sleep for a month, then maybe I can try for them.

Chel leans forward and holds out her hand. I reach out mine too, and let her pull me up, and hug me before she goes, even if I can't respond properly yet.

EPILOGUE

yantsinmypants.rabbithole.com
8 January 15:32

This is the new personal blog of the late isga-bites-u. I'm going to talk about hats, life, and InSaNiTy, Because to hell with stigma.

So . . . *drum-roll* *fart noise* As of a few days ago, I officially have a diagnosis of bipolar, type II. Bipolar I is when you get manic and maybe psychotic and think you're god or Elvis. Type II is when you're *hypo*manic, i.e. not mental enough to *think* you're god, but you still feel like it. Until the depression from hell kicks in. Bipolar I is best for destroying your life by accident, and bipolar II is best for witnessing the mess you're making and getting so miserable you kill yourself. 0/10, I do not recommend either.

End of general public service announcement.

AND ME . . .

I'm sitting here on my bed, with @tomtartoes writing fanfic on the windowseat, so I'd have to say things are back to normal to a degree. I got hypo in the summer when I was in London. I think some of you probably noticed that. But what goes up has to splat back down, so in autumn I had to spend a few days in hospital. Unless you like jigsaws with missing pieces, that is not the place to be, even with toes visiting and people emailing support (thank you).

But to cut a long story short-ish, I got referred to therapy – you can get a few sessions on the NHS, though it's pretty limited – and I got MEDSSS. If I just take lithium I still get brainshred hell depression (technical term) and if I just take antidepressants I get wonkypants hypo (another technical term). But on both together I am PERFECTLY NORMAL!

For me. There's a normal amount of yants in my pants. I still get moodswings, but it's nice not to want to either lie down and die, or hammer on the walls. Not gonna lie, being level is strange, but I get so much more done. ~~Only I miss the hypo sometimes.~~ Ahem.

My mum accepts it now, though she's not exactly comfortable. I've exchanged a couple of emails with my dad and I probably will see him again, but that isn't my priority at the moment. Telling my grandparents . . . maybe not.

Meanwhile, @tomtartoes' Oxford interview results come through in mid-January. How can she fail? But keep everything crossed anyway . . .

And I have a decision to make. If I'm going to apply to St Martin's, it has to be very soon. Should I go for it, or give myself a break? I do have a portfolio ready, but is it good enough? I can re-apply next year if I fail this time, but I don't know if I can take the rejection right now.

Anyway. I'm going to update this blog pretty regularly because I don't want to lose touch with my Nordhelm friends, even if I'm not into the show as much as toes is any more.

Follow me if you relate to the bipolar content, or if you're an interesting person, or if you like amazing hats. I'm getting plenty of ideas now, and they are definitely going to get made.

🏯16:02 **far-oceans:** Aw bitey (pantsy? lol) it's so cool that the meds work. Re college, I don't think you should rush. You've been aiming at St Martin's for a long time.

🗡 16:18 **idris-elbow:** 👍

🎯16:27 **vikinghusbands:** I'm sorry, but no one will forget about blackm00ds. Or toes' false accusation that I doxxed her when it was you, her 'best friend'.

  ♟ 16:43 **freaksjustkillyrselves:** Yeah.

  🎏16:44 **ships-kitty:** @vikinghusbands . . . maybe we could move on from that. 'blackm00ds' was obvs really ill.

    👑16:46 **longboat_life:** @vikinghusbands . . . shut up.

🏛 17:07 **anonymous:** i really appreciate you talking about this stuff. i'm bipolar ii as well and I've been having a difficult time. please keep posting.

🏯19:27 **far-oceans:** OH MY GOD <u>CHECK IT OUT</u>

---

hollywoodbuzz.com

HUANG TO STAR IN JBC'S *VISIONARIES*

Florence Huang, best-known for playing the mermaid queen Isga in JBC's *Nordhelm*, has been confirmed as the lead in *Visionaries*, the network's new headline sci-fi drama . . . <u>Click to read more</u>

🖊19:28 **yantsinmypants:** OMG AAAAAAAAAAAAAAAAA-
AAHHHHHHHHHHHHHH!

MARVEL AT USKAAR'S MUSCLES!

PLUMB THE DARK SECRETS
OF ROTHGERN'S SOUL!

GET BITTEN BY QUEEN ISGA!

IT'S ALL IN
CHELSEA'S GUIDE TO NORDHELM

AVAILABLE SOON AS AN EBOOK

FEATURING . . .

CHARACTER PROFILES

Lord Rothgern

On a rabbithole thread about describing Rothgern in five words, someone wrote, 'the broodiest brooder everto brood' (which mostly provoked a lot of discussion about cheating with the five words). That's not entirely fair, though. Rothgern has some good reasons for being in a bad mood. His wife was killed by a vittra while out hunting not long before the show begins, and he's in charge of holding Nordhelm together. He really did love her, too. ♡

At first glance he looks like a bit of a tyrant, but he's enlightened in his way. He's a sharp operator and will do 'good' things if they keep Nordhelm running better than 'evil' ones. He's about thirty-two, has dark hair, perpetual stubble and wears black leather ALL THE TIME because . . . well, let's be real, because it's gorgeous. OMG WHAT'S HAPPENING TO MY PANTS? (Sorry, I know this guide is supposed to be impartial.) He's a competent fighter though not as bulky as Uskaar, who would probably be able to beat him in a wrestling match. I can recommend a lot of fics about this. He also keeps his dungeons in very good repair considering the amount of other business he has to attend to.

Rothgern has some kind of mysterious connection with the fire spirits worshipped by the Nordhelmers, and his right forearm was badly burned as part of sealing this deal. He

can sometimes do fire magic but it's not quite clear when/
why/how.

BEHIND-THE-SCENES RUMOURS

⊷➤A leak from the studio suggested that Ethraig the dragon
was originally going to be a giant evil tomte. Nobody is sure
whether the showrunners were just trolling the fandom, or if
it was really planned.

SERIES NOTES

⊷➤People have counted (it's important, right?) and Gunsten
Berg and his family suffer from twenty-one individual
instances of bad luck during the first three seasons.

MEMES

⊷➤Fandom decided early on that Uskaar lives entirely on
a real Swedish delicacy called sour herring (well, that and
things you can quaff). This is in spite of the fact that he eats
all sorts of food in the episodes. Eventually the showrunners
picked up on it, and we saw him about to down an entire tub
of the stuff . . . before the Jaarv were attacked and he used it
as a weapon instead, because it smells *that* bad.

SPIRIT OF FIRE
A FANFIC BY TOMTARTOES
CHAPTER 1

It was a dark and stormy night in Nordhelm and Rothgern's fire kept going out.

This particular spell was always difficult, but after the nixxi occupation of the castle (the maids still hadn't been able to get the smell of seaweed out of the throne-room curtains) he'd realised he had to raise his game. So here he was, practising every night in the stone courtyard, far from the flammable wood and furnishings indoors.

The gate guards watched warily as Rothgern conjured another elegant curl of yellow-white power in the air above the battlements making the falling rain sizzle and steam. What did the Jaarv, down there in their valley camp, make of this? Hopefully it would remind them who they were truly dealing with.

Satisfied with the results of his exercise, Rothgern jogged lightly up the stone staircase to the battlements and looked down at the lights of the Jaarv camp in the valley, pushing his dark, sopping hair out of his eyes. The damn pirates had started out by raiding his villages, but now the Jaarv and the locals were practically best friends. What was it about Uskaar that made people like him? Well, Rothgern would never lower himself to –

Wait. There was a dark shape moving down there on the road leading up to the castle.

No, surely not. Who'd be out on a night like this?

But as Rothgern watched, the shape moved closer. He could have summoned an archer and bade her shoot it, but some instinct or perhaps weakness made him hesitate. Instead he withdrew from the battlements and, ignoring the questioning looks of the guards, quietly approached the slit window in the base of the gate tower that looked out onto the road.

What he saw made him stifle a gasp. It was Uskaar himself, drenched, blond hair slicked back, muscular arms gleaming in the fitful moonlight. As Rothgern watched, Uskaar raised his mighty fist to hammer on the gate.

'OPEN UP! LORD ROTHGERN, I SEEK YOUR AID!'

To be continued in

Chelsea's Guide to Nordhelm,

available soon.

ACKNOWLEDGEMENTS

Reader, I would like to thank you for sticking with Yan. I would also like to thank:

Gill Armstrong, Alex Norrish and Jarita Rutkowski for endless hours spent feeding back on my fiction and believing it would eventually see the light of day; Philip Cotterell for the thudding, and for really doing his best to get his head around Yan; and Jude Ellison, Silvia Gasparini, Emily Johnson, Natalia Savana Muñoz and Yulia Serdyukova for bonus cheerleading over the years.

My agent Jenny Savill of Andrew Nurnberg and my publisher Elaine Bousfield for noticing that my writing is quite good; and Jane Tait and Melissa Hyder for the eagle-eye editing.

Ludi Price, China and Inner Asia Librarian at SOAS (and prodigious fanficcer!) for an invaluable sensitivity read; Lucy Miller-Sheen, and Xueting Christine Ni of Snow Pavilion (www.snowpavilion.co.uk) for their advice on Anglo-Chinese culture; and Bahira for her insights on Ras's origins.

My younger self, for hanging on through the twenty years between bipolar onset and diagnosis.

Elyssa Warkentin, Rosamund Taylor and Saathi for their advice on LGBTQ+ issues, and just being my friends.

RESOURCES FOR
YOUNG PEOPLE

If you are concerned about your mental health, we recommend speaking with a trusted, caring adult and going to see your GP. You can also use some of the resources below.

Young Minds is the leading UK charity for young people's mental health. You can find information and resources on bipolar disorder and other conditions on their website. There is also information on medication, access to treatment and support and a helpline for parents who have children, teenagers or young adults who may be struggling with their mental health.

youngminds.org.uk

The Royal College of Psychiatrists has put together an animated film about bipolar disorder for young people, describing the symptoms and experiences you might have with the illness. If you don't want to read lots of blurb about bipolar, you might find this film more interesting.

rcpsych.ac.uk

Bipolar UK is the national charity dedicated to supporting people of all ages with bipolar. It was formed in the 1980s and is a campaigning organisation as well as a supportive service offering peer support and contact with their team.
bipolaruk.org

Rethink is another organisation offering factsheets and guidance on what to expect and where to get help in your local area. We would recommend their website for readers aged 18+.

rethink.org

The Anna Freud Centre has information on a whole range of conditions, and access to films made by young people on their experiences of mental health challenges.
annafreud.org

Kooth is the UK'S leading digital mental health service for children and young people. Anonymous at the point of entry, Kooth offers safely moderated peer support channels, content and access to counsellors. They cannot diagnose you but they are linked into the NHS so can help you find more specialised care. They offer online counselling and support.

kooth.com

The Mix is a digital mental health and advice service open to young people from 16 to 25 years of age. They offer online support through webchat and social media, plus telephone support. They cannot diagnose you but they can offer you guidance on a range of issues.

themix.org.uk

For more insightful books you'll love,

head to

zuntold.com